JOURNEY FROM ST. PETERSBURG TO MOSCOW

RUSSIAN LIBRARY

R

The Russian Library at Columbia University Press publishes an expansive selection of Russian literature in English translation, concentrating on works previously unavailable in English and those ripe for new translations. Works of premodern, modern, and contemporary literature are featured, including recent writing. The series seeks to demonstrate the breadth, surprising variety, and global importance of the Russian literary tradition and includes not only novels but also short stories, plays, poetry, memoirs, creative nonfiction, and works of mixed or fluid genre.

■ □ ■

For a list of books in the series, see page 263

Columbia University Press / *New York*

Published with the support of Read Russia, Inc., and the Institute of Literary Translation, Russia

Columbia University Press
Publishers Since 1893
New York Chichester, West Sussex
cup.columbia.edu

Library of Congress Cataloging-in-Publication Data
Names: Radishchev, Aleksandr Nikolaevich, 1749–1802 author. | Kahn, Andrew, translator. | Reyfman, Irina, translator.
Title: Journey from St. Petersburg to Moscow / Alexander Radishchev; translated by Andrew Kahn and Irina Reyfman.
Other titles: Puteshestvie iz Peterburga v Moskvu. English
Description: New York : Columbia University Press, [2020] | Series: Russian library | Translated from the Russian.
Identifiers: LCCN 2020002496 (print) | LCCN 2020002497 (ebook) | ISBN 9780231185905 (cloth) | ISBN 9780231185912 (paperback) | ISBN 9780231546393 (ebook)
Subjects: LCSH: Serfdom —Russia. | Russia—Social conditions—To 1801.
Classification: LCC HN525 .R313 2020 (print) | LCC HN525 (ebook) | DDC 306.0947—dc23
LC record available at https://lccn.loc.gov/2020002496
LC ebook record available at https://lccn.loc.gov/2020002497

Cover design: Roberto de Vicq de Cumptich
Book design: Lisa Hamm

CONTENTS

ACKNOWLEDGMENTS

While translating Alexander Radishchev's travelogue, we benefited from the generous help of many individuals. First of all, we would like to express our gratitude to Christine Dunbar, the editor of the Russian Library series at Columbia University Press. She was the person with whom we first discussed this project, and has remained enthusiastic and supportive from beginning to end, answering our questions and helping to solve problems, small and large. We particularly appreciate her reading the entire manuscript, both the introduction and the translation, and coming up with many helpful suggestions at the revision stage. We also thank friends and colleagues who read either the entire manuscript or parts of it at different stages and helped us to revise and improve our translation. Our deepest gratitude goes to Kelsey Rubin-Detlev and Nicholas Cronk for reading the entire manuscript. Their meticulous and learned help was inestimable. Avi Lifschitz and Thomas Wynn generously read selections and offered valuable feedback on aspects of Radishchev's sources and his style. We would also like to acknowledge the generosity of colleagues who responded to our queries about sometimes very complex aspects of the Russian eighteenth-century economy, legal system, and social system. We could not have managed without their expertise. Robert H. Davis, librarian for Russian, Eurasian and East European Studies at Columbia University, helped to search for hard-to-find books and articles. Robert H. Scott, head of the Electronic Text Service, Columbia University Libraries (retired), has our gratitude for making it possible to copy the microforms of rare eighteenth-century publications. We also owe profound gratitude to the anonymous reader of our manuscript for the Columbia University Press. We found her or his careful reading and thoughtful and wise suggestions tremendously useful while giving our manuscript one last round of revisions. Ben Kolstad and Leslie Kriesel provided valuable help with production, and Peggy Tropp with copyediting, for which we are extremely grateful. The opportunity to present our work at the X International Conference of the Study Group on Eighteenth-Century Russia (Strasbourg) in July 2018 afforded feedback from our fellow participants that proved invaluable to the development of our translating strategy. We are grateful to them.

INTRODUCTION

ANDREW KAHN AND IRINA REYFMAN

The *Journey from St. Petersburg to Moscow* is the work that made Alexander Radishchev an underground celebrity. Confiscated when Radishchev published it in late May 1790, this work of travel literature and political critique is one of the most notorious books of the eighteenth century. Banned until nearly the end of the Imperial period, it was read in manuscript copies that circulated clandestinely (there are about seventy extant copies dating from 1790, many with readers' comments), in the few rare copies of the first edition that survived (Alexander Pushkin acquired such a copy), or finally, in copies published by the émigré press outside Russia starting in 1856. Radishchev's arrest, on June 30, 1790, came at the start of the third decade of a reign that began in 1762, when Catherine II took the throne. Because her clash with this dedicated civil servant and gifted freethinker came toward the end of the epoch, it overshadowed her long record of accomplishment. Radishchev's sentence of exile looked like an act of despotic intolerance, casting doubt on Catherine's commitment to the improvement of social welfare and other progressive tenets of the Enlightenment. Russian historians have continued to debate whether the principles of toleration, reform, and rational government that Catherine had made cornerstones of her reputation were real or mere virtue signaling. The historical irony is that Radishchev's intellectual qualities and philosophical views were very much the product of the values of toleration, Westernization, and reform that Catherine had championed for much of her reign.

THE MAN AND HIS WORK

Born in Moscow in 1749, Radishchev was the scion of a wealthy and well-educated provincial nobleman, a descendant of a Tatar prince who entered Russian service under Ivan the Terrible. The future writer spent the first years of his life on one of his father's numerous estates and was taught at home; beginning in 1756 or 1757, he lodged in the Moscow house of a relative on his mother's side, Mikhail Argamakov, the director of Moscow University, to be taught together with his children.[1] Their education was first-rate: Moscow University professors gave them private lessons, they had access to the university library, and they were able to attend public lectures at the university. In 1762, the young Radishchev entered state service as a page to the newly enthroned Empress. He spent the first year in Moscow, where the court had relocated for Catherine's coronation, and then moved with the court to St. Petersburg. His education continued at the Corps of Pages, where he studied physics, mathematics, geography, and languages. He also learned music, dance, and fencing. The duties of a page required Radishchev to appear at court, and his first attempt at creative composition, the synopsis of a one-act comedy in French cowritten with his classmate P. I. Chelishchev (the Ch. of the chapter "Chudovo"), was staged at the court theater.[2]

In 1766, Radishchev was one of a select group of twelve young noblemen sent to Leipzig University to further their education. Each of them was given room and board and a bursary of eight hundred rubles, a substantial sum. The young people studied natural philosophy, law, logic, geography, physics, and mathematics; they also learned languages—German, French, and Latin. Among their instructors were first-rate European scholars and scientists, including the philosopher Ernst Platner and poet Christian Gellert. Radishchev also studied medicine. The connections he makes in his major writings between forms of sensibility and sensation may have been rooted in his education at Leipzig University. The Age of Reason was also an Age of Sensibility, and the human propensity for sympathy and empathy was seen as a matter of hardwiring in the body as much as a product of a refined education (discussions of pedagogy in this period in Russia, as well as in Western Europe, considered these parallel influences). The foundation for Radishchev's knowledge of a wide range of Enlightenment ideas about the body and soul, as well as about political economy and the law, was laid during his Leipzig years.

The period of study at Leipzig was formative not only educationally but also politically and emotionally. Radishchev developed firm friendships with some of his fellow students, most especially Fyodor Ushakov (1748/49–1770), whom he would later commemorate in an important biography, *The Life of Fyodor Ushakov* (1789). The biography recounts how Russian students, with Ushakov as their ringleader, rebelled against their corrupt supervisor to protest poor living conditions. This experience was seminal for Radishchev, who later traced his mature thinking about political action and legitimate forms of protest back to this event. *The Life of Fyodor Ushakov* also describes the titular character's death from venereal disease, stressing his courage in the face of death and connecting his firm behavior with his leadership qualities. Radishchev is unusually frank about Ushakov's libido and the sexually transmitted disease that prematurely killed him. The topic of prostitution and syphilis recurs in episodes of the *Journey* that consider passions, including sexual passions, as an important factor in human behavior.[3] The friendship with Ushakov was thus a turning point for Radishchev, providing both a political and an emotional education.

On his return to Russia, Radishchev and two others of his cohort, including his friend Alexei Kutuzov, the future Freemason and eventual dedicatee of the *Journey*, served briefly in the Senate before entering military service. Radishchev served as a military lawyer until his retirement in 1775. Soon after retirement, Radishchev married Anna Vasilyevna Rubanovskaya (who died prematurely in 1783). He resumed his service career in January 1778 as a civil servant in the Commerce College, with the rank of collegiate assessor. He held this post under Alexander Vorontsov, the well-educated, progressive nobleman, diplomat, and brother of Catherine's confidante Ekaterina Dashkova. At the time, Vorontsov was president of the Commercial College and had recruited Radishchev to work for the Commission on Commerce. He remained a loyal patron to Radishchev during his career and, especially, after his arrest and exile in 1790.

A civil servant of distinction and ability who had a practical grasp of policy implementation (he visited the port cities on the Baltic to see things with his own eyes), Radishchev seems never to have put a foot wrong. When the government passed gubernatorial reforms in 1780, Radishchev was seconded to State Councillor Dal, the director of St. Petersburg Customs, and assumed oversight for trade entering the port at St. Petersburg. In this capacity he was said to have commanded the respect of his colleagues for his incorruptibility, a conspicuous virtue when contrasted with the venality of officialdom much illustrated in the *Journey*. He made steady progress up the ranks, achieving several promotions in the early 1780s. In 1789 he was designated director of St. Petersburg Customs.

Arrested a month after the publication of the *Journey*, Radishchev was imprisoned in the notorious Peter and Paul Fortress, investigated, and condemned to death in late July. In early September, Catherine commuted the death sentence, replacing it with exile to Siberia. On September 8, 1790, in chains and under guard, Radishchev began his journey to Ilimsk, a small fortress not far from the Angara River. Thanks to Vorontsov, the chains were soon removed, and on his way to Siberia Radishchev spent significant time in Moscow, Nizhny Novgorod, Tobolsk, and Irkutsk, which eased his journey. His sister-in-law, Ekaterina Rubanovskaya, and his two younger children joined him in Tobolsk. Rubanovskaya became Radishchev's common-law wife (marriages between in-laws were prohibited), with whom he had three children. She died on the family's way back to European Russia in 1797.

Radishchev arrived in Ilimsk in January 1792 and left in February 1797, having been granted permission to live in Nemtsovo, one of his estates, by the new ruler, Paul. After Paul was assassinated in March 1801, Alexander I fully pardoned the writer and offered him a position on the Legislative Commission to work on the codification of Russian law. Steeped in Western legal theory and knowledgeable about Russian legal practice, Radishchev joined the commission's work with enthusiasm. Several of his pieces on jurisprudence date from his year and a half with the commission. In September 1802, however, he committed suicide by drinking nitrohydrochloric acid. His motivation remains a mystery. It has been conjectured that he may have taken his life either because he feared another period of Siberian exile, as his son Pavel suggests in his biography of his father, or out of his general disillusionment with the constitutional project in which he was involved at the time. It is significant, however, that he had been thinking and writing about suicide ever since Fyodor Ushakov voiced his desire to kill himself instead of dying a slow and painful death during his illness in Leipzig.

From early on, Radishchev found in writing a medium to explore his thoughts about personal and public matters of concern. During his time in Leipzig and for several years after his return to Russia, he was chiefly engaged in translations from French and German; most important among these was Abbé de Mably's *Observations sur les Grecs*, which was published anonymously in 1773. Around the same time, Radishchev turned to literature. In 1779–82 he worked on the metrically innovative "oratory" "Creation of the World"; he included it in the early version of the *Journey*, where it followed the excerpts from the iambic ode "Liberty," written around 1783. In its full form, the ode discusses the social contract and the right it gives the sovereign people to protest against a corrupt monarch. Radishchev's examples of champions of liberty include Cromwell against the Crown and, for the American colonies, Washington's revolt against the British Empire.

While in the Peter and Paul Fortress, Radishchev began writing a work that perhaps provides some insights into his authorial motives for the *Journey*. It is based on the *Life* of St. Philaret the Merciful, who lived in the first century AD in Asia Minor. A prosperous and charitable man, Philaret lost his estate to robbers and became a pauper.

Nonetheless, he continued his charitable work, and God eventually rewarded him. Radishchev uses this *Life* as a canvas for his own biography, to communicate with his family and to explain his actions. It is significant that he chose the *Life* of the saint who, like the author of the *Journey*, was sensitive to the sufferings of humanity.

Most of Radishchev's works of literature (excluding the *Journey*) were made available to the reading public when his sons Nikolai and Pavel published an edition in six volumes (1806–11). Literary activities were clearly just as important to him as his political interests. His diverse writings included a work of natural philosophy on the nature of the soul and the body, *A Historical Song* about the idea of historical change, a long poem, *Bova*, based on folk traditions (inspired as well by Voltaire's burlesque epic *The Maid of Orleans*), and another long poem, *Songs Sung at the Competition in Honor of the Ancient Slavic Divinities*, written in tribute to the Russian medieval epic the *Lay of Igor's Campaign*. Yet Radishchev was not much appreciated as a writer by the generation that followed. His openness to experimentation and the use of highly idiosyncratic forms stymied most readers. There were some exceptions. Pushkin, for instance, admired both Radishchev's experiments with meters and his poetry. His 1836 essay "Alexander Radishchev" is often cited for its criticism of Radishchev's "barbaric" style, but Pushkin also paid tribute to Radishchev's "honesty of intention" in the *Journey* and this work's comprehensive summation of "all French philosophy of the period." Radishchev's persecution and the initial hostility to his ideas were instrumental in shaping how readers interpreted the work's political goals in the last century of Imperial Russia, as well as in Soviet Russia, where virtually from the 1917 revolution Radishchev was lionized as a proto-Bolshevik.

THE *JOURNEY*: ITS PUBLICATION AND RECEPTION

Textual studies of the composition of Radishchev's *Journey*—his second longest work after the complex quasi-materialist treatise he wrote in exile on the body-soul duality—suggest that he began writing when Catherine's policies were more permissive and she still had a reputation as a reformer. The first part of the *Journey* written was "An Oration About Lomonosov." The other chapters followed, and by the end of 1788 the version that Radishchev submitted to the censor was complete. The censor approved this short version for publication. Censorship, both state and church, in the Catherine period was unsystematic and sporadically applied; in general, the 1780s were a period of flourishing for small presses and of growth for university presses.

V. A. Zapadov calculated that Radishchev added about 40 percent more material after the book was approved by the censor.[4] Many of the added passages were the ones that particularly enraged Catherine. Had Radishchev deliberately sought early permission in order to evade censorship? That seems unlikely for at least two reasons: first, because it assumes that the censor would have been vigilant, whereas the evidence suggests that he may not have read the shorter version with any attention; second, and more important, there is no basis on which to claim that Radishchev expected his work would be received as an outrage or as a "personal attack" on the monarch. His superior and old friend Vorontsov regarded the book as no more than an "incautious blunder," while Catherine saw it as an attempt to foment, as stated in the official charge of July 1790, "disobedience and social discord."[5] Everything suggests, in fact, that the Empress's fury and her personal involvement in Radishchev's arrest took him and others by surprise.

Radishchev published the *Journey* anonymously and at his own expense in May 1790, using his own hand press, obtained the previous year. At 650 copies, the number he confessed in the transcript of his interrogation, the print run was large, especially as Radishchev undoubtedly knew that, at the time, few books sold more than 300 copies. He must have hoped his work would attract wide interest among the educated elite. He clearly expected to recover some of the costs via sales through the bookshop of G. K. Zotov. Some copies were sold, and Radishchev sent several to his friends and acquaintances, including Vorontsov's sister, Catherine's longtime friend and ally, Princess Dashkova; and the great poet and senator G. R. Derzhavin, who also fell under suspicion and distanced himself from Radishchev by writing a poem in which he condemned him as "a Russian Mirabeau."[6] The rest Radishchev destroyed when he learned that the authorities were looking for the book's author. Catherine acquired her own copy—which survived with her marginal notes harshly condemning many of the book's ideas and denouncing the author as a dangerous rebel.

By June 1790, Catherine had determined to her own satisfaction Radishchev's authorship (her initial suspicions that he had an accomplice coauthor were rejected) and that he was, in her words, "a rebel even worse than Pugachev."[7] His arrest followed an investigation directed by Count Alexander Bezborodko, one of Catherine's most valued statesmen and a man of cultivated sensibility, who argued for leniency. On the one hand, he believed that Radishchev had not violated the letter of the law, since free presses were permitted by a decree of 1783; on the other hand, the immediate context of the French Revolution was impossible to ignore, as were passages in Radishchev's book urging the establishment of equality and praising the regicide Cromwell. It was no help to Radishchev that the rumor mill about French spies in St. Petersburg had gone into overdrive, including allegations about a suspected plot to assassinate the Empress attributed to the Masonic Martinists, with whom the work's dedicatee Andrei Kutuzov had links.[8] Evidence that the book was a *succès de scandale* in demand by readers (the documented investigation speaks of "the great curiosity of the public for the book"); that perhaps as many as fifty copies had gone unaccounted for; and that a translation into German was already in preparation (untrue, as it happened) exacerbated tensions. Radishchev was imprisoned in the Peter and Paul Fortress, his interrogation conducted by S. I. Sheshkovsky, who, as the dreaded head of the Secret Chancery, was nicknamed "knout-flogger." In mid-July Radishchev addressed to Sheshkovsky a letter of extenuation and apology intended for the ruler. The questions put to Radishchev were in effect scripted by Catherine; they asked Radishchev to explain whether he felt "the significance of his crime" and to gloss the meaning of passages regarded as explicitly of criminal intentionality.[9] The official charge spoke of a "personal affront" to the Empress and a "determination to stir up the people against their masters." The death sentence decreed on July 24th was confirmed by the Senate in early September, after Radishchev had been stripped of his rank (legislation forbade the execution of nobles). Catherine commuted the sentence to ten years of Siberian exile. This second decree noted the exceptional gesture of "clemency" (*miloserdie*), one of the Enlightenment values that differentiated the Enlightened autocrat from the tyrant, in sparing Radishchev, who was then sent east under armed convoy.

In 1811, when Radishchev's sons published their edition of his works, they omitted the *Journey* because of the ongoing censorship ban. For most of the nineteenth century, the *Journey* remained a clandestine book, notwithstanding the anonymous publication of a sporadic chapter or two in journals in Russia and Germany and mentions in works of reference such as Bantysh-Kamensky's *Dictionary of Memorable People* (1836). After the political turmoil of 1825, Radishchev's name was taboo for a decade, and precious few readers had access to his writings. Among them was Alexander Pushkin, who may have read Radishchev's book in manuscript even before purchasing a rare copy in 1835 (only sixty-seven copies of Radishchev's printing have been accounted for). One indicator of Pushkin's engagement with Radishchev's book can be found in the title of his essay "Journey from Moscow to Petersburg" (1833–35, unfinished). The piece examines the chapters of Radishchev's *Journey* in reverse order, providing a set of revisionist commentaries for which Radishchev's text is always the departure point. It was a sign of the times that in 1837 the minister of education, Count S. S. Uvarov, excluded Pushkin's article "Alexander Radishchev" from the third volume of his literary journal *The Contemporary*, extending the ban to the posthumous edition of his works. The ban remained in force until Pavel Annenkov's important edition of Pushkin's works in 1857, when the novelist Ivan Goncharov, no less, was the censor.

In 1858, Nikolai Ogarev and Alexander Herzen, exiles based in London and often dubbed the fathers of Russian socialism, published in effect the second edition of Radishchev's *Journey* in *The Bell* (*Kolokol*) of 1858, their famous radical journal. Although full of errors and unauthorized editorial interventions, this notable edition (reprinted with its distortions in Leipzig in 1876) stimulated Pavel

Radishchev in 1859 or 1860 to apply to Tsar Alexander II for permission to publish this and other works by his father. He had published in 1858 his own memoir of his father, partly drawing on rare materials, including a manuscript copy of the *Journey* provided by the historian Mikhail Pogodin. Pavel succeeded against enormous resistance in publishing his memoir (the censor, reputed to be a secret friend to radicals, lost his job over the matter). However, his efforts to publish the *Journey* met with refusal in 1860 and again in 1865, during which time he sent Herzen a copy of Radishchev's massive ode "Liberty" for publication. The ban on the *Journey* was lifted by the Tsar in March 1868. Rumors of new editions proliferated, and a memoir by Radishchev's other son, Nikolai, was allowed to appear, while some mentions of Radishchev as the author of the *Journey* in reference works were tolerated (a fuller version of memoirs by both sons would be banned until 1912). An 1872 edition of the *Journey* was advertised, but it never appeared, and the print run was destroyed in 1873. Radishchev's most important work remained taboo in nineteenth-century Russia, and signs of a thaw were scarce. The continued suppression of this work only enhanced its reputation among budding radicals in post-Emancipation Russia.

THE *JOURNEY* AS A NEW FORM OF POLITICAL LITERATURE

In his introduction to the first and only translation of Radishchev's *Journey* into English, Roderick Page Thaler articulated a view long held in the West and in Soviet criticism of Radishchev as one of "the earliest of the liberal Russian intelligentsia" whose main purpose in writing the book was to condemn serfdom and convince Russian landowners to abolish it before the serfs revolted.[10] Indeed, Radishchev was one of the first—if not the first—proponents of individual rights in Russia, a position based on his extensive reading of natural law theorists who argued for the equality of all in the state of nature (although some also contended that separate national histories proved that the class structures that emerged were natural for those societies). Radishchev opposed serfdom—even though he never attempted to free his own serfs. He advocated greater humanity in the management of estates, but his stance also looks defensive of an autocracy that put itself at risk by failing to undertake some reform. Recruiting Radishchev to the ranks of the "liberal intelligentsia" speaks very much of a Cold War outlook. Radishchev wrote toward the end of a reign that had in many respects been progressive in legislating reforms of Russia's political economy and, in certain peripheral areas, experimenting with the emancipation of state serfs. Catherine the Great was one of the intellectual stars of the European Enlightenment, a celebrity correspondent of many great thinkers such as Voltaire and D'Alembert, as well as host to Diderot in 1774 in St. Petersburg. Given the fear caused by the French Revolution, 1790 was a bad time to agitate for further reforms to Russia's highly top-down power structure, in which the monarch ruled almost at the grace of the wealthiest nobles, whose fortunes in turn were vested in the land. The *Journey* contains two "projects for the future," and while they have a utopian quality, they are also rooted in present circumstance and hint at the possibility that Catherine might reform the Table of Ranks, the hierarchical system Peter had created for staffing the imperial bureaucracy, and create financial incentives for the better treatment of serfs by the landed gentry.

A purely political reading of Radishchev's rich, complex, multifaceted, and profoundly innovative book would be reductive, however. For all the evidentiary value Radishchev's *Journey* has for historians, it is of course not a straightforward piece of documentation or social analysis. There is much more in his *Journey* than an exposition of his political beliefs, condemnation of serfdom, and criticism of the contemporary Russian monarchy. Most important, it is not a political treatise but a work of literature whose genre is unique. Despite the heated arguments about Radishchev's political intentions that have persisted since its first publication, the *Journey* remains not fully appreciated as a work that uses its multiple types of discourse and polyphonic style of narration to offer perspectives on questions about Russian civilization at the end of Catherine's reign, when the European Enlightenment had come under assault from the French Revolution. The different perspectives of the literary characters from across the social spectrum, including serf and conscript narrators as well as landowners and high-ranking civil servants, emerge in how they tell their stories. There are also narrators who offer perspectives from outside the system by imagining a better future in the language of the allegorical dream and by offering utopian visions of progress.

Radishchev structured his work in twenty-five chapters, each of which is named for a post station where the traveler stops to rest and change horses. The chapters are preceded by a dedication whose addressee is Radishchev's boyhood friend Alexei Mikhailovich Kutuzov. The dedication addresses two of the most important human capacities: to engage in close observation of the world around one and to feel compassion by virtue of empathy. The former makes the latter possible. Wherever the traveler goes, he must be ready to keep his eyes open and actually see and not turn away from injustice but feel the pain it inflicts. By averting his gaze, man overlooks suffering and condones its existence. Outward observation is not the only mode of viewing, however, because the book also contains allegorical visions and dreams. They enlighten the traveler and allow him to see the failings, his own and mankind's, that lead to cruelty toward fellow humans.

While sometimes read as a work of political satire and brutal realism, the *Journey's* picture of Russia is anything but straightforwardly realistic (any more than Gogol's *Dead Souls* is simply a mirror held up to economic reality). Radishchev's debt to other writers—whether Vasily Trediakovsky for linguistic experimentation, the French anticolonial writer Abbé Raynal for models of slave rebellion stories, or Rousseau for his focus on one's own heart as a touchstone of virtue—makes it a highly literary work. Although Radishchev read pioneering writers of the social sciences, such as Condorcet and Adam Smith, and drew lessons on political economy and social justice from them, reading Radishchev is not like reading Adam Smith—certainly not the Adam Smith of *The Wealth of Nations*. For one thing, while Radishchev was expert at administrative memoranda, here his primary rhetorical mode is the story.

Radishchev understood the human self as an empirical being. While he does not deny that goodness may be an innate propensity, he believes that individual values are conditioned by a range of social, scientific, economic, and intellectual forces, and his use of a literary form aims to see how characters respond to competing interests. Travel literature was among the eighteenth century's most flexible literary modes, and it proved the optimal form for an inquiry into the state of Russian life—mostly rural life, but also life in the capitals—at that time. Episodes provide an opportunity to perform, in virtuous and sympathetic acts, the principles that the narrator holds to be universal. The *Journey* contains many stories intended to arouse emotional responses from readers, mainly indignation at injustice. Displays of philanthropy, fellow feeling, and sympathy provide essential narrative moments for demonstrating how sensibility is meant to work. But Radishchev's manner is not to let readers, or participants, indulge their feelings simply as an emotional reflex without considering the cause of their indignation. Sentimental fiction of the period encouraged readers to weep openly, because the shedding of tears was a display of feeling and affirmation of sensibility that required cultivation. For the historian Lynn Hunt, the seeds of revolution in France lay in the gradual development of sensibility brought on by literary movements.[11] For Radishchev, the facile demonstration of virtue was insufficient, and the difficult manner he devised for the *Journey* may strive to promote reading of a particularly thoughtful kind. One role of Radishchev's narrator is to bring home the social component in roused feeling by framing it in the conceptual vocabulary of sensibility, social contract, and the law. Does this reflect a mistrust of the efficacy of fiction? Radishchev most likely did not share the view, widespread in the eighteenth century (and enshrined in Russia by the neoclassical theorist Alexander Sumarokov in his "Epistle on Poetry," 1748), that fiction corrupted. His Sternean moments of digression and plotting are not a facile imitation of the sentimental style. They show a commitment to the underlying belief that narration can re-create empirical reality and affect sensibility especially strongly when written in a style that is antisentimentalist or at the very least not Karamzinian or Sternean.

Journey narratives require some form of itinerary and movement in time and space as an axis of development. The form is highly flexible, permitting embedded stories, anecdotes related second- or even thirdhand, and multiple forms of place description, such as historical excursus or a highly aesthetic type of picturesque. Stories in Radishchev's *Journey* do not extend beyond the book's basic unit of the chapter. Yet over the course of the book, a set of case studies develops in the demonstration of moral principles advocated by the narrator and other storytellers. Like the picaresque, the travel narrative depends on the staging of random encounters and stories told or overheard before the voyager can continue. For instance, in the chapter "Spasskaya Polest," when the narrator parts with the victim of a shipwreck whose extended tale has been reproduced in the previous chapter, "Chudovo," he overhears the conversation of an official and his wife concerning a corrupt boss and his taste for oysters. Listening is just as important as observing; the narrator must remain attuned to the stories he hears from others, anecdotes that expand the range of topics treated. In the same chapter, after the narrator meets an unfortunate passenger who is being ruined in the law courts, he responds to his interlocutor's distress physiologically, which results in an allegorical dream that affords an interior vision. Sometimes, as it happens, the narrator need not go anywhere to become a witness to tales about miscarriages of justice.

For Radishchev, forms of discourse and forms of discovery go together. In travel literature, we frequently see that tenets held to be universal face challenges in local practices and customs, forcing the narrator to raise questions about beliefs, their origins, and their validity. Performativity is one important technique in the way the work lays bare the epistemological foundations of certain ideas. In the chapter "Bronnitsy," the narrator has a religious experience we could call a revelation. One effect of the scientific revolution that preceded the Enlightenment—in which no discoveries were more important than Newton's theories of light—was to generate religious controversy, questioning whether revelation afforded a privileged verification of the divine in the workings of man or whether the only basis for explanation of natural effects was empirical and scientific. Reconciling science or natural philosophy and Christian dogma occupied much of the intellectual energy of the period, and Radishchev was well informed on the range of heterodox views, from deism to materialist atheism, that faced Christian theology (topics he treated later in his treatise *On Man, His Mortality, and Immortality*). In "Bronnitsy," the traveler arrives at a place that had once been the location of a pagan cult in the pre-Slavic period and where now a small church stands. His travel in this instance becomes imaginary as he envisions himself "transported to antiquity." The purpose of his time travel and indulgence in an imagined act of divination is to learn the future. In his emotional stupor, the traveler enters a state similar to that of the initiate into Masonic mysteries. He hears a divine voice reproaching him for trying to pierce the "impenetrable shield of unknowability" and explaining that limits in human knowledge are a form of self-protection designed by a divinity to preserve man in a state of blissful ignorance. Thunder, the sign of the pagan god Perun, peals and seemingly confirms the truth of this conclusion. However, it impels the traveler to meditate further on the nature of names for the divine, from the Eastern and classical gods to the Christian God, and to end with an evocation of "O my God!" The traveler's declaration of his monotheistic faith is nondenominational and based on an inner belief that spells the difference, he states, between the believer and the atheist. The institutions of religions, their practices and their buildings, are transient and therefore an insufficient basis for belief in the divine. Ultimately, the traveler concludes, as did Plato and Rousseau, that religion is a personal matter based on an individual aptitude to hear "a secret voice." That affirmation, however, is not the last word. The chapter ends with a quotation adapted from Joseph Addison's *Cato* that presents a vision of cosmic destruction in which "something" will persist even beyond the extinction of the stars and the cooling of the sun. What Radishchev means exactly is a matter for speculation, but he does not call this energy "God" and seems to associate it with Nature. In mentioning "the crush of worlds," Addison's lines seem to side with an idea fashionable in the eighteenth century, starting with the French philosopher Fontenelle (whose treatise *On the Plurality of Worlds* was translated into Russian in 1728 by the highly European and pro-Petrine prince Antiokh Kantemir) that there is a multiplicity of worlds. This concept was long seen as a challenge to Christian dogma. How could one reconcile the idea of multiple worlds with the account of Genesis? Did it mean that there were multiple gods? In this chapter, Radishchev acknowledges that historically there have been many names for a supernatural power but finds that since empirical proof for the existence of God cannot be produced definitively, it is one's own spiritualism that convinces best. This short chapter turns out to be a demonstration of the anthropology of religion and a typical example of Radishchev's method in making plots out of philosophical inquiry.

Traditional readings of Radishchev's book have seen it largely as a damning satire, a critique of serfdom and the serf economy, and there is no denying the force with which it exposes all sorts of social ills and evils that arise from abuses of power. These range from corporal punishment and the corruption of the judicial system to sexual exploitation and bribe taking. Far from blaming Catherine for all these ills, Radishchev focuses attention on the newly ennobled—small landowners who advanced up the social ladder through service to the state in the reigns of monarchs from Peter to Catherine II. But Radishchev's fall from grace was arguably more a story of aspirations disappointed than tyranny opposed: he was not an advocate of revolution and preferred reform, even hoping that Catherine would take to heart his advice on renovating Russian laws to address human exploitation, economic and often sexual. For all his use of sad stories to illustrate the types of exploitation brought about by fundamental inequalities of class, economic situation, and gender, Radishchev keeps alive a more positive undercurrent. In two chapters bearing the subtitle "Project for the Future," he imagines the promise of a virtuous monarch and state. Radishchev employs here one of his favorite words, a term that is hard to translate: *blazhenstvo*. Meaning "bliss," "prosperity," "the common good," and "felicity," and distinct from "good fortune" (*schastie*), it comes up time and again as a reminder that the human condition has the potential for much happiness when social conditions are reasonable. Late in life, Radishchev became a reader of Condorcet, a great advocate of the rationalist reform of society, whose belief in gender equality and the progress of the human spirit he seems to have shared. The optimism of his century may have been one reason for a critique of Russia born of aspirations for improvement. In 1790, after serving under a monarch who had enshrined social reforms in several important legislative packages, Radishchev hoped for more, and the *Journey* can be read as his attempt to synthesize in one complex literary work a lifetime spent in various forms of study—of natural and comparative law, the laws of the Russian Empire, and systems of taxation, as well as natural philosophy, as science was called in the eighteenth century.

TRANSLATING THE *JOURNEY*

Until the eighteenth century, the written form of the Russian language derived strongly from the ecclesiastical Church Slavonic. The rise of a secular literature accompanied the development of a new vernacular idiom marked by a more modern vocabulary, conversational tone, and varied patterns of syntax. While Radishchev can be an effective storyteller, he did not adopt for the *Journey* the newer style that had become the norm in Russia in the 1790s, famously crafted by the other great prose writer of the age, Nikolai Karamzin (1766–1826). On the contrary, for his *Journey*, Radishchev developed an artificially archaic and difficult style, not only using and overusing existing Church Slavonic forms but also creating his own "Slavonicized" expressions. This linguistic oddity has occasioned much comment and criticism, and even native Russians find the laborious syntax, neologisms, and pseudo-Slavonic register a challenge.

The only English translation of Radishchev's 1790 travelogue was published by Harvard University Press in 1958. Two translators worked on it: first Leo Wiener (1862–1939), who died before publishing his translation; and then Roderick Page Thaler, who edited Wiener's translation and supplied it with an introduction, notes, and index. As Thaler informs the reader in his preface, the Harvard historian Michael Karpovich served as his chief consultant during this work. Thaler labeled Radishchev a poor prose writer, seeing the style of his *Journey* as monotonous, repetitive, uneven, awkward, and often old-fashioned against Karamzin as a benchmark. Such a characterization indicates that Thaler (and, most probably, the original translator Leo Wiener as well) never suspected that Radishchev's idiosyncratic writing was a consciously created stylistic device, part of his design to make his travelogue effective as a literary work.

All readers of the *Journey* know that it is a difficult read. Anyone who has looked at other writings by Radishchev will have seen ample counterevidence that he was also entirely able to write clear prose. The question is why Radishchev devised a style designed to make the reader work hard at the meaning. Many passages in the *Journey* are not simply outdated (as Thaler believed) but artificially archaic, as has been demonstrated by a number of scholars who have examined Radishchev's linguistic choices. The fact that some chapters of Radishchev's book are written in a language that does not present any difficulties to the reader, while others are almost beyond comprehension—so difficult are their word choice, grammar, and syntax—indicates that Radishchev intentionally changed the degree of difficulty to influence his readers in a certain way. It is significant, for example, that the most linguistically obscure chapters and passages usually present the most provocative ideas. Finally, as has been pointed out by historians of the Russian literary language, Radishchev's reputation as a bad writer originates with Karamzin and his supporters, who used his archaized style as an example of incorrect linguistic choices in a quarrel that took place in the early nineteenth century with the cultural conservative Alexander Shishkov (1754–1841) and his followers.

Radishchev thus wrote in a Russian that was deliberately awkward. He is not, whatever anyone says about the literariness of the final product, a writer without a style or a theory of style. To be sure, norms of prose idiom in the period remained in flux, with translators and original writers still experimenting with German and Latin syntactic forms as well as other prosodic features. Yet Radishchev's purpose was not to experiment with style for its own sake. He wished to create a distinctive medium to convey his ideas and to manipulate the reader. One of the most curious and innovative chapters in the work is "Tver." It brings together, for a rare change, both prose and poetry and represents an extended critique of poetic forms in Russia, as illustrated by the many stanzas excerpted from Radishchev's much longer poem *Liberty*. It is almost needless to say that a poem with that title, while presented under the guise of a lesson in style, also has a political message, and stanzas cited for their rhetorical verve vividly denounce tyranny. Much of what has been said about Radishchev's prose holds true of his poetry. In the hope of preserving that sense of a form overloaded with drama and abstraction, we have translated the excerpts in verse, approximating the ten-line stanza and rhyme scheme. And while Radishchev's narrative mode can be fleet, the sometimes turgid style and strained idiom function as a tool for focusing the reader's mind on his sometimes abstract philosophical vocabulary and on the highly visual element of his prose, which relies on anecdote, episode, and verbal painting as a way of aligning emotional and intellectual content. Radishchev took his epigraph for the *Journey* from Trediakovsky's *Tilemakhida*. That work was a poetic resetting of an important didactic prose work by the French archbishop Fénelon, used as a textbook in the education of princes. In his foreword to *Tilemakhida*, Trediakovsky stressed the idea that poetic language not only has to differ from colloquial language but also has to correspond to the content of the work and, furthermore, to impart wisdom to the reader. By the late eighteenth century, the work's neoclassical style and Trediakovsky's highly artificial idiom struck readers as passé. The epigraph signaled that the *Journey* would combine narrative and didacticism in the manner of

Fénelon's original educational treatise-cum-novel and that Radishchev, in spite of popular opinion, intended to emulate Trediakovsky in devising a work of linguistic and stylistic idiosyncrasy.[12]

Certain aspects of Radishchev's style cannot be reproduced in a translation. But can a translator completely disregard the stylistic complexion of the *Journey* and not try at least to indicate the strangeness of Radishchev's word choice, grammar, and syntax? A smooth Radishchev would be a contradiction in terms. But once syntactic effects specific to Radishchev are acknowledged as daringly disjointed in the original, and once it is accepted that only some of these are eligible to be transferred formally intact into English, stretching translation to be the faithful re-creation of all aspects would be self-defeating (the most notorious example of such translation perhaps being Vladimir Nabokov's *Eugene Onegin*). We recognize that the *Journey*'s stylistic opacity is part of its meaning and have aimed to retain it where that can be done without undue stretching of the norms of English. At the same time, we have also aimed to use a more straightforward English syntax where understanding is little changed by ironing out syntactic knots in isolated phrases. The question is about the overall reading experience, and we trust that the effects of Radishchev's idiosyncratic style and voice, where they have been captured, will give a sufficient cumulative sense of what kind of writer he is.

The reader may find it helpful, then, to have an outline here of the problems posed and solutions offered. These can be discussed in terms of layout, syntax, and lexicon. Radishchev's paragraphing has been retained in this translation. The original printed punctuation of the *Journey* is very much that of an eighteenth-century work, sometimes with very long sentences broken up by commas alone or cast in a succession of verbal phrases choppily strung together. Following the example of Laurence Sterne, an important model in the writing of sensibility across Europe including Russia, Radishchev makes expressive use of the dash. He also uses the dash inconsistently to indicate dialogue and direct speech, and our practice has been to modernize and substitute quotation marks and also delineate voices where long dashes are originally missing.

Syntax is the most challenging feature for the reader and the translator. The complexities relate to the length and structure of subordinate clauses; the framing of scenes with near formulaic expressions to indicate arrivals and departures; and nonstandard word order. There are certainly meaningful instances in which chapters adopt a more formal tone and periodic syntax commensurate with serious topics. It is to be expected that Radishchev would formulate complex observations about the law, social justice, institutions, and other matters in complex ways, just as many of the writers of the period he read on these topics did. Some of the challenges posed by Radishchev's syntax are not unique to him and are familiar from much prose of the period. The page-long sentences to be found sometimes in the *Journey* are no more archaic than the majestic sentences typical of eighteenth-century English prose masters such as Samuel Johnson, Edward Gibbon, or David Hume. In English translation, preserving all of the far-ranging sentences that spool into the nesting of clauses would prove counterproductive. There are times when little of the sense has been lost, in our view, by dividing a page into a succession of shorter sentences or by shaping clauses made up of a string of phrases joined by commas with the more explicit divisions of semicolons, colons, and dashes to stave off syntactical implosion. We have generally preferred to normalize the Russian syntax to produce a readable English version. In some instances, the result is an English text that is actually more accessible than a knotty piece of Russian.

Length is not the only syntactic feature that is difficult to preserve. Radishchev's use of gerunds and participles in setting up narrative sequences looks overcomplicated by the standard of Karamzin and Pushkin. Typically, "having arrived," "having approached," "having driven up," characters then speak or act. This is a point of grammar that, arguably, conveys how consistently Radishchev emphasizes process—action and reaction—and his technique in setting up encounters and moving characters on and off is to underscore the beginnings and endings of speech acts. Similarly, Radishchev piles up clauses when creating coordinated actions, as in the following sentence, given here literally: "The having arrived detachment rescued this barbarian from the hands of peasants raging against him." Our translation turns gerundive and participial clauses into the more modern prepositional clauses that suit contemporary English, as seen in this example: "When it arrived, a detachment of soldiers rescued this barbarian from the hands of his angry peasants." Radishchev can also string together a series of separate subject-predicate combinations, punctuated only with commas. He condenses into a short space entire chain reactions of perception, feeling, and response. These are the moments that are meant to lead to moral realizations, in the reader if not always in the fictional characters. Our translation imitates his pattern, separating successive verbs only with commas.

The rules of word order in Russian, while not absolutely fixed, had acquired a more regular shape by the late eighteenth century. The freedom Radishchev exercises creates an unsettling impression and is undoubtedly one of his most effective devices for slowing down the reader. In these instances, the translator can decide on a case-by-case basis how much of the original wording can be conveyed—or, essentially, how much strain can be tolerated. In general, it is our assumption that when readers open a translation, they accept that there is a barrier of a kind between them and the original and wish for accuracy of meaning without constant stylistic reminders of how remote the original stands from the present idiom. This may be all the more so with a text removed in time by a couple of centuries. The matter is not simple, however, given our firm belief that form and content are inextricably linked in Radishchev's travelogue. For that reason, we have also sought, at least in some places, to retain an element of syntactic irregularity when the formal complication of the original underpins the message. The bookish language Radishchev uses, especially his insistence on nouns emphasizing process, focuses attention on the internal physical, moral, and psychological processes that define human action, reaction, and interaction in the *Journey*. The translator into English has some flexibility in choosing between noun forms based on a single root to express action—e.g., "attaining the shore" versus "the attainment of the shore." We have followed the English preference for nouns based on participles such as "attaining" but have tried to retain denominative nouns where the effect isn't grossly stilted, because Radishchev's point is to turn the mundane into some larger category (and vocabulary is a tool of defamiliarization). The clumsiness typical of this text should, however, feel like bumps in the road and not like obstacles, as Radishchev's narrative often hits its stride to achieve momentum and focus.

Ultimately, a modern translation cannot imitate closely Radishchev's style and remain readable; at the same time, the translator cannot disregard entirely the artificial idiom Radishchev created for the *Journey*. We have aimed to provide the readability of an accurate but accessible modern version while also making reasonable efforts to convey an impression of the stylistic dimension of a work of extraordinary historical importance.

NOTES

1. *Biografiia A. N. Radishcheva, napisannaia ego synov'iami*, ed. D. S. Babkin (Moscow: Izdatel'stvo Akademii nauk SSSR, 1959), 37.
2. *Biografiia A. N. Radishcheva*, 54.
3. M. I. Sukhomlinov, *A. N. Radishchev, avtor "Puteshestviia iz Peterburga v Moskvu"* (St. Petersburg: Izdatel'stvo Imp. Akademii nauk, 1883), 6.
4. See V. A. Zapadov, "Istoriia sozdaniia 'Puteshestviia iz Peterburga v Moskvu' i 'Vol'nosti,'" in A. N Radishchev, *Puteshestvie is Peterburga v Moskvu. Vol'nost'* (St. Petersburg: "Nauka," 1992), p. 518. Radishchev expanded "Spasskaya Polest," "Podberezye," "Novgorod," "Zaitsovo," "Edrovo," "Torzhok," and "Chornaya Gryaz."; see *Slovar' russkikh pisatelei XVIII veka*, vol. 3 (St. Petersburg: "Nauka," 2010), p. 21.
5. Cited in Sukhomlinov, *A. N. Radishchev, avtor*, 54, and *Biografiia A. N. Radishcheva*, 65.
6. Sukhomlinov, *A. N. Radishchev, avtor*, 31, 43. Honoré Gabriel Riqueti, comte de Mirabeau, was a French nobleman who supported the revolution but was later disgraced when he was found to be in the pay of France's enemies.
7. *Biografiia A. N. Radishcheva*, 64. Yemelyan Ivanovich Pugachev had led a peasant uprising earlier in Catherine's reign.
8. Sukhomlinov, *A. N. Radishchev, avtor*, 36.
9. The life written by Pavel Radishchev, as published in the *Biografiia A. N. Radishcheva*, amply draws on the documentary sources concerning Radishchev's case ("delo o Radishcheve").
10. In Aleksandr Nikolaevich Radishchev, *A Journey from St. Petersburg to Moscow*, trans. Leo Wiener, edited with an introduction and notes by Roderick Page Thaler (Cambridge, MA: Harvard University Press, 1958), vii. Leo Wiener (1862–1939) began teaching at Harvard in 1896 and eventually became the first American professor of Slavic literature. He was a prolific translator (including of the works of Tolstoy). As Thaler reports in the preface to the book, this "translation was first prepared by Professor Leo Wiener of Harvard University, who unhappily did not

live to see it published" (vii). Thaler then reports that he "thoroughly revised" Wiener's translation and supplied the introduction and notes (viii). The Cold War position on Radishchev as a radical and early advocate of "liberal" values, meaning broadly republican or specifically democratic, was a view that took hold in scholarship of which David Marshall Lang, *The First Russian Radical. Alexander Radishchev, 1749–1802* (London: Allen & Unwin, 1959) is an example.

11. Lynn Hunt, *The Family Romance of the French Revolution* (Berkeley: University of California Press, 1992).
12. Radishchev's interest in Trediakovsky as a stylistic rule giver was genuine, informing his *Monument to a Dactylic-Trochaic Knight* (*Pamiatnik daktilokhoreicheskomu vitiaziu,* 1801). A formally heterogeneous work, part dialogue, part treatise, concerning aspects of versification and earlier influential writers such as Trediakovsky and Lomonosov, it can be read as an extension of the exploration of norms of Russian prosody versus prosody adapted from European models to which the chapter in the *Journey* "Tver" is dedicated.

NOTE ON THE TEXT

Our source for this translation is the text published in A. N. Radishchev, *Puteshestvie iz Peterburga v Moskvu. Vol'nost'*, ed. V. A. Zapadov (St. Petersburg: Nauka, 1992). While we have followed this edition's paragraphing and punctuation, we have departed from its tendency to print certain words (usually religious in meaning, such as "God" and related pronouns) in lowercase and normalized according to standard English practice. In this regard, the first edition as printed by Radishchev has been of somewhat limited use because the book, like many eighteenth-century editions, is typographically inconsistent, although in most instances these words appear in uppercase. While we have also consulted the edition published by Andrei Kostin, generally based on Zapadov's text, and taken note of his more liberal use of uppercase, we have preferred to follow the usage in the original 1992 publication.

All notes in the backmatter are by the translators. The footnotes in the text are of two kinds: simple translation glosses, indicated by "—Trans.," and Radishchev's own footnotes, some of which include lengthy passages from his source documents. The transliteration of Russian words in English follows house style and in most instances omits the soft-sign and other diacritics. Chapters are not numbered in Radishchev's original; that numbering is added for the readers' convenience.

JOURNEY FROM ST. PETERSBURG TO MOSCOW

A monster stout, wicked, huge, with a hundred maws, and barking.

Tilemakhida, vol. II, book XVIII, verse 514

A.M.K.

To my dearest friend

Whatever my heart and mind should wish to create, O! you who share all my feelings, may it be dedicated to you! While our opinions differ in many respects, your heart beats in tune with my own—and therefore you are my friend.

I glanced about myself: my soul became lacerated by the sufferings of humanity. I directed my gaze to my inner being and beheld that the woes of man come from man, and often only because we do not inspect closely what surrounds us. Can nature treat its children so meanly, I said to myself, that it has hidden truth forever from a person who strays innocently from the right path? Can it be that this fearsome stepmother has created us to feel woes alone and never bliss? My reason flinched at this idea, and my heart thrust it far away. I found man's consoler inside himself. "Tear away the veil from the eyes of natural feeling—and I shall be gratified." This voice of nature reverberated loudly through my constitution. I rose up from the desolation into which empathy and the capacity to feel had cast me. I felt within myself strength enough to resist error; and—unspeakable joy!—I sensed that everyone has the ability to participate in doing good for his equal.—This thought prompted me to write what you are about to read. But if, I told myself, I find someone who approves my intention, who for the sake of this good goal will not fault the unfortunate representation of my thought, who will suffer together with me over the woes of his brethren, who will fortify me in my progress—will not, then, the fruit of the work I have undertaken be greater? . . . Why, why indeed should I seek far for such a person? My friend! Near my heart do you dwell, and may your name illuminate this beginning.

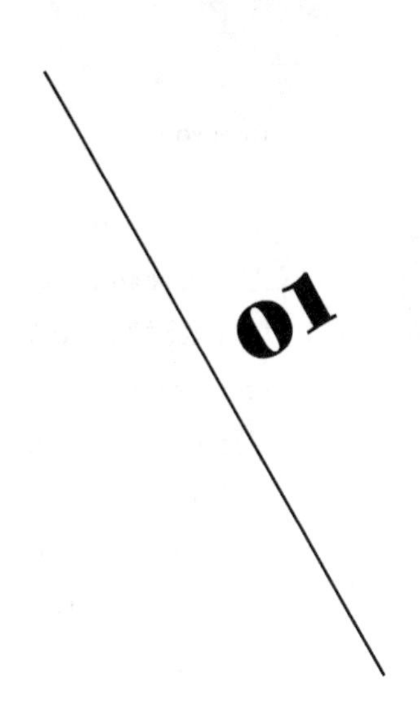

DEPARTURE

After supping with my friends, I settled in the carriage. As was his habit, the coachman drove the horses at full pelt, and within a few minutes I was already outside the city. Parting from one who has become essential to every minute of our existence is difficult, even for a short time. Parting is difficult. But blessed is he who is able to take his leave without smiling: love or friendship secure his comfort. As you pronounce "farewell," you weep. But remember that you will return and let your tears at this imagining vanish like dew before the face of the sun. Blessed is he who weeps while hoping for a consoler;[1] blessed is he who sometimes lives in the future; blessed is he who lives in a reverie. His being is enriched, his joys multiply, and tranquility preempts the gloom of sadness by placing images of rejoicing in the mirrors of the imagination.—I lie in the carriage. At last the din of the postal carriage's bell, grown wearisome to my ears, summoned beneficent Morpheus. The sorrow of my departure, pursuing me into my deathlike state, represented me to my imagination on my own. I beheld myself in an expansive valley that had lost all pleasantness and variety of greenery owing to the heat of the sun. No source of freshness could be found here, there were no shady trees for the alleviation of the heat. Alone, abandoned, a hermit in the middle of nature! I shuddered. "Wretch," I cried, "where are you? Where has everything that used to entice you vanished? Where is that which made your life pleasant? Could it be that the enjoyments of which you partook were a dream and fancy?" When the carriage hit the rut that happened to be in the road and woke me up it was a lucky stroke.—The carriage stopped. I lifted my head a bit. I see: in a deserted place stands a house of three stories. "What have we here?" I asked my driver. "The postal station." "Where then are we?" "In Sofia." He was meanwhile unharnessing the horses.

SOFIA

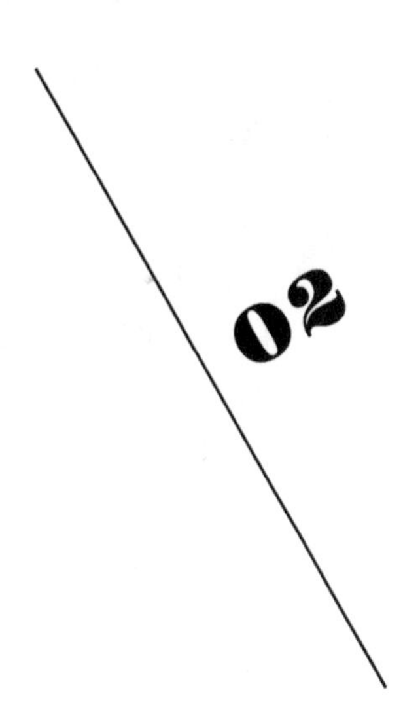

Silence everywhere. Plunged as I was in my ruminations, I failed to note that my carriage had long been standing without horses. The coachman who took me there drew me out of my pensiveness. "Sir, Master, a tip!" Although such a collection is not legal, everyone pays willingly in order not to travel according to the decrees.[2] The twenty kopecks served me well. Anyone who has traveled by post coach knows that a voucher for horses is an indemnifying letter without which there is a cost to every purse (excepting that of a general, possibly). Taking it out of my pocket, I walked with it in the way people sometimes walk holding a cross to protect themselves.

The stationmaster was snoring when I lightly took him by the shoulder. "Who the devil is pestering me? What an idea it is to travel out of the city at night. There are no horses; it is still very early. Why don't you go over, then, to the tavern, drink some tea or have a sleep?" Once he spoke, Mr. Stationmaster turned to the wall and again began to snore. What to do? I shook him again by the shoulder.[3] "Damn it, as I've already said there are no horses," and Mr. Stationmaster covered his head in the blanket and turned away from me.—"If the horses are all in use," I reflected, "then it is unfair to be disturbing the sleep of the stationmaster. But if the horses are in the stable. . . ."—I decided to find out whether Mr. Stationmaster was telling the truth. I went out to the courtyard, found the stable, and there discovered up to twenty horses; and while it is true that their bones were showing, they would have dragged me as far as the next station. From the stable, I returned to the stationmaster, shook him much harder. It seemed to me that I had the right to do so after discovering that the stationmaster had lied. He jumped up hastily and before he managed to force his eyes open asked, "Who has arrived? It isn't. . . ." But he came to his senses when he saw me and said, "Apparently, young fellow, in the past you acquired the habit of treating drivers this way. They used to be beaten with sticks. Times have changed." The stationmaster lay down in the bed angrily. I wanted to treat him like those drivers of olden times were treated when they were exposed as liars. But the generosity I had exercised in giving a gratuity to the city driver aroused the drivers of Sofia to harness horses for me as fast as possible, and just as I was planning to take it out on the back of the stationmaster, a little harness bell chimed in the courtyard. I remained a good citizen. That is how twenty copper kopecks spared a peace-loving man from prosecution, my children from the example of intemperance in anger; and from this I learned that reason is a slave to impatience.

The horses hurry me along. My coachman has launched into song, a mournful one, as usual. Anyone who knows the melodies of Russian folk songs will admit that they contain something that expresses spiritual anguish of the soul. Practically all the melodies of songs of this kind have a soft tone.—One could learn from the people's ear for music how to govern. You can find the composition of our nation's soul in these songs.[4] Consider the Russian person: you will find him to be thoughtful. If he wants to dispel boredom or if, as he himself calls it, he wants to have good time, he goes to a tavern. When in his cups he is spontaneous, bold, disagreeable. Should something cross him, he will quickly begin an argument or a fight.—The barge-hauler who visits a tavern with his head hanging and returns bloodied from fisticuffs is able to explain a lot of the Russian history that until now was enigmatic.

My coachman sings.—It was the third hour of the morning. Just like the little bell earlier, now his song effected sleep in me.—O Nature, having wrapped man at birth in the swaddling cloth of bitter sorrow, dragging him through the length of his entire life span across the harsh ridges of fear, grief, and sadness, you gave him sleep as a joy.—One goes to sleep, and everything has ended.—To an unhappy man waking up is unbearable. Oh, how pleasant death is for him. If it truly is an end to bitter sorrow.—All-benevolent Father, would you really avert your gaze from a man who bravely ends a troubled life? To you who are the source of all blessings a sacrifice of this kind is proffered. You alone give strength when one's nature, shaken, falters. This is the voice of the Father summoning His child to Him. You gave me life, to You I return it, it has already become futile in this world.

TOSNA

03

When departing from Petersburg, I thought the road would be top quality. All who traveled on it following the sovereign thought so.[5] And so it truly was, but only for a short spell. In dry weather, the dirt scattered on the road gave it a smooth surface; once soaked by the rains, it produced heaps of mud in the summer that made the road impassable. . . . Bothered by the bad road, I quit my carriage and entered the postal cabin with the intention of resting. In the cabin, I found a traveler who, seated at the usual sort of long rustic table in the front corner, was sorting papers and asking the postmaster to order that his horses be provided as soon as possible. In response to my question as to who he was, I learned he was solicitor of the old school, heading to Petersburg with a mass of tattered papers that he was reviewing at that moment. I entered unhesitatingly into conversation with him, and this is the talk we had: "Kind Sir! I, your most humble servant, was a registrar in the Service Archive[6] and had occasion to use my position for my own advantage. To the best of my modest ability, I compiled genealogies of many Russian lineages, based on clear deductions. I can prove their princely or noble lineage for several hundreds of years.

I can restore practically any person's princely standing, having traced his origin from Vladimir Monomakh or Rurik himself.[7] Kind Sir!," he continued, pointing to his papers, "the entire nobility of Great Russia ought to purchase my work, and pay for it sums not paid for any merchandise. But if your Excellency, your Honor, or Most Honorable—I do not know what your honorific is—will allow, these people do not know what they need. You are aware just how much the pious Tsar Fyodor Alexeyevich of blessed memory offended the Russian nobility when he abolished *mestnichestvo*. This strict law placed many distinguished princely and royal clans on equal footing with the nobility of Novgorod.[8] But then our pious ruler, the Emperor Peter the Great, brought about their total eclipse with his Table of Ranks.[9] He opened the path for everyone to the acquisition of a noble title through military and civil service and trampled in the dirt, so to speak, the ancestral nobility. Our Reigning Most Gracious Mother, ruling most kindly, confirmed these earlier ordinances with a supreme regulation on the nobility, that alarmed just about all our lineal nobles since ancient families were ranked lower than all the rest in the register of nobles.[10] But a rumor is going round that soon an additional decree will be published and that those families whose noble origins can be proven for either two hundred or three hundred years will be awarded the title Marquess or some other eminence, and that they will enjoy before other families a certain distinction. For this reason, kind Sir, my work ought to be thoroughly agreeable to the entire ancestral nobility. But everyone has his detractors.

"In Moscow I found myself in the company of some young whippersnapper lordlings and offered them my work in order to recoup, thanks to their generous attention, the paper and ink I had wasted, if nothing else. But instead of a favorable reception I met with mockery and, having out of grief left behind this capital city, I embarked on the road to Piter[11] where, as we know, there is much more enlightenment." Having said this, he bowed deeply from the waist,[12] drew himself up and stood before me in an attitude of great reverence. I understood his meaning, got . . . out of my wallet . . . and once I'd given that money to him, advised him that when he came to Petersburg he should sell his paper by the weight as wrapping to peddlers, since many would have their heads turned by the imaginary title of Marquess, and he would be the reason for the rebirth in Russia of an evil that had been abolished—bragging of an ancient pedigree.

LYUBANI

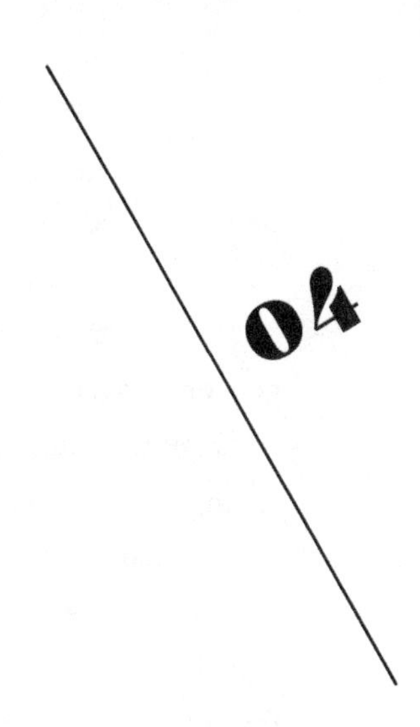

It is all the same to you, I think, whether I was traveling in the summer or winter. Perhaps it was both winter and summer. This happens not infrequently with travelers: they go out on a sleigh and come back in a cart.—It is summer.—The road paved with logs wore out my sides; I got out of the carriage and continued on foot. While I was lying in the carriage, my thoughts were turned toward the immeasurability of the world. Detaching myself spiritually from earth seemed to alleviate the bumps of the carriage.—But spiritual exercises do not always distract us from corporeality; and for the preservation of my sides I went on foot.—At a distance of several paces from the road I saw a peasant plowing a field. It was hot out. I looked at my watch.—Forty minutes past noon.—I set out on Saturday.—Today is a day of rest.—The peasant at the plow surely belongs to a landowner who does not take quitrent from him.[13]—The peasant plows with great diligence.—The field is evidently not the landlord's.—He turns the plow with unbelievable ease. "Godspeed," I said as I approached the plowman who, without stopping, completed the furrow that had been started. "Godspeed," I repeated. "Thank you, Master," said the plowman, shaking out the plowshare and moving the plow over to a new strip. "You must be a Schismatic if you plow on Sundays."[14] "No, Master, I make the sign of the cross in the straight fashion," he said, showing me three fingers held together.[15] "But God is merciful, when one has strength and family, He does not will one to die of hunger." "But can it be that during the entire week you have no time to work so that you cannot skip Sundays, not even during the hottest period?" "In the week, as it happens, Master, there are six days, and six times a week we go to work for the master;[16] and toward evening we bring the hay left in the forest to the landowner's courtyard if weather permits; and on holidays the womenfolk and gals go for walks into the forest for mushrooms and berries. May God grant (making the sign of the cross) some rain this evening. Master, if you, too, have peasants then they are praying for the same thing from the Lord." "I have no peasants, my friend, and that is why no one curses me. Is your family large?" "Three sons and three daughters. Going on ten years is the eldest little one." "How do you manage to provide their bread if you are free only on holidays?" "Not only the holidays are ours, since the night is ours too. If the likes of me are not lazy, then we will not die of hunger. Do you not see that one horse is resting, and when this one grows tired, I will then take the other; this way the work goes smoothly." "Do you work this way for your owner?" "No, Master, it would be sinful to work the same way. At the plowing he has a hundred hands for each mouth, while I have two for seven mouths, you know how to count. Why, even if one busted a gut working for the landowner they'll never say thank you. The landowner will not pay the poll tax[17] for you; he will not let you off the hook for a single sheep or chicken; nor a piece of canvas or butter. For us it's a good life when the master collects the quitrent, even better if he does not have an estate manager. It is true that sometimes even good owners collect more than three rubles per soul; but still, this is better than the corvée. Now a new arrangement has also come into use, it is called *letting villages out for rent.* But we call this 'complete betrayal.' A poor tenant skins the peasants alive, he even helps himself to our best season. In the winter he bars us from the carrier trade and from seeking work in the city. You work no end for him because he pays the poll tax for us. What a diabolical idea it is to lend one's own peasants to another for work. At least you can complain about a bad estate manager, but to whom do you complain about a renter?" "My friend, you are mistaken, the laws prohibit the tormenting of people." "Tormenting? This is true; nonetheless, Master, I venture you would not want to be in my skin." Meanwhile the plowman harnessed the other horse to the plow and, after starting another strip, parted from me.

The conversation of this landworker aroused in me a multitude of thoughts. The first to come to mind were the inequalities within the peasant estate. I compared state peasants with serfs.[18] Both one and the other live in villages; but one group pays a fixed amount, while the other must be prepared to pay what the owner wishes. One set are judged by their equals, while the others are dead in the eyes of the law except in criminal matters.—It is only when he breaks the social bond, when he becomes a malefactor, that a member of society acquires the recognition of the government that protects him! Such an idea made my blood boil.—Be afraid, hard-hearted landowner, I see your condemnation on the brow of each of your peasants.—Plunged into these meditations, I unwittingly turned my gaze to my servant who, seated in front of me in the carriage, was swaying from side to side. Suddenly, I felt coursing through my blood a rapid chill that, by driving the heat upwards, forced it to spread across my face. The shame I felt in my very innards caused me nearly to weep.—In your rage, I said to myself, you are fixated on the proud owner who wears out his peasant in his field. But do you not do the same, if not worse? What crime has your poor Petrushka committed so that you prevent him from availing himself of sleep, the sweetener of our woes, the greatest gift of nature to an unfortunate man?—He receives payment, is fed, clothed, I never whip him with birches or a truncheon (O moderate man!)—and you think that a piece of bread and scrap of woolen cloth give you the right to treat a being who is your equal like a spinning top, and the only thing of which you can boast is that you do not strike him so often as to make him spin faster. Do you know what is written in the first law code of all, in the heart of each person? If I strike someone, he too may strike me.—Recall that day when Petrushka was drunk and was not in time to dress you. Recall the slap you gave him. Oh, if he had come to his senses while drunk and answered you in proportion to your demand!—And who gave you power over him?—The law.—The law? And you dare abuse this sacred name? Unfortunate one! . . .—Tears trickled from my eyes and this was the state I was in when the postal nags dragged me to the next station.

CHUDOVO

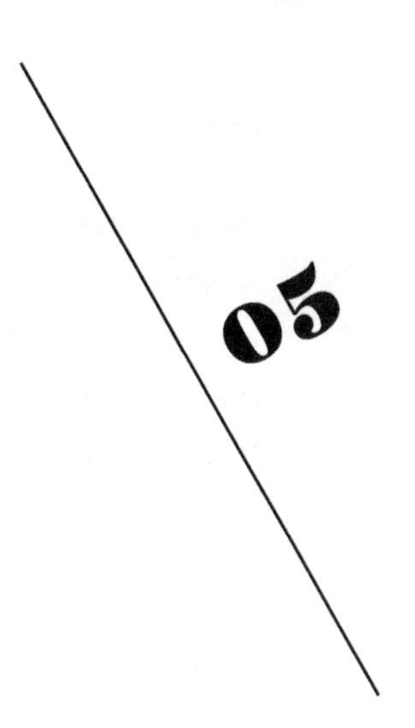

No sooner had I entered the postal cabin than I heard from the street the sound of the postal bell, and several minutes later my friend Ch...walked into the cabin. When I left him behind in Petersburg he had had no intention of leaving there immediately. An extraordinary event had prompted a man with the quick temper of my acquaintance to leave Petersburg, and here is what he recounted to me:

"You were already set for your departure when I left for Peterhof. I spent the holidays enjoyably, insofar as it is possible to enjoy oneself amidst hubbub and intoxication. But eager to turn my journey to benefit, I took the decision to make the trip to Kronstadt and Sisterbek[19] where I had been told great changes had taken place. In Kronstadt, I stayed for two very pleasurable days, feasting my eyes on the multitude of foreign ships, the stone-clad fortress of Kronstadt, and the buildings that were going up rapidly. I had been curious to see the plan of the new Kronstadt and with pleasure envisaged the beauty of the projected construction. In a word, the second day of my visit ended happily and pleasantly. The night was calm, clear and the salubrious air filled my feelings with a certain tenderness that is easier to feel than to describe adequately. I decided to turn the beneficence of nature to my advantage and, for at least once more in my life, to take pleasure in a magnificent view of a sunrise, one which I had not yet managed to catch on a smooth watery horizon. I hired a twelve-oar sloop and departed for S...

"We sailed successfully for about four *versts.** The monotonous sound of the oars incited in me a doziness, and my languid gaze barely came to life at the passing shimmer of drops of water as they fell from the tips of the oars. My poetic imagination was transporting me to the lovely pastures of Paphos and Amathus.[20] Suddenly the sharp whistle of a wind arising from afar drove sleep away, and my drowsy eyes met the sight of densely packed clouds whose dark mass, it seemed, drove them toward our heads and threatened to crash down on us. The glassy patina of the water began to ripple, and calm gave way to an incipient splashing of the swells. I was glad about this sight as well; while I observed the magnificent features of nature, I can say without boastful arrogance that what had begun to terrify others gladdened me. From time to time, like Vernet, I exclaimed, "Oh, how pleasing!"[21] But the wind, as it gradually strengthened, compelled me to think about reaching the shore. The sky became completely dark from the thickening of somber clouds. The strong surge of the waves crippled control of the helm, and the gusty wind, now forcing us upward onto wet ridges, now plunging us into the clifflike ruts of watery swells, sapped the rowers' forward-moving force. Involuntarily going with the flow of the wind we were borne along randomly. That was when we began to dread

* two and two-thirds miles—Trans.

even the shore; and then what might have comforted us on a successful voyage began to drive us into despair. Nature at that hour looked mean to us, and we now grew angry with her for not displaying her awesome majesty by flashing lightning bolts and disturbing our hearing with peals of thunder. But hope, which accompanies man into extremes, fortified us, and we bucked one another up as best we could.

"Borne by the waves, our vessel suddenly stopped, immobile. All our joint efforts were insufficient to shift us from the spot where it stood. While essaying to dislodge our vessel from what we thought was a shoal, we did not notice that, meanwhile, the wind had almost completely died down. Bit by bit the sky was cleared of the clouds obscuring the deep blue. But incipient dawn, instead of bringing us joy, revealed our dismal position. We perceived clearly that our sloop was located not on a shoal but rather wedged between two large rocks, and that no amount of effort would suffice for its rescue from there undamaged. Imagine, my friend, our situation. No matter what I can say, it would pale by comparison with my feeling. And even if I were able to give sufficient outline of each movement of my soul, it would still be too feeble to reproduce in you sensations similar to the ones that arose and crowded in my soul at that moment. Our vessel stood in the middle of a stone ridge encircling the bay and extending to S... We were positioned about one and a half *versts** from the shore. The water had begun to enter our vessel from all sides and threatened to submerge us completely. In the final hour, when the light begins to depart from us and eternity yawns, then all distinctions erected between people by convention fall away.

* one mile—Trans.

Man becomes simply man: hence, as we saw our end approaching, each of us forgot his status, and each thought about our salvation as we bailed out water, as handily as each could. But what was the use of that? As much water accumulated again as was sluiced by our combined efforts. To our most heartfelt distress, there was no passing vessel in sight either nearby or far off. Even had one appeared to bring joy to our stares, it would have intensified our despair on distancing itself from us in order to avoid the same fate as our own. In the end, our captain was more accustomed than the rest to the hazards of marine accidents because he had, perhaps unwillingly, coldly stared at death during various naval battles in the last Turkish War in the Archipelago.[22] For that reason, he resolved either to save us by saving himself or to perish in this virtuous attempt. By staying put, we were certain to perish. He left the boat, and, stepping from stone to stone, aimed his advance toward the shore, attended by our heartfelt prayers. Initially, he progressed quite confidently, hopping from stone to stone, wading through the water in the shallows or swimming across when it got deeper. Our eyes never left him. At length, we saw that his strength had begun to give out, since he traversed the stones more slowly, frequently stopping and sitting down on a rock to rest. It seemed to us that he was sometimes deliberating and uncertain about the continuation of his way. This roused one of his companions to follow him to give him aid should he see that he was exhausted in trying to reach the shore; or to reach it himself if the captain failed. Our gaze was trained now on one, now on the other, and our prayer for their safety was unfeigned. At length, the second of these imitators of Moses in the crossing of depths of sea on foot without a miracle halted on a rock, while we lost the first from view altogether.

"Each one's agitations, until now hidden and trapped as it were by terror, became overt with the disappearance of hope. Meanwhile, the water level in the vessel rose, and our increasing labors to evacuate it began noticeably to exhaust our strength. A person of a violent and impatient constitution tore at his hair, bit his fingers, cursed the very hour of his departure. A person of meek spirit who had long felt, perhaps, the impact of stultifying slavery, sobbed, dousing with his tears the bench on which he lay prostrate. Another, in remembering his home, children, and wife, sat as if petrified, considering not his own but their destruction, since they were fed by the fruits of his labor. Since, my friend, you know me reasonably well, you can divine the state of my soul. I shall tell you only that I prayed to God assiduously. Finally, we all began to give way to despair, for our boat was more than half inundated, and we stood in water up to our knees. Not infrequently we considered whether to quit the vessel and to walk along the stone reef to the shore; however, that one of our fellow passengers had already been on the rock for several hours and that another had disappeared from view suggested to us that the danger of walking across was greater than might have actually been the case. Amidst these sorts of woeful ponderings, we spotted on the water near the opposite shore, at some distance from us that was hard to define precisely, two black specks that appeared to be moving. The black something seen by us, and it was moving, seemed gradually to get bigger; finally, as it approached, it presented clearly to our eyes two small ships heading straight for the place where we were located in a state of despair that exceeded hope by a hundred times. As when in a building sealed off from light suddenly a door opens and a ray of daylight, having swooped rapidly into the middle of the gloom disperses it, expanding to the furthest boundaries of the entire building, so a ray of hope in salvation suffused our souls when we saw the ships. Despair turned to rapture, woe into jubilation, and there was a danger lest our joyous movements and clapping bring disaster upon us before we could be wrested from danger. But a hope of living, returning to our hearts, again roused thoughts that slumbered during our peril about the difference in ranks. This time it served the common good. I cut short excessive rejoicing, being liable to turn harmful. After a bit of time, we saw two large fishing boats approaching us and at their reaching us we saw that in one of them was our savior who, having walked along the stone reef to the shore, had sought out these boats in order to extricate us from certain death. Without dawdling one bit, we left our boat and sailed to the shore in the boats that had come to us, not forgetting to retrieve from the rock our fellow companion who had spent about seven hours there. No more than half an hour passed before our boat, wedged in the rocks, relieved of the weight, floated up and disintegrated completely. While we sailed to the shore in a state of rejoicing and the raptures of salvation, Pavel—that was the name of the fellow passenger who saved us—told us the following:

"'Having left you in imminent danger, I hastened along the rocks to the shore. The wish to save you gave me unnatural strength, but about one hundred *sazhen*[*] from the shore my strength began to give out, and I began to despair for your salvation and my life. Yet after I lay for half an hour on a rock, I rose with renewed vigor and with no further rest crawled, as it were, all the way to the shore. There I sprawled on the grass, and after I rested about ten minutes, got up and raced

* two hundred yards—Trans.

with all my might along the strand to S... And while the depletion of my energy was considerable, by remembering you I made it to the spot. It seems as though the Heavens wanted to test your resolve and my patience, since I had found no boat for your rescue on the strand or in S... itself. Finding myself practically in despair, I thought there was no better place to seek help than from the superior officer there. I ran to the house where he lived. It was already the seventh hour. In the entrance room I found the sergeant of the local guard. Having briefly told him why I came and of your situation, I asked him to awaken Mr..., who was still resting. Mr. Sergeant said to me, "My friend, I do not dare." "What! You do not dare? When twenty people are drowning, do you not dare to wake up one who can save them? You good-for-nothing are lying, I will go myself. . . ."—Mr. Sergeant grabbed me by the shoulder not very courteously and shoved me out the door. I almost burst with indignation. But thinking more about the danger you were in than about the insult to me, and about the hard-heartedness of the man in charge and his deputy, I rushed off to the sentry station at a distance of about two *versts*[*] from the wretched house from which I had been ejected. I knew that the soldiers living there kept boats in which while sailing around the bay they collected cobbles for sale as paving stones. I was not mistaken in my hopes. I found these two small boats and my rejoicing was indescribable: you shall all be saved! If you had drowned, then I would have thrown myself into the water after you.' Pavel was dissolving into tears while saying this. Meanwhile, we had reached the shore. When I got out of the boat I fell on my knees, raised my hands to the sky. 'Almighty Father,' I cried out, 'it pleased You that we should live.

* one and one-third miles—Trans.

You led us to a test, may it be Your will.' This, my friend, is a weak depiction of what I felt. The terror of the last hour had pierced my soul; I saw the moment when I would cease to exist. What would I be? I know not. A terrifying unknown. Even now I can feel it: my hour has struck; I am dead; motion, life, feeling, thought, all vanish instantly. Imagine, my friend, that you are on the edge of the grave, wouldn't you feel the spasmodic chill pouring through your veins and prematurely cutting off your life. O my friend!"—But I have digressed from my narrative.

My prayer completed, rage entered into my heart. Is it possible, said I to myself, that in our age, in Europe, near the capital, in sight of a great ruler such inhumanity has occurred? I recalled the Englishmen incarcerated in the jail of the Bengal Subedar.*[23]

"I groaned in the depths of my soul.—In the meantime, we arrived at S... I thought that the superior officer, once up, would punish his sergeant and grant respite at least to those who had suffered

---

* The English took under their protection in Calcutta a Bengal official who defected to them when liable to execution for taking bribes. The Subedar was offended, rightly so, gathered a force, attacked the city and took it. He ordered the English prisoners of war to be thrown into a crowded dungeon in which they expired in half a day. Of their total only twenty-three people remained. These unfortunate ones promised great sums of money to their guards to get them to tell the ruler of their plight. Their cries, their groans reached the people who felt anguished for them, but nobody wished to tell the ruler. "He is resting" was the answer given to the dying Englishmen; and not a single person in Bengal thought he must disturb momentarily the sleep of this tyrant to save the lives of one hundred fifty unfortunate men.

What is a tyrant? Or rather what sort of people is it that has become accustomed to the yoke of tyranny? Is it reverence or fear that keeps them bowed down? If it is fear then the tyrant is worse than the gods to whom man sends either a prayer or a lament during the night or in the hours of day. If it is reverence, then one can induce man to respect the contributors to his woes: a miracle that is possible only because of superstition. What is there to wonder at more, the ferocity of the sleeping nabob or the cravenness of him who does not dare to wake him?—Raynal, *Histoire des Indes*, vol. 2.

on the water. This was my hope when I went straight to see him at home. But I was so exasperated by the action of his deputy that I was unable to moderate my words. When I saw him, I said, 'Sir! Have you been informed that several hours previously twenty men were in danger of losing their lives at sea and requested help from you?' He responded to me with the greatest indifference as he smoked tobacco: 'I was told about this just now, but I was sleeping at the time.' Thereupon I began to tremble in a humanity-incensed rage. 'If your sleep is so sound you should have given the order to be roused with a hammer to the head when people are drowning and in need of your aid.' Guess, my friend, what his reply was. I thought I was going to have a stroke when I heard it. He said to me, 'That is not my duty.' I lost patience: 'As if it were your duty to kill people, wretch. And you wear decorations, you are in charge of others! . . .' I was unable to finish my speech, practically spat in his mug, and walked right out. I tore my hair from indignation. I was devising a hundred schemes for taking revenge on this beastly superior officer not for myself but on behalf of humanity. When I regained control, by rehearsing in my memory many examples I grew convinced that my vengeance would be fruitless; that I would then get the reputation for being either mad or an evil person. I became resigned.

"Meanwhile, my people called on a priest who greeted us gladly, warmed and fed us, gave repose. We spent an entire twenty-four hours with him, benefitting from his hospitality and refreshment. The next day, after finding a large sloop, we arrived safely in Oranienbaum.[24] In Petersburg, I recounted this to one person and another. All empathized with the danger I had been in, all disparaged the hard-heartedness of the superior officer; no one wanted to broach the matter with him. If we had drowned then he would have been our murderer. But someone said: 'It was not prescribed as his duty to save you.' Now I shall part with the city forever. There is no way I shall return to this den of tigers. Their only enjoyment is to maul one another; their joy is to torment the weak till they croak and to kowtow to power. And you wanted me to settle in the city! No, my friend," said my storyteller, jumping up from his seat, "I shall go where people do not go, where they do not know what man is, where his name is unknown. Farewell." He got into his carriage and galloped off.

SPASSKAYA POLEST

06

I galloped in pursuit of my friend at such speed that I reached him while he was still at the next postal station. I attempted to persuade him to return to Petersburg, attempted to demonstrate to him that the small and partial flaws of a society will not destroy its bonds, just as a speck that falls into the expanse of the sea is unable to trouble the surface of the water. But he answered me brusquely: "If I, a small speck, sank to the bottom, it is of course clear that no storm would occur in the Bay of Finland. I'd be off to swim with seals, though." Taking his leave of me with obvious indignation, he sat in his carriage and departed hastily.

The horses were already harnessed, I had already lifted my leg to climb into the carriage when it suddenly began to rain. "Not a terrible misfortune," I thought, "I shall take cover under a piece of coarse fabric and stay dry." No sooner had this thought flown into my brain than I felt like I was plunged into an ice hole. Without asking my view, the sky burst a cloud open and the rain came bucketing down.—Nothing to be done about the weather. As the saying goes, "the slower you travel, the farther you go." I dismounted from the carriage and ran into the nearest cabin. The owner was going to bed and it was dark in the cabin. Nonetheless, even in the dark I asked leave to dry off. I removed my wet clothing and, placing what was drier under my head, soon fell asleep on a bench. My bedding was not exactly fluffy and did not afford me a chance to luxuriate for long. Awakening, I overheard a whisper. I could distinguish two voices having a chat between themselves. "Well, husband, give us a story then . . . ," said a female voice. "Listen, wife."

"Once upon a time. . . ." "And it's just like a fairy tale; not that one can believe a fairy tale," said the wife in a soft voice, yawning from sleep, "as if I could believe that there used to be a Polkan, Bova, and Nightingale-Robber."[25] "Well, who is browbeating you; believe if you like. But it is true that in olden times physical strength was held in respect and certain strongmen abused their powers. That's where Polkan comes in. And on Nightingale-Robber, mother mine, read the interpreters of Russian antiquity. They will tell you that he was named Nightingale thanks to his eloquence. . . . Do not interrupt my speech. And so, once upon a time somewhere there lived a governor-general.[26] In his youth he bummed around foreign lands, learned to eat oysters for which he had a keen appetite. For as long as he had little moolah of his own he refrained from his craving, eating about ten at a time, and then only when he happened to be in Petersburg. As soon as he climbed in rank the number of oysters on his table began to increase. As soon as he joined the ranks of governors-general and then had a lot of his own money, and a lot of government money at his disposal, concerning oysters he became like a pregnant female. He sleeps and dreams of eating oysters. When they are in season nobody gets any rest. His subordinates, all, become martyrs. He will eat oysters—no matter what! He sends an order to the Department to supply a courier whom he intends to dispatch to Petersburg with important reports. Everyone knows the courier will go off at a gallop to fetch oysters. No matter what, just fork out the travel costs. The departmental purse is full of holes. A messenger, equipped with a pass, travel expenses, fully prepared, wearing britches and a riding jacket, comes before His Excellency. 'Make haste, my friend,' he intones, medal-laden, 'make haste, take this envelope, deliver it to Bolshaya Morskaya Street.'[27] 'The order is to whom?' 'Read the address.' 'His . . . His. . . .' 'That's not how you should read.' 'To my Lord . . . Lor. . . .' 'Wrong . . . to Mr. Korzinkin, honorable shopkeeper in St. Petersburg on Bolshaya Morskaya.' 'I know, Your Excellency.' 'Get on with it then, my friend, and return as soon as you receive it, delay not an instant; I shall say more than one thank-you.'

"Giddy up to all three horses all the way to Piter, and direct to Korzinkin at his business. 'Welcome. That Excellency is a veritable joker, he is, sending for such rubbish from a thousand *versts*.* A good master though. Happy to serve him. The oysters here are straight from the Exchange. Tell him that they are not less than one hundred fifty a barrel, no discount, they cost us a lot. But we, I and his grace, will settle up.' A barrel was dumped into the carriage. Heading back, the courier gallops once again; he had only enough time to pop into a tavern and down two thimbles of moonshine.

"Ding-ding. . . . As soon as the bell of the postal carriage was heard at the city gates the watch officer dashes off to the governor-general (isn't it good when everything works) and reports to him that from a distance the carriage is visible and the ring of the little bell audible. He had scarce managed to get the words out when the courier darted through the door. 'Your Excellency, I have brought them.'

* six hundred and sixty miles—Trans.

'Very timely.' (Turning to the assembled:) 'A genuinely good man, responsible and not a drunkard. Quite a few years now that he makes the journey twice a year to Petersburg, and as for how many times to Moscow—I cannot fathom. Secretary, write a recommendation for promotion: "For his numerous deeds in dispatches and his most accurate completion thereof I reward him with promotion by a rank. . . ." '

"In the treasurer's expenditure ledger there is an entry: 'by the motion of his Excellency to the courier N.N. dispatched to S.P. with the most important documents is granted from the reserve budget travel expenses in both directions for three horses. . . .' The ledger of the accounts department has gone off for an audit but there's not a whiff of oysters.

"On the recommendation of the General Sir etc. IT WAS ORDAINED: Sergeant N.N. is to be a warrant officer. . . . Well, wife," said the male voice, "this is how to progress in the ranks, and what do I gain by serving flawlessly? I shall not get ahead by one jot. According to the rules, it is mandated that competent service be rewarded. A Tsar's generosity is only as good as his ministers. That's the way it is here with our Mr. Treasurer. Once again, for the second time by his order, I am being sent for criminal trial. If we had been more hand in glove, that would have been like being a pig in clover."[28] "Enough, Klementich, of talking nonsense. Do you know why he doesn't like you? Because you take payments for the exchange from everyone and don't share round with them."[29] "Shush, Kuzminichna, quiet, what if someone is listening." Both voices fell silent, and I fell asleep again.

In the morning I learned that a treasury clerk and his wife, who departed for Novgorod before daylight, had slept in the same cabin with me.

While the horses were being harnessed for my cart, another carriage drawn by three horses arrived. A man wrapped in a large cape got out, and the hat he wore, its floppy brim pulled down, hindered me from seeing his face. He demanded horses even though he did not have a pass, and since lots of coach drivers swarmed round him and haggled, he did not wait for them to finish their bargaining and impatiently said to one of them, "Harness up quickly, I shall give you four kopecks per *verst*."* The coachman ran for the horses. The others, seeing that there was nothing left to negotiate about, all walked away from him.

I stood not more than five *sazhen*† from him. Without removing his hat, he approached me and said, "My dear sir, give an unhappy man whatever you can." This astonished me exceedingly, and I could not refrain from telling him that I was surprised by his request for aid when he had not bargained over the fee for the relay horses and paid twice as much as others did. "I see," he told me, "that in your life nothing untoward has crossed you." So firm a response I liked a good deal and I readily pulled out my wallet. . . .: "Do not disapprove of me," I said, "I cannot do any more for you right now; but if we travel to our destination then perhaps I shall do something more." My intention in this respect was to make him come clean, and I was not wrong. "I see," he said to me, "that you still possess sensitivity, that mixing in society and the quest for your own advantage have not closed your heart to it. Allow me to take a seat in your carriage, and

* two-thirds of a mile—Trans.

† ten yards—Trans.

bid your servant to take a seat in mine." Meanwhile, our horses were readied, I fulfilled his wish—and off we go.

"Ah! dear sir, I find it hard to fathom that I am unfortunate. No more than a week ago was I cheerful, gratified, had no want, was loved, at least so it seemed since my house daily was full of people sporting marks of distinction already conferred; my table was always like some magnificent celebration. But if my vanity was greatly satisfied, the genuine bliss the soul enjoyed was its equal. After repeated, initially fruitless efforts, approaches, and failures, finally I had acquired for a wife her whom I desired. Our mutual passion, delighting feeling and soul, presented everything to us in a bright guise. We never saw a cloudy day. We attained the zenith of our bliss. My spouse was pregnant and the hour of her delivery approached. Fate had decided that all this bliss would collapse in a single instant.

"I hosted a luncheon, and a multitude of so-called friends, having gathered, were sating their idle appetite at my expense. One of those present, someone who privately did not like me, began to speak to someone next to him, albeit in a low voice though still sufficiently loud so that what was spoken could be audible to my wife and many others. 'Are you not aware that our host's case in the criminal court has already been decided. . . .'

"You will think it odd," said my fellow traveler, addressing his speech to me, "that a man not in service and in the situation I describe could become subject to a criminal trial. That is how I thought for a long while—indeed, until the moment when my case, after wending its way through the lower courts, reached the highest one. This is what it was about. I belonged to the merchant estate. In putting my capital into circulation, I took a share in a private concession. My inexperience was the reason I trusted a devious man who, having personally been caught in a crime, was banned from a business concession and, supposedly on the evidence of his accounts, it seemed a substantial liability had accumulated against him. He vanished, I remained available, and it was decided to recover the financial shortfall from me. After doing calculations the best I could, I found that the sum for which I was liable either did not exist; or, if it did, was very small, and for that reason asked that a final account be struck with me, since I was the guarantor. But instead of complying with my request, it was decided to seek the arrears from me. This was the first unjust ruling. To this a second one was added. At the time I became the guarantor of concession, I owned no property; but, as was customary, a forfeit was issued on my property in the civil court. A strange matter it is to prohibit the selling of property that does not exist as an actual possession! Afterwards, I bought a home and made other acquisitions. At this very time, chance allowed me by rising in rank to move from the merchant estate into that of the nobility. Seeing an advantage, I had an opportunity to sell my home on good terms, having completed its purchase in the very same court of justice where the forfeiture of my belongings was established. This was attributed to me as a crime, for there were people whose satisfaction was overshadowed by the blessings of my life. The solicitor of fiscal matters produced a denunciation of me to the effect that I evaded payment of the liability when I sold the house, I swindled the civil court of justice, by having identified myself by the status to which I belonged rather than the one in which I was at the time of the purchase of the home. It was to no effect that I said that no prohibition could exist against something that was not my property; it was to no effect that I said that at the very least any remaining property had to be sold first and the payment of the debt had to be financed through that sale before resorting to other means, and that I had not hidden my social position since I bought the house when already a nobleman. All this was rejected, the sale of the home was annulled, for a fraudulent deed I was condemned to be stripped of my rank. 'And they are now demanding that,' said the narrator, 'our host be brought to court so that he be placed under arrest until the case has been concluded.'

"While narrating the last part, the storyteller raised his voice. As soon as my wife heard this, she embraced me, cried out: 'No, my friend, I am going with you.' She was unable to speak any more. Her limbs went all weak and she fell senseless into my arms. I lifted her from the chair, carried her into the bedroom, and have no idea how supper ended.

"On reviving after a bit of time, she began to feel pains auguring the approaching birth of the fruit of our passion. No matter their severity, the thought that I would be under arrest caused her such alarm that she just said over and over: 'I too will go with you.' This unhappy event hastened the birth of the baby by an entire month, and all the efforts of the midwife and doctor summoned to help were in vain and could not prevent my wife from giving birth the next day. Far from calming down with the birth of the child, the movements of her soul greatly intensified and caused her a fever.—Why should I carry on in this narration? On the third day after delivery my wife died. You will well believe that seeing her suffering I did not leave her for a minute. In my grief, I altogether forgot my legal case and condemnation. The day before the death of my darling, the unripe fruit of our passion also died. The illness of the mother had completely absorbed me and this loss was at the time not great to me. Imagine," said my storyteller, clutching at his hair with both hands, "imagine my situation when I saw that my beloved was parting from me forever.—Forever!" he cried in a wild voice. "But why do I flee? Let them put me in prison. I am already insensate; let them torture me, let them deprive me of life.—O barbarians, tigers, fierce serpents, gnaw at this heart, release into it your excruciating poison.—Forgive my frenzy, I think that I shall soon lose my mind. As soon as I imagine the minute when my darling was leaving me I become oblivious to everything and the light in my eyes goes dark. But I shall complete my tale. When I was prostrate in such dire grief over the lifeless body of my beloved, one of my sincere friends ran to me: 'They have come to take you into custody, the police are in the courtyard. Flee from here, a carriage is ready at the back gates, be on your way to Moscow or another place of your choosing and live there until it becomes possible to alleviate your lot.' I didn't heed what he was saying but he overcame me by force and took and carried me out with the help of his servants and placed me in the carriage; and remembering then that I needed money gave me a purse in which there were only fifty rubles. He went into my study to find money there and bring it out to me; but on discovering an officer in my bedroom he had time only to send word to me to leave. I do not recall how I was driven the distance to the first station. My friend's servant, having told me all that had happened, took his leave, and at present I am travelling wherever my eyes lead, as the saying goes."

The tale of my fellow traveler moved me ineffably. Is it possible, I said to myself, that under a government as lenient as our present one, such acts of cruelty could have been committed? Is it possible that there were judges mad enough that for the enrichment of the Treasury (which is what in reality one could call every unfair confiscation of property for the satisfaction of the Treasury's need) they deprived people of their property, honor, life? I considered the way in which such an occurrence might reach the ears of the supreme power. For I thought justly that in an absolute government only the very top can be dispassionate in relation to everyone else.—But can I not assume myself his defense? I will compose an official petition to the highest level of government. I shall give a detailed account of the incident and shall present the miscarriage of justice of those who judged and the innocence of the victim.—But they will not accept a petition from me. They will ask what right I have to do it, will require of me power of attorney.—What right do I have? The right of suffering humanity. The right of a man deprived of his property, honor, deprived of half of his life who is in voluntary exile in order to avoid shameful incarceration. And for this one needs power of attorney? From whom? Is it insufficient that my fellow citizen suffers?—There is no need even for that. He is a human being: there is my right, my power of attorney.—O God-Man! Why did You write Your law for barbarians? Even while they cross themselves in Your name, they make bloody sacrifices to malice. Why were You so clement to them? Instead of a promise of future punishment, You should have exacerbated their current punishment; and by inflaming conscience commensurate with their evildoing You would have given them no peace day and night until through their suffering they expunged the evil they committed.—Such thoughts so exhausted my body that I fell into a deep sleep and did not wake up for a long time.

Juices stirred up by my thoughts flowed to the head while I slept and, disturbing the tender substance of my brain, stimulated in it the imagination.[30] Countless pictures appeared to me in my sleep, but vanished like thin vapors in the air. Finally, as can happen, some sort of mental fiber, strongly stirred by the vapors rising up from the internal vessels of the body, vibrated longer than the others, and this is what I saw in my dream.

It appeared to me that I was the Tsar, Shah, Khan, King, Bey, Nabob, Sultan, or something else from these designations for one sitting in power on the throne.

The place of my enthronement was made from pure gold and, cleverly clad with precious stones of different colors, shone radiantly. Nothing could compare with the brilliance of my raiment. My head was adorned with a laurel wreath. Around me were disposed signs attesting my power. Here a sword lay on a column carved from silver. On it were depicted naval and land battles, the conquest of cities, and more in that vein. Everywhere at the top one could see my name, borne by the Genius of Fame, flying over all these triumphs. Here my scepter was visible, laid out on sheaves laden with wheaten spokes carved out of pure gold and imitating nature perfectly. Hung on a firm beam scales were showing. On one of the scales lay a book with the inscription "Law of Mercy"; on the other there was also a book with the inscription "Law of Conscience." The royal orb, carved out of a single stone, was being supported by a gaggle of cherubs carved from white marble. My crown was elevated higher than everything and reposed on the shoulders of a mighty giant, its edging supported by Truth. A serpent of enormous proportion, forged from shining steel, lay entwined round the entire base of the royal seat and, clasping the end of its tail in its maw, represented eternity.

But these inanimate depictions did not declare my might and majesty on their own. The ranks of government stood around my throne, catching my glances with timid obsequiousness. At a certain distance from my throne an innumerable multitude of people thronged: their motley clothes, facial expressions, deportment, appearance, and bearing heralded the difference between their tribes. Their nervous silence assured me that they were all subject to my will. On the sides, on a somewhat elevated spot, women in great numbers stood in the most enchanting and magnificent clothes. Their glances revealed their pleasure in beholding me, and their desires would have been quick to anticipate my own if they happened to recur.

The most profound silence presided in this assembly. It seemed that all were in expectation of some important event upon which the peace and welfare of the entire society depended. Turned inward and feeling within my soul deeply rooted boredom arising from a monotony that quickly palls, I rendered my debt to nature and stretching my mouth from cheek to check yawned with all my might. All understood the emotional workings of my soul. Suddenly, dismay cast its gloomy veil over the features of merriment, the smile flew off the mouth of tenderness, and the gleam of jubilation from the cheeks of satisfaction. Twisted glances and glaring round revealed an unexpected onset of horror and pending woes. Sighs were heard, the piercing harbingers of sorrow; and groaning, restrained by the presence of terror, had begun to resound. Already with swift steps did despair progress in the hearts of all, and mortal convulsions, worse than death itself.—Moved to the depths of my heart by such a sorrowful sight, the muscles of my cheeks imperceptibly stretched toward my ears and by distending my lips produced in the features of my face a crookedness similar to a smile, after which I sneezed very loudly. Just as when a ray of the midday sun pierces a gloomy atmosphere thickened by a heavy fog, its vital heat disperses the moisture condensed into steam and decomposes it, whereupon the lighter part rises rapidly into the immeasurable space of the ether and another, retaining in itself only the mass of its earthly particles, rapidly falls downward: darkness, omnipresent in the nonexistence of the luminous globe, instantly, entirely disappears and, having hastily cast off its impenetrable mantle, flies off on the wings of the momentary, leaving behind not even a trace of its presence.—The look of sadness, settled on the faces of the entire assembly, dispersed, then, with my smile, elation speedily penetrated the hearts of all and not a single sideways look of dissatisfaction remained. All began to exclaim: "Long may our great ruler flourish, long may he live!" Similar to a gentle afternoon breeze that sways the foliage of trees and produces in the oaks a concupiscent rustling was the joyous murmuring that carried across the entire meeting. One in a low voice uttered, "He pacified external and internal enemies, expanded the boundaries of the fatherland, subjugated to his might thousands of different nations." Another exclaimed, "He enriched the state, he expanded internal and external commerce, he loves the arts and sciences, encourages tillage and manufacture." Women tenderly proclaimed, "He did not permit thousands of useful citizens to perish, saving them from a fatal end before they could suckle." Another person with grave demeanor declared, "He increased the revenue of the government, relieved the people of tax burdens, supplied them secure nourishment." The young, extending in ecstasy their hands to the sky, spoke, "He is merciful, just, his law is the same for all, he considers himself its first servant. He is a wise lawgiver, a righteous judge, a zealous upholder of the law, he is greater than all kings, he grants liberty to all."

Speeches of this kind, striking the tympanum of my ear, reverberated loudly in my soul. These praises looked plausible in my mind, since they were accompanied by external displays of sincerity.

Taking them to be such, my soul rose above the usual field of vision; it expanded in its essence and, by encompassing all things, touched degrees of Divine wisdom. But nothing was comparable to the pleasure of self-approval that came with the issuing of my orders. The chief commander I ordered to proceed with a large army to the conquest of a land separated from me by an entire zone of stars. "Sire," he responded to me, "the very fame of your name alone will vanquish the peoples populating this terrain. Fear will precede your arms, and I shall return bearing the tribute of mighty kings." To the chief admiral of the navy I uttered, "Let my ships scatter across the seas, let the unknown peoples espy them, let my flag be known in the North, East, South, and West." "I shall fulfill it, Sire." And off he flew to do my bidding like a wind created to fill the sails of a ship. "Proclaim to the most distant limits of my realm," spake I to the guardian of the laws, "that today is my birthday, let it be marked forever in the annals as a general amnesty. Let the prisons be opened so that criminals may walk out and return to their homes as if they had strayed off the righteous path." "Your mercy, Sire, is the image of the All-Beneficent Being. I hasten to announce the joyous news to fathers who grieve for their children and wives for their husbands." "May there be erected," spake I to the Chief Architect, "the most magnificent buildings as shelters for the Muses, may they be adorned with multifaceted imitations of nature; and may they prove indestructible, like these heavenly dwellers, for whom they have thus been made ready." "O most wise," he responded to me, "if the elements were to obey the commands of your voice and, mustering their might, were to establish in deserts and wastelands vast cities that surpass in their grandeur the most famous of antiquity, how insignificant then will the labor of the zealous implementers of your commands be. You spake, and the raw supplies of construction already obey your voice." "Let," spake I, "the hand of generosity be opened forthwith to shower the remains of excess on the helpless, so that superfluous treasures may be returned to their source." "O most generous Sovereign, given to us by the Almighty, a father to your peoples, enricher of the pauper, may your will be done." At my every utterance all those standing before me exclaimed joyously, and not only did a clapping of hands accompany my speech, but even anticipated my thought. Only one woman from the entire assembly, leaning steadily against a column, emitted sighs of woe and displayed a look of scorn and indignation. The features of her face were stern and her dress simple. Her head was covered in a hat although all the others stood bareheaded. "Who is she?" I inquired of someone standing near me. "She is a wanderer we do not know; she calls herself Straight Seer and Eye Doctor. She is, though, a most dangerous magician, bearing poison and venom, she rejoices in grief and destruction; always gloomy, she scorns and curses everyone, she does not spare in her abuse even your sacred head." "Why, then, is such a villain tolerated in my realm? But about her—tomorrow. This day is a day of mercy and joy. Come, collaborators in supporting the heavy burden of ruling, take up a generous recompense for your labors and triumphs." Whereupon, rising from my seat, I conferred various signs of honor on those present; and the absent were not forgotten, but those who when called presented themselves with a pleasant expression had a larger share in my benefactions.

Following this I continued my speech: "Let us go, pillars of my power, fundaments of my might, let us go take delight after work. It is befitting for one who toils to partake in the fruit of his labors. It befits a Tsar to partake in joys, for he showers many on everyone.

Show us the path to the jubilee you have prepared," spake I to the organizer of festivities. "We shall follow you." "Halt," declared the female wanderer from her place. "Halt and approach me. I am a physician sent to you and others like you so that I might cleanse your vision.—What cataracts!" she exclaimed.—An unknown force compelled me to walk to her despite the fact that everyone surrounding me hindered me, even to the point of using force.

"On both of your eyes," said the wanderer, "there are cataracts, but you passed judgment on everything so decisively."[31] And then she touched both my eyes, and removed from them a thick film like a corneous layer. "You see," she said to me, "that you were blind, you were completely blind.—I am the Truth. The Almighty, moved to pity by the groaning of people over whom you reign has sent me from the heavenly sphere so that I could remove the darkness hampering the penetration of your gaze. I have fulfilled this. All things now will appear in their natural guise to your eyes. You will penetrate to the inmost of hearts. The serpent secreted in the crannies of souls can no longer hide from you. You will know your faithful subjects, those who far from you love not you but love their Fatherland: those who are always ready for your defeat if it will avenge the enslavement of man. But they will not stir up civic order untimely or needlessly. Summon them to you as friends. Banish the arrogant mob who surrounds you and who hide the disgrace of their soul with gilded raiments. For they are the real villains who obscure your vision and block my entrance to your halls. I appear to kings only one single time during their reign so they might recognize me as I am; but I never abandon the dwellings of mortals. My residence is not in the halls of kings. A guard that rings them round and keeps vigil day and night with a hundred eyes blocks my entrance into them. If I should penetrate the massed crowd, then by raising the scourge of banishment everyone around you will try to drive me from your dwelling; hence beware that I not retreat from you again. Then the words of flattery, by exhaling poisonous fumes, will restore your cataracts again, and a scab that light cannot penetrate will cover your eyes. Then your blindness will redouble; your gaze will barely penetrate as far as a step. Everything will have a cheerful appearance. Your ears will not be disturbed by groans, but your hearing will hourly rejoice in sweet song. Sacrificial incense will abide in your soul, opened to flattery. Only smoothness will fall within your sense of touch. Beneficial roughness will never shred your tactile nerves. Tremble now at such a state! A cloud will rise over your head and arrows of a vengeful thunder will be readied for your defeat. But I declare to you that I shall live in the confines of your realm. If you should ever wish to see me, if besieged by intrigues of flattery your soul thirsts for my gaze, summon me from a distance. You shall find me where my firm voice can be heard. Never fear my voice. If from the popular sphere a man arises to criticize your deeds, know then that he is your sincere friend. A stranger to hopes of reward, a stranger to servile trepidation, he will announce me to you in a firm voice. Take care and do not dare to punish him as though he were a common troublemaker. Bid him come, host him like a wanderer. For everyone who reproves the absolute power of a king is a wanderer in a world where everything trembles before him. Host him, I declare, venerate him so that, upon return, he might be able again and again to give voice unflatteringly. Hearts of such firmness, however, happen to be rare, and scarcely a single one will appear in the worldly arena in an entire century. But so that the ease of power not dull your vigilance, I make a gift to you of this ring that it might reveal your own falseness to yourself should you challenge it. For know: you have the potential to be the worst killer in society, the worst bandit, the worst traitor, the worst violator of the general peace, the fiercest enemy directing your malice at the innards of the weak. If a mother weeps for a son killed on the battlefield, or a wife for her husband—you will be to blame; for the threat of captivity can hardly justify the murder known by the name of war. If the field becomes barren, if the children of the tiller of the soil lose their lives because their mother's breast is dry without healthful food—you will be to blame. So divert your gaze onto yourself now and on all those before you, check the implementation of your orders, and if your soul does not shudder from horror at such a sight, then I shall leave you and your palace will be effaced forever from my memory."

The visage of the wanderer after speaking seemed cheerful and of a radiance of material brilliance. Looking at her poured joy into my soul. No longer did I sense in her swells of vanity or the pomposity of arrogance. I sensed in her peace; the turmoil of worldly vanity and overwhelming lust for power did not affect her. My garments, brilliant as they were, seemed spattered with blood and drenched in tears. On my fingers I could see the remains of a human brain, my feet stood in mire. Those standing around me looked even more vile. Their entire innards looked black and consumed by the dull flame of insatiability. They trained on me, and on one another, ravaged glances dominated by rapaciousness, envy, cunning, and hatred. My commander, sent off to conquer, was drowning in luxury and making merry. There was no discipline among the forces; my soldiers were treated worse than cattle. Nobody cared for their health or nourishment; their lives were worthless; they were deprived of their statutory pay, which had been used for elaborate uniforms, which they did not need. The majority of new soldiers were dying from the neglect of their leaders or their unnecessary and untimely severity. Funds allocated for maintenance of the militia were in the hands of the organizer of festivities. Medals were not the prerogative of bravery but rather of vile obsequiousness. Before me, I saw one commander renowned by word of mouth whom I had honored with the distinctive marks of my favor; now I saw clearly that all his excellent distinction consisted in the fact that he had been the instrument of the satisfaction of the lust of his superior, and that there was no occasion when he might have shown bravery since he had not seen the enemy even from afar. These were the sorts of soldiers from whom I was expecting new crowns of laurel for myself. I averted my gaze from the thousand woes arising before my eyes.

My ships, those designated to cross the most distant seas, I saw sailing about the mouth of the harbor. The commander, who had flown on the wings of the wind to fulfil my commands, his limbs spread out on a soft bed, was indulging in voluptuousness and sex in the embraces of a hired female arouser of his lusts. On a map he commissioned of a journey undertaken in his imagination could be seen new islands in all parts of the world, abounding in the fruits appropriate to their climate. Vast lands and multiple peoples had come to life from the paintbrush of these new travelers. A majestic description of this journey and acquisitions in a flowery and magnificent style was already sketched by the gleam of nocturnal torches. Gold boards were already prepared as a cover for such a significant composition. O Cook! Why did you spend your life in toils and privation?[32] Why did you finish it in such a lamentable way? On board these ships, having begun the journey happily and completed it happily, you would have made as many discoveries while sitting in the same spot (and in my kingdom) and would have been equally celebrated, since you would have been honored by your sovereign.

The suspension of punishment and the amnesty of criminals were the triumphs in which in the blindness of my soul I, too, had most pride—and they scarcely figured on the scale of civic activities. My command was either undermined completely because of misguided directions, or did not have the desired effect because its application was perverse and implementation slow. Clemency became a commercial matter: the gavel of pity and magnanimity struck for the one who paid more. Instead of being renowned among my people as merciful in the pardoning of guilt, I acquired the reputation of a deceiver, hypocrite, and baleful joker. "Refrain from your clemency," cried thousands of voices, "do not make an announcement of it in a magnificent discourse if you do not intend to fulfil it. Do not add sarcasm to insult, burden to the feeling. We slept and were calm, you disturbed our sleep; we did not wish to keep vigil since it would have been over nothing." In the establishing of cities I saw only the squandering of public money, not infrequently bathed in the blood and tears of my subjects. In the erection of magnificent buildings there was often coupled with extravagance a failure to understand true art. I saw interior and exterior designs that were utterly tasteless. Their appearances belonged to the age of the Goths and Vandals.[33] In the dwelling prepared for the Muses I did not see the springs of Castalia and Hippocrene flowing beneficially;[34] this reptilian art hardly dared to lift its gaze above a horizon delimited by routine. Architects, hunched over the sketch of a building, did not think about its beauty, but about how they would acquire thereby a fortune for themselves. I felt disgust at my overblown vanity and averted my eyes.—But the outpouring of my generosity wounded my soul worse than anything.

In my blindness, I had thought that one could do no better than use public money that was surplus for governmental needs on helping the destitute, clothing the naked, feeding the hungry, supporting the victims of an adverse accident, or rewarding the dignity of someone indifferent to gain and merit. But how grievous it was to see my acts of generosity showered on the rich, on the flatterer, on the perfidious friend, on a sometimes secret murderer, on the traitor and violator of the social contract, on the panderer to my predilections, on the indulger of my weaknesses, on the woman flaunting her shamelessness. The feeble sources of my generosity barely rewarded modest merit and shy distinction. Tears poured from my eyes and hid from me such pitiful images of my thoughtless generosity.—I now saw clearly that the signs of honor conferred by me were always given to the undeserving. Struck by the glitter of such sham bliss, inexperienced merit always ended up following the same path as flattery and baseness of spirit in the hope of honors, that coveted fancy of mortals; but by dragging its feet unevenly it always became weak with its initial steps and was condemned to find satisfaction in the approval it gave itself, convinced that worldly honors are ash and smoke. Seeing in everything such depravity caused by weakness and the cunning of my ministers; seeing that my tenderness was directed to a woman who in my love sought to satisfy only her vanity and who arranged only her appearance to my delight even as her heart felt disgust for me—I roared in a fury of anger: "Unworthy criminals, villains! Declare why you abused the trust of your master? Come now before your judge. Tremble in the hardness of your villainy. How can you justify your deeds? What can you say in your own excuse?" There he is, I shall summon him from an abode of humiliation. "Come," I said to the elder whom I observed hiding on the edge of my demesne at the bottom of a hut covered in moss, "come to lighten my burden; come and restore peace to a pained heart and disturbed mind." Once I said this, I directed my gaze on my station, I understood the extent of my obligation, I understood wherefrom derive my right and power. I was shaken to the core of my being, I felt dread at my office. My blood went into severe tumult and I awoke.—Scarcely coming to, I grabbed myself by the finger but no ring of thorns was on it. Oh, if only it had been even on the little finger of kings!

Ruler of the world, if in reading my dream you should smile sarcastically or furrow your brow, know this: the female wanderer I saw has flown away far from you and shuns your palace.

07

PODBEREZYE

I awoke with difficulty from a mighty sleep in which I had so many dreams.—My head was heavier than lead, worse than sometimes happens to drunks with a hangover after spending a week or so on a binge. I was in no condition to continue my trip and be shaken up on wooden axles (my carriage did not have springs). I got out a book of household remedies, searched whether there might be a recipe for headache caused by delirium in sleep and in a waking state. Although medication always traveled with me just in case, it was according to the proverb "each wise man has his share of foolishness": I was not forearmed against delirium, which is why my head, when I arrived at the postal station, was in worse shape than a wig stand.

I remembered that in the old days my nanny of blessed memory, Klementevna, Praskovya by name and therefore called Friday,[35] was a coffee lover and used to say that it gave relief from the headache. "If I drink about five cups," she used to say, "I then see the light, but without it I would die within three days."

I set about getting nanny's medicine, but not having the habit of drinking at once five cups or so, I offered the leftovers of what had been prepared for me to a young man who sat on the same bench albeit in a different corner by the window. "I thank you in earnest," he said, having taken the coffee cup.—His amicable look, plucky glance, polite bearing, it seemed, did not go with the long demi-caftan and hair slicked down with kvass. Pardon me, reader, for my conclusion, I was born and grew up in the capital, and if someone is not curly-haired and powdered then I reckon him to be a nonentity. If you are a country bumpkin yourself and do not powder your hair do not blame me if I were to walk past you and not even look.

My conversation with my new acquaintance about this and that settled down. I learned that he was from a seminary in Novgorod and was on foot to Petersburg to pay a visit to an uncle, who worked as a clerk in the administration of the province. His main aim, though, was to find an opportunity for acquiring learning. "Our store of means to enlightenment is deeply inadequate," he said to me. "A knowledge of the Latin language on its own is unable to satisfy the mind's reason for learning. I know practically by heart Virgil, Horace, Livy, even Tacitus, but when I compare the knowledge of seminarians with what I have had the chance to learn thanks to good fortune I consider our school to be a relic of past centuries. We are familiar with all the classical authors, but we better understand critical commentaries of texts than know what at present makes them pleasant, what has secured eternity for them. We are taught philosophy, we study logic, metaphysics, ethics, theology, but to cite the words of Kuteikin in *The Minor*: let us complete our philosophical education and start all over again.[36] No surprise in this: Aristotle and Scholasticism to the present day reign supreme in seminaries. I, to my good fortune, being a familiar in the house of one functionary of the provincial administration in Novgorod, had the opportunity there to acquire a smatter of learning in the French and German languages and used the books of the owner of that house. What a difference in enlightenment between times when the Latin language exclusively was used in schools and the present period! What an aid to learning when knowledge is taught in the national language and are mysteries open only to initiates in the Latin language! But why," he continued after an interruption of his speech, "why have we not established institutions of higher learning in which the sciences are taught in the vernacular, in Russian? Learning would be more intelligible to all; enlightenment would be attained all the more quickly; and after a generation, for each Latinist you would have two hundred enlightened people. At the very least, in every tribunal you would have perhaps at least one member who understands what jurisprudence or legal education is. My God!" he continued with an exclamation, "if it were possible to adduce examples from the reflections and ravings of our judges about cases! What would Grotius, Montesquieu, Blackstone say?"[37] "You've read Blackstone?" "I read the first two parts that were translated into Russian. It would do no harm to compel our judges to have this book instead of the calendar of saints and to compel them to take a peek at it more often than at the court almanac.[38] How not to regret," he repeated, "that we do not have educational establishments where the sciences are taught in the vernacular language."

The stationmaster disturbed the continuation of our conversation when he came in. I managed to tell the seminarian that his wish would soon be fulfilled, that there was already a decree about the establishment of new universities where the sciences were going to be taught as he would wish. "High time, Sir, high time. . . ."

While I was paying the stationmaster the travel allowance, the seminarian walked out. As he left he dropped a small bunch of paper. I picked up what had fallen and did not hand it to him. Do not accuse me, dear reader, of theft: on that condition, I shall inform you what I filched. Once you do read it I know for sure that you will not then reveal my theft to the outside world. For as is written in the Russian law, the thief is not only the one who stole but also the one who did the accepting. I confess that I have sticky fingers. Where I see something that looks a little reasonable I immediately swipe it.—Look, do not leave your ideas lying about. Read what my seminarian says:

"The person who likened the moral world to a wheel—this is a person who, in speaking a great truth, did perhaps no more than glance at the round image of the earth and other great bodies circulating in space and express only what he saw. When mortals advance the knowledge of the physical universe, they will perhaps discover the hidden connection of spiritual or moral entities with corporeal or natural entities; that the cause of all changes, transformations, vicissitudes of the moral or spiritual world depends, perhaps, on the rounded form of our habitation and other bodies that belong to the solar system that just like it are circular and revolve. . . ." This resembles a follower of Saint-Martin,[39] a pupil of Swedenborg. . . .[40] No, my friend! I do not drink and eat only in order to survive but because I find in eating and drinking no small pleasure for the senses. And I must confess to you like a spiritual father: I would rather spend an entire night with a most enticing girl and fall asleep in her arms sated by voluptuousness than after burying myself in Hebrew or Arabic letters, ciphers, or Egyptian hieroglyphs, attempt to separate my spirit from body and, like the spiritual knights, modern and ancient, prowl in the vast fields of mental ravings. When I die there will be plenty of time for the imperceptible and my little soul can wander all it likes.

Look back: it seems that the time is only just behind us when superstition together with its full complement reigned: ignorance, slavery, the Inquisition, and much else. It was not long ago, was it, that Voltaire railed against superstition till he was hoarse; it was not long ago that Frederick was its implacable enemy not only in word and deed but more worryingly for it by way of his sovereign example.[41] However, in this world everything reverts to its previous stage since everything has its origin in destruction. An animal, a plant, grows in order to produce others like it, then to die and cede them its place. Nomadic tribes gather in cities, establish kingdoms, grow strong, become famous, grow weak, falter, fall apart. Their dwellings disappear; even their names will perish. Initially, Christian society was humble, meek, cloistered away in deserts and caves; then it gained strength, reared its head, lost its way, succumbed to superstition. In this state of frenzy, it followed a path typical of peoples: it elevated a leader, expanded his authority, and the Pope became the most powerful of kings. Luther began the Reformation, launched a schism, seceded from the Pope's leadership, and had many followers. The edifice of prejudices about papal power began to crumble, and superstition began to disappear; truth found enthusiasts, trampled on the enormous stronghold of prejudice but lasted only briefly on this path. Freedom of thought turned into a lack of restraint. Nothing was sacred, everything was under threat. Having reached a possible extreme, freethinking drew back. Our age faces a change in the manner of thinking. While we have not yet reached the final frontier of unbounded freethinking, many are already beginning to turn to superstition. Open the most recent occult works, you will think you have returned to the age of Scholasticism and logical disputes, when human reason was concerned with locutions and gave no thought to whether there was any sense in the locution; when the task of philosophy was, and when seekers of truth were asked to ponder the question: how many souls could fit on the head of a pin?

If delusion lies ahead for our descendants; if, in giving up to the system of nature they set about chasing after chimeras, then there would be great utility in the work of the writer who could show from previous activities the progress of human reason when, once the fog of prejudice was dispelled, it began to pursue truth to its heights; and when, wearied by its period of vigor, so to speak, once again began to dissipate its strength, grow tired, and decline into the vapidness of prejudice and superstition. The work of this writer will not be useless, for in exposing the course of our thoughts toward truth or delusion it will head off at least a few people from a dangerous path and hamper the rise of ignorance. Blessed is the writer if he is able to enlighten even one person through his creation, blessed is he if he has sown virtue in even a single heart.

We can call ourselves fortunate not to be witness to the extreme disgrace of rational beings. Our immediate descendants might be even luckier than we. But having lain dormant in the loathsomeness of filth, vapors are already floating up and are predestined to shroud the field of vision. Blessed shall we be if we do not see a new Mahomet; the hour of error will become more distant. Know that when in our speculations, when in our judgments about moral and spiritual matters, a ferment begins and a resolute man arises, one enterprising in the service of truth or deception, that is the time when a change in kingdoms will follow, when there will be a change in religious confessions.

On the ladder down whereby human reason is obliged to decline into the murk of error, if we can reveal anything that is funny and do a good deed with a smile, we shall then be considered as blessed.

In wandering from speculation to speculation, O beloved ones, take care not to enter onto a path of investigation like the following.

Akibah[42] relates: "Having entered on the path of Rabbi Jehoshua to a clandestine place, I had a triple recognition. I learned firstly: one is bidden to turn not to the east and not to the west but to the north and south. I learned, secondly, one should defecate not standing on one's feet but seated. I learned thirdly: one should wipe one's behind not with the right hand but with the left." To this Ben Gazas objected: "How far have you brought disgrace on your own head when you looked at your teacher in the act of defecating?" He answered: "These are the mysteries of the law; and it was to recognize them that I had to act in this way."

See Bayle's Dictionary, article Akibah.[43]

NOVGOROD

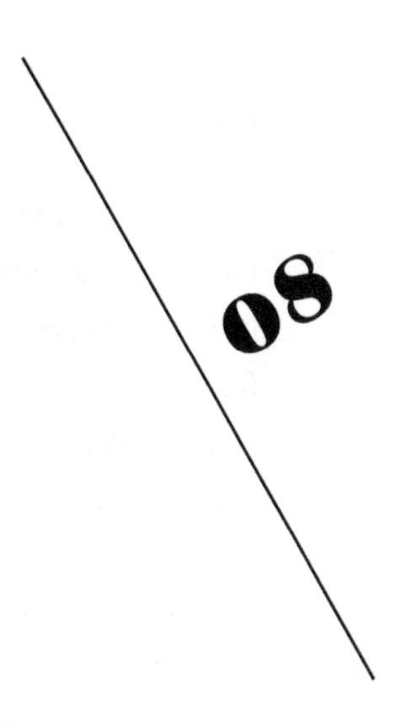

Take pride, vain builders of cities, take pride, founders of states; dream on that the glory of your name will be eternal; pile up stone upon stone until you reach the very clouds; carve out depictions of your triumphs and inscriptions proclaiming your deeds. Lay firm foundations of government in immutable law. With its sharp row of teeth, Time laughs at your boasting. Where are the wise laws of Solon and Lycurgus that affirmed the liberty of Athens and of Sparta?—In books.—In the place where they dwelled slaves graze under the scepter of despotism.—Where is wealthy Troy, where Carthage?—Scarcely visible is the place where they proudly stood.—In the famed temples of Ancient Egypt, is there an imperishable sacrifice burning mysteriously to a unique being?—Their magnificent ruins serve as a haven for bleating cattle during the midday heat. They are not bedewed by joyous tears of gratitude to the Almighty Father, but rather by the stinking emissions of their animal bodies.—O pride! O human arrogance, look at this and know what a low-life you are!

These were my thoughts as I drove up to Novgorod, looking at the many monasteries situated around it.

They say that all these monasteries, even those located at a distance of fifteen *versts** from the city, were enclosed within; that from its walls up to one hundred thousand troops could exit. It is known from the chronicles that Novgorod had a democratic government.[44] Whilst they had princes, their power was scant. The power of administration was vested in the mayors and the military commanders.[45] The people, assembled in the *veche*,[46] was the true ruler. The province of Novgorod extended north even farther than the Volga. This free state was a member of the Hanseatic League. The old saying: "Who can stand up to God and Novgorod the Great?" serves as proof of its might. Trade was the cause of its rise. Internal disagreements and a rapacious neighbor sealed its fall.

On the bridge, I got out of my carriage in order to enjoy the spectacle of the flow of the Volkhov. There was no way the deed of Tsar Ivan Vasilyevich after the capture of Novgorod could not come to mind.[47] Stung by the resistance of this republic, this proud, savage but intelligent ruler wished to raze it to its very foundations. He appears to me standing with his cudgel on the bridge subjecting to his fury, as some accounts narrate, the elders and superiors of Novgorod. But by what right did he rage against them? What right did he have to annex Novgorod? Was it because the first Grand Princes of Russia lived in this city? Or because he styled himself the Tsar of All Russia? Or because the Novgorodians were of the Slavic tribe? But when power acts what is the use of a right? Can a right exist when the blood of peoples seals an outcome? Can the law exist when the power to implement it is lacking? Much has been written about the law of nations. Reference is frequently made to it but law-givers

---

* nine miles—Trans.

have not considered whether there can be a judge between peoples. When enmities arise among them, when hatred or greed incite them against one another, the sword is their judge. Whoever falls dead or disarmed, he is guilty; he obediently capitulates to the outcome and there is no appeal.—This is why Novgorod belonged to Tsar Ivan Vasilyevich. And this is why he destroyed it and usurped its smoking ruins.—Necessity, a wish for security and preservation create kingdoms; discord, scheming, and power destroy them.—What then is the right of the people? Peoples, say the law experts, are positioned in relation to one another just like individuals in regard to one another in a state of nature.—Question: in the state of nature what rights does man have? The answer is: look at him. He is naked, hungry, thirsty. Everything he is able to grab to satisfy his needs he acquires. If anything should try to hinder him, he would remove the hindrance, destroy it, and would take what he wants. Question: if on the way to satisfying his needs, a person encounters his equal, if for example two men, feeling hunger, seek to assuage it with one morsel, which of the two has the greater claim? Answer: the one who will take the morsel. Question: and who will take the morsel? Answer: the one who is stronger.—Is this really natural law, is this really the basis of the right of the people?—Examples of all ages demonstrate that right without force was always thought at a practical level to be empty language.—Question: what is civil law? Answer: he who is journeying on postal horses does not busy himself with trivialities and thinks about how to get horses faster.

From The Novgorod Chronicle[48]

The Novgorodians fought a war with Grand Prince Yaroslav Yaroslavich and concluded a written peace accord.—

> The Novgorodians drafted a charter to defend their freedoms and confirmed it with fifty-eight seals.—
>
> The Novgorodians forbade the circulation in their state of coined money introduced into circulation by the Tatars.—
>
> In 1420 Novgorod began to strike its own coinage.—
>
> Novgorod was in the Hanseatic League.—
>
> There was a bell in Novgorod to the sound of which the people gathered at the *veche* to consider public affairs.—
>
> Tsar Ivan confiscated the charter and bell of the Novgorodians.—
>
> Later in the year 1500—and in 1600—in 1700—in the year—in the year—Novgorod remained in its previous location.

But one should not always think about olden times, not always think about the day that comes tomorrow. If I constantly gaze at the sky without considering what is under foot then I shall soon stumble and fall into the mud . . ., thought I. No matter how much you grieve you will not repopulate Novgorod as it used to be. What will be in the future is God's will.—It is now time to dine. I shall go to Karp Dementich.

"Hey hey hey! Welcome, whence has the Lord brought you?" said my friend Karp Dementich, previously a merchant of the third guild and now an eminent citizen.[49] "As the saying goes, 'a lucky one comes in time for lunch.' We invite you graciously to take a seat." "But why such a feast?" "Benefactor mine, yesterday I married off my lad." Benefactor thine, thought I, he's not puffing me up without a reason. Like others, I helped him join the ranks of eminent citizens. From 1737, it seems as though my grandfather had a debt by bill of exchange to someone—who I don't know—for 1000 rubles. In 1780 Karp Dementich purchased the bill of exchange, somewhere, and initiated a complaint for forfeiture on an obligation. He and an experienced legal fixer came to me, and at that time they graciously got off me only the interest payments for 50 years, and made a gift of all the capital that had been borrowed.—Karp Dementich is a grateful fellow. "Daughter-in law, some vodka for our unexpected guest." "I do not drink vodka." "Well, at least have a sip." "Health to the newlyweds . . ." and we sat down to eat.

On my one side sat the host's son, and on the other Karp Dementich seated his young daughter-in-law. . . . Let us interrupt the account, reader. Give me a pencil and sheet of paper. I shall draw to your satisfaction the entire honorable company and that way I shall make you a participant in the wedding feast even if you happen to be on the Aleutian Islands catching beavers. Even if I do not copy out exact portraits I shall be contented with their silhouettes. Lavater teaches how to use them to recognize who is intelligent and who stupid.[50]

Karp Dementich has a grey beard of eight *vershok** counting down from his lower lip. His nose is like a stubby stick, eyes grey, sunken, a pitch-black brow, he bows deeply from the waist, he smooths his beard, he greets all flatteringly as "my benefactor."—His dear wife is Aksinya Parfentyevna. At sixty years of age, white as snow, and ruddy as a poppy flower, she always purses her lips in a circle, before supper drinks half a cup of Rhine wine in the presence of guests and also a glass of vodka in the pantry. Her husband's domestic manager keeps track. . . . At the request of Aksinya Parfentyevna, the annual store of three *poods*† of ceruse from Rzhev and 30 pounds of myrtle for rouge

* fourteen inches—Trans.

† one hundred and nine pounds—Trans.

is purchased. The husband's domestic managers are Aksinya's chamberlains.—Alexei Karpovich is my neighbor at the table. Not a whisker nor yet a beard but his nose is already crimson, his brows twitch, his hair is cropped round, he bows like a goose, shaking his head and primping his hair. In Petersburg he was a shopkeeper's boy. He deducts a *vershok** from every *arshin*† of fabric he sells. For that reason, his father loves him like himself. When he was fourteen going on fifteen, he gave his mother a slap.—Paraskovya Denisovna, his newlywedded wife, is white and rosy. Teeth like coal.[51] Eyebrows are thread-thin, blacker than soot. In company, she keeps her eyes lowered, but entire days she spends at the window and stares at every man. In the evening she stands by the gate.—She has one black eye. The gift of her darling little husband on their first day—your guess as good as mine for what.

But dear reader, you yawn already. Enough of my taking silhouettes, clearly. You are right: there will be nothing more than noses and lips, lips and noses. And for that matter I have no idea how you distinguish ceruse and rouge on a silhouette.

"Karp Dementich, what are you trading in nowadays? You don't travel to Petersburg, do not transport flax, and you are buying neither sugar nor coffee nor pigments. It seems to me that your business was not unprofitable." "I almost went bust from it. God saved us by a narrow squeak. In the one year in which I received adequate revenue I built this very house for my wife. The next year there was no harvest in flax and I was unable to deliver what my contract required.

---

* one and three-quarters inches—Trans.

† twenty-eight inches—Trans.

That's why I ceased to trade." "I recall, Karp Dementich, that in return for the thirty thousand rubles collected in advance you sent your creditors a thousand *poods** of flax to be distributed among them." "By God, more was impossible, trust my conscience." "Of course, in the very same year the failed crop affected the trade in imported goods. You collected about twenty thousand worth of . . . Yes, I recall: that was some headache." "Truly, my benefactor, my head ached so I thought it would burst. Yet what complaints could creditors have against me? I gave them my entire estate." "At about three kopecks on the ruble." "No way, not at all, it was about fifteen." "And your wife's house?" "How could I touch it? It's not mine." "Tell me then, what business are you doing?" "Nothing, swear to God, nothing. Since I entered a state of bankruptcy my boy has been doing the business. This summer, thank God, he delivered flax to the value of about twenty thousand." "In future, of course, he will sign contracts for fifty thousand, will take half the money up front and will build his young wife a house. . . ." Alexei Karpovich just smiles. "You are an old joker, my benefactor. Enough shooting the breeze: let's get down to business." "I don't drink, you know." "Well, just have a sip."

Have a sip, have a sip—I sensed that my cheeks had begun to redden and that toward the end of the feast I would, like the others, be completely sozzled. But fortunately, one cannot sit at the table forever just as it's impossible to be clever all the time. And for the very same reason I sometimes play the fool and rave I was sober at a wedding feast.

After leaving my acquaintance Karp Dementich, I fell to thinking. I had reckoned until then that the law of the promissory note

---

* thirteen tons—Trans.

introduced everywhere, that is the rigorous and expedient indemnification of commercial obligations, was a protection guaranteeing trust; I considered it a fortunate invention of modern times that had not occurred to the minds of ancient peoples for the enhancement of rapid turnover in commerce. But if the one who issues the credit note is less than honest, why is this little scrap of paper worthless? If the rigorous settlement of debt did not exist would trade vanish? Is it not for the creditor to know whom to trust? Whom should legislation be obligated to protect more, the creditor or the debtor? Who in the eyes of humanity deserves more respect, the creditor who forfeits his capital because he did not know the person to whom he entrusted it; or the debtor who is in chains and in prison? On the one hand, gullibility, on the other, practically thievery. The former gave his trust because he was relying on the law to be strict, but the latter. . . . But if the settlement of debentures was not so strict? There would be no place for ready credulity, perhaps there would be no chicanery in matters of credit. . . . I began to think again, the previous system had gone to the devil, and I went to bed with an empty head.

BRONNITSY

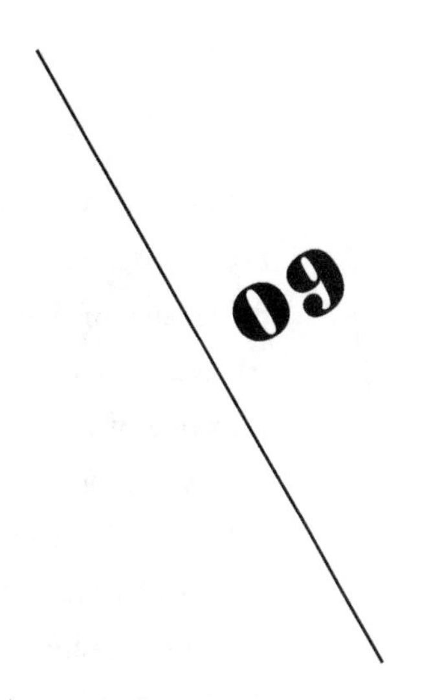

Meanwhile as the horses to my carriage were being changed I conceived a wish to visit the tall mountain located near Bronnitsy on which, they say, in ancient times before the advent of the Slavs, I think, there stood a temple famed at the time for the prophesies it issued and to hear which many northern lords used to come. On this spot, it is recounted, where the village of Bronnitsy now stands, was the city of Kholmograd, famous in the ancient history of the north. Now a small church stands on the spot of this celebrated ancient temple.

In ascending the mountain, I imagined myself transported to antiquity, arriving so that I might learn the future from the majestic deity and bring calm to my uncertainty. Divine terror grips my limbs, my chest begins to heave, my gaze goes dull, and the light dims. I hear a voice, like thunder, proclaiming: "Mad man! Why do you wish to discover the mystery that I have obscured from mortals by the impenetrable shield of unknowability? Why, O arrogant one! do you crave to discover that which only eternal thought is able to grasp? Understand that the unknowability of the future is proportional to the fragility of your organism. Understand that bliss known beforehand loses its sweetness owing to overlong anticipation; that the delight of present pleasure, finding the organism's energy depleted, is unable to produce in the soul as nice a quiver as pleasure receives from a surprise. Know that extinction revealed beforehand robs one of equanimity in an untimely way, poisons the pleasure you would enjoy if you were still ignorant of their termination. What is it that you seek, unreasonable child? My superior wisdom has instilled what is needed in your mind and heart. Consult them on days of sadness and you will find comforters. Consult them on days of rejoicing and you will find a curb on impudent happiness. Return to your home, return to your family; calm your disturbed thoughts; enter into your inner realm, there you will discover my godhead, there you will hear my prophesy." And the cracking of a strong blow by Perun[52] thundering in his domain resounded in the distant valleys.—I came to my senses.—I reached the summit of the mountain and, having spied the church, I raised my arms to the sky. "Lord," I shouted out, "this is Your temple, this is the temple, they declare, of the true, one God. On this spot, on the spot where You dwell at this moment in time, they say there used to stand a temple of error. But I cannot believe, O! Almighty, that man sent his heartfelt prayer to some being other than to You. Your mighty right hand, invisibly outstretched everywhere, compels even the denier of Your omnipotent will to acknowledge the architect and keeper of Nature. If a mortal in his error names You with strange, unbecoming, and beastly names, his reverence, all the same, flows to You, everlasting, and he quivers before Your might. Jehovah, Jupiter, Brahma; the God of Abraham, God of Moses, God of Confucius, God of Zoroaster, God of Socrates, God of Marcus Aurelius, Christian God, O my God! You are the same everywhere. If in their error mortals seemingly did not reverence You alone, they still worshipped Your incomparable powers, Your inimitable deeds. Your might, felt everywhere and in everything, was everywhere and in everything worshipped. By acknowledging the law of nature as constant, the atheist who renounces You in that very way bears You praise, praising You even more than our hymns. For moved to his inner core by the gracefulness of Your creation he faces it, trembling. "All-Generous Father, You seek a sincere heart and innocent soul; they are everywhere open to Your advent. Descend, Lord, and ensconce Yourself in them." For several moments I was detached from the objects around me, withdrawing deep into my interior self—My eyes then raised, my gaze directed on the settlements nearby, I pronounced: "These huts are a degradation on the spot where once a great metropolis elevated its walls. Not even the smallest trace of them remains. Reason that so craves convincing and empirical proofs balks at belief in the very story." And all that we see will pass; all will collapse, all will be dust. But some secret voice declares to me: something will continue to exist alive forever.

> In the course of time all sounds will darken,
> The brilliance of the sun will go out; nature, worn out
> With the frailty of the years, falls
> But you in immortal youth will flourish
> Steadfast amidst the battle of the elements,
> The ruins of matter, the destruction of all the worlds.*[53]

---

* *Death of Cato,* Addison's tragedy, act V, scene 1.

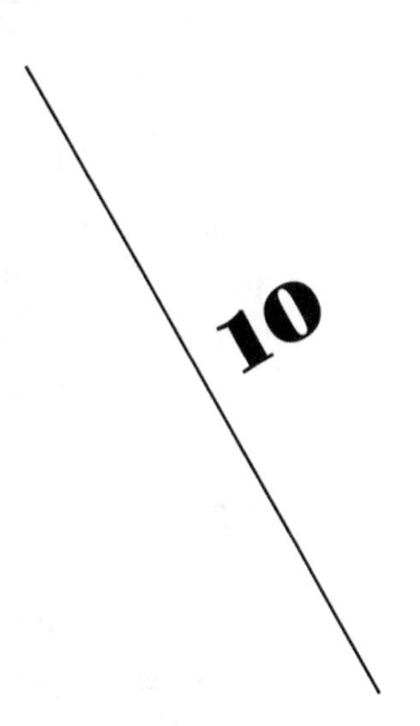

ZAITSOVO

At the postal station in Zaitsovo, I came across my old acquaintance Mr. Krestyankin. We had known one another since our childhood days. It was rare for us to be in the same city, but while our conversations were infrequent they were sincere. Mr. Krestyankin had spent long years in military service, and having tired of its cruelties especially during war when great acts of violence are covered up as legitimate acts of war, moved into the civil service. To his misfortune even in the civil service he could not avoid the very thing he sought to distance himself from in quitting the military. The soul he possessed was very sensitive, and his heart was philanthropic. These excellent qualities, already recognized, gained him a position as a presiding judge in the criminal court. Initially, he was reluctant to assume this title. Having given it some thought, however, he told me: "My friend, what a broad field of action opens before me for the satisfaction of the fondest inclination of my soul! What an activity for tenderheartedness! Let us break the cruel scepter that so often weighs upon the shoulders of innocence. Let the prisons go empty, so that distracted weakness, careless inexperience may never see them; and bad luck never be treated as criminality. O my friend! My duty fulfilled, I shall shed parents' tears for their children, the sighs of spouses for each other. But these tears shall be tears of renewal for the sake of good, while the tears of suffering innocence and simpleheartedness will dry up. How very much this thought delights me. Let us go and hasten my departure. It may be that my arrival there is needed and that any delay might turn me into a murderer should I fail to head off incarceration or accusations, by granting pardon or by freeing someone from their bondage."

It was with these thoughts that my friend departed to his place of service. How very surprised I was to learn that he had quit his position and intended to spend his life in retirement.

"I thought, my friend," said Mr. Krestyankin to me, "that I would find an abundant harvest, one rewarding to reason, in performing my job. Instead all I found was gall and thorns. Wearied of this, no longer strong enough to do any good, I have ceded my post to a truly predatory beast. In a short period, he has garnered praise by the prompt resolution of cases that have piled up, whereas I had the reputation of being on the slow side. Others considered me to be venal because I was in no rush to aggravate the lot of the miserable who had fallen into criminality often through no choice of their own. Before entering state service, I had acquired the reputation, flattering to me, of a philanthropic commander. Now, the very same quality that gladdened my heart so greatly—now it is regarded as a sign of lenience or unforgivable indulgence. I saw my decisions mocked for the very thing that made them perfect; I saw them left unimplemented. While my superior did not have the power to compel me to free a genuine villain and a dangerous member of society or to punish alleged crimes with the confiscation of property, honor, and forfeiture of life; or to encourage me to undertake illegal covering up of a crime or to prosecute innocence, I regarded with scorn that he succeeded in recruiting other members of the criminal chambers for this purpose. And so it was not rare for me to see my benevolent intentions go up like smoke disappearing into the air. As a reward for their deplorable complicity these members, however, received distinctions whose wrongness made them as lackluster in my eyes as they were appealing to the others. In difficult cases, when belief in the innocence of a person deemed to be a criminal aroused my inclination to be softhearted, it was not rare for me to resort to the law to brace myself against hesitation. But I often discovered in the law cruelty instead of love of mankind, and cruelty had its origin not in the law as such, but rather in the fact that the law was obsolete. Disproportion of punishment to crime frequently extracted tears from me. I saw (and how could this be otherwise) that the law forms judgments about actions without regard for the causes that bring them about. Indeed, it was a final instance relating to this type of action that obliged me to quit service. Unable as I was to save the people who were dragged into guilt by the powerful hand of fate, I had no wish to be a participant in their punishment. Unable as I was to ease their fate, in my innocence I washed my hands and shunned hardness of heart.

"In our province there lived a nobleman who had resigned from the service several years earlier. Here is his service record. He began service at court as a stoker, was promoted to lackey, then a lackey of the bedchamber, and then a butler.[54] I have no idea what special qualities are required for advancement up these rungs of court service. But I do know that he loved wine more than his life. After about fifteen years in service as a butler, he was transferred to the

Office of Heraldry to be appointed in accordance with his rank. However, sensing his own lack of competence, he made a request to take retirement and was rewarded with the rank of collegiate assessor, with which he arrived in the place where he had been born, that is, to our province, about six years ago. It is not rare for vanity to be the cause of notable affection for one's homeland. The person of low social origins who has achieved distinction; or a poor man who has acquired wealth, once having cast off the inhibition of shame, which is the last and weakest root of virtue, prefers the place of his birth for the display of his grandeur and pride. There, soon enough, the assessor found occasion to buy a village in which he settled with his not small family. Had there been born among us a Hogarth he would have found in the family of Mr. Assessor a rich vein of caricature. I am but a poor artist. However, if I were able to discern the inner characteristics of a man in the features of his face with the same penetration of a Lavater,[55] even then a portrait of the assessor's family would be noteworthy. Lacking these talents, I will make their deeds speak for themselves—these are always the true indicators of a moral disposition.

"Mr. Assessor, descended from the lowest class, found himself to be the master of several hundred of his fellow human beings. This turned his head. He would not be the only one to protest that the exercise of power turns one's head. He regarded his own rank as the highest, regarded the peasants as livestock given to him to be deployed as labor at his discretion (it is not unlikely that he considered that his power over them derived from God). He was mercenary, squirreling away money, cruel by nature, querulous, base, and therefore arrogant toward the very weakest. You can judge from this how he got on with the peasants. Under the previous landowner they had been on a quitrent basis; he settled them on a tillage basis. He confiscated all their land, bought from them their livestock at a price he set himself, obliged them to work the entire week for him, and, to prevent them from dying of starvation, fed them in the courtyard of the manor house, and then not more than once daily, and to some he gifted a monthly charitable allowance. If anyone looked lazy to him, he birched, whipped, clubbed, and beat them with a cat-o'-nine-tails calibrated to the degree of indolence. When it came to real crimes such as theft from others than himself, he said not a word. It looked as though he wanted in his village to revive the ways of ancient Sparta or the Zaporozhian Host.[56] It came to pass that for subsistence his peasants robbed one traveler and then later killed another. He did not surrender them to justice but hid them at home, telling the authorities that they had fled. He maintained that he would not profit if a peasant of his were to be lashed with the knout and sent to do hard labor for a crime. If one of his peasants committed robbery against him, he whipped him as he did for indolence or for making a bold or witty challenge and in addition put them in the stocks, clapped their legs in chains, and put a harness around their neck. I could tell you many a tale of the clever orders he gave, but this will suffice to introduce you to my hero. His consort maintained total power over the womenfolk. Her abettors in implementing her orders were her sons and daughters, as they were for her husband. This was because they had made it a rule on no account to distract their peasants from work. For domestic staff, they had a boy purchased in Moscow, a hairdresser for their daughters, and an elderly female cook. They had neither a coachman nor horses; they always used the draft horses to travel. The sons personally birched the peasants or whipped them with a cat-o'-nine-tails. The daughters slapped the women and girls on the face, or pulled their hair. In their free time, the sons roamed the village or the fields to flirt and to debauch girls and women, and none could escape being raped by them. Because the daughters did not have suitors, they vented their frustration on the spinning women, many of whom they disfigured. My friend, judge for yourself what outcome deeds like these might have. From a large number of cases, I have established that the Russian people are extremely patient and will remain patient to the very limit. But when their patience is at an end then nothing can avert them from turning to cruelty. This is precisely what happened with the assessor. The terrible and senseless—or perhaps it would be better to say beastly—act of one of his sons provided such a cause.

"In his village there lived a young peasant wench. She was not bad looking, and promised in marriage to a young peasant of the same village. The middle son of the assessor fancied her, and he did everything he could to woo her affections. But the peasant girl was faithful, having plighted her troth to her groom, a rare thing that does occasionally happen among the peasantry. The wedding was due to take place on a Sunday. According to the custom introduced by many landowners, the father of the groom accompanied his son to the manor house and brought with him two *poods** of honey as a bridal tribute to his master. This was the moment the young master decided to use in order to satisfy his own lust. He took along his two brothers, used a strange boy as intermediary to lure her into the courtyard, gagged her while dragging her into a pen. Unable to cry out, she resisted with all her might the ferocious intention of her young master. Overwhelmed in the end by all three, she was coerced

* thirty-two pounds—Trans.

into submitting to their violence, and thus it was that when the horrid monster was on the brink of satisfying his intention, the bridegroom returned from the manor house, entered the courtyard, and, spotting one of the young masters near the pen, became suspicious about their evil plan. He called for his father to come help and then quicker than lightning flew to the pen. What a sight awaited him! As he approached, the door to the pen closed shut but the combined strength of two brothers was unequal to contain the headlong charge of the enraged groom. He grabbed a stake lying nearby, jumped into the pen and bashed on the back his bride's predator. They were about to grab him but when they saw the groom's father running, also with a stake in hand, to his aid, they abandoned their prey, scampered out of the pen, and ran. But the bridegroom caught up with one of them and with his stake bashed him on the head, smashing it in. These villains, wishing to avenge their injury, went straight to their father and told him that they had been walking around the village when they had met the bride and joked with her; and that when her bridegroom saw this he attacked them, aided by his father. As proof they showed him one of the brothers' smashed-in head. Enraged to the innermost part of his heart by the injury to his own born, the father boiled over with the wrath of fury. At once he ordered that the three villains, as he called the groom, bride, and groom's father, be brought before him. When the three were in his presence, his first question was as to who had smashed open his son's head. The groom did not deny what he had done and gave an account of the entire incident. 'How did you dare,' said the old assessor, 'to lift a hand against your master? Even if he had spent the night before your wedding with your bride you should have been grateful for this to him. You shall not marry her. She will remain in my home and you will be punished.' The decision made, he ordered that the groom, having given him over to his sons to do as they please, be whipped mercilessly with a cat-o'-nine-tails. Bravely did he withstand their beating, and his spirit was unflinching as he watched them begin to torture his father in the same way. But he was unable to bear it when he saw the master's servants make to remove his bride into the house. The punishment was being delivered in the courtyard. In a split second he wrested her from the hands of her captors; freed, the pair of them fled the yard. Seeing this, the master's sons stopped whipping the father and gave chase. Sensing they were catching up with him, the groom grabbed a plank and fought back. Meanwhile, the noise attracted other peasants to the courtyard of the manor house. Sympathizing as they did with the plight of the young peasant, and their hearts filled with rancor against their masters, they took his side. Seeing this, the assessor rushed there, began to chew them out, and with his walking stick landed such a blow on the first person he saw that he fell to the ground senseless. This was the signal for a general assault. All four of the masters were surrounded and, to put it succinctly, beaten to death on the very spot. They were all so reviled that not a single person wished to be denied the chance to participate in this killing, as they admitted themselves later. It was just at that moment that the chief of police of this district was passing through with his squad. He was an eyewitness to some of what occurred. He arrested the guilty men—and half the village was guilty; the investigation he conducted eventually went to the criminal court. The case was laid out very clearly and the guilty confessed to everything. In their defense, they cited only the excruciating deeds of their owners about which the entire province already knew. Such was the case on which, by virtue of my position, I was obliged to establish a final verdict: to condemn the guilty to a death sentence, commuted to a public beating and the life sentence of hard labor.

"In reviewing the case, I did not find sufficient or convincing grounds for conviction of the criminals. The peasants who killed their master committed murder. But was this murder not coerced? Was not its cause the dead assessor himself? Just as a third number obviously follows two numbers arithmetically, in this case, too, the consequence was necessary. The innocence of the killers was, at least to me, a mathematical certainty. If while I am walking a villain attacks me and, raising a knife above my head, wants to stab me, would I be considered a murderer if I prevent the crime and knock him down lifeless at my own feet? If some present-day fop should want to get even with me for well-deserved disdain and, on meeting me in an isolated place, draws his sword to attack me either to deprive me of my life or at the very least to wound me, would I be guilty if, having pulled out my sword for my own defense, I were to relieve society of a member causing a disturbance to the peace? Can we consider that such a deed violates the safety of a member of society if I commit it for my own salvation, if I do it to preempt my demise, if without it my own welfare would be irretrievably pitiable?

"Imbued with these thoughts, I felt, as you can imagine, a torment in my soul when considering the case. With my customary frankness, I disclosed my thoughts to my fellow justices. They raised their voices unanimously against me. They considered clemency and philanthropy a culpable defense of criminal deeds. They called me a fomenter of murder; they called me an accessory to the murderers. Their opinion was that all domestic security would vanish if my opinions were to spread. 'Would any nobleman,' they said, 'henceforth be able to live securely on his estate? Would he see his commands fulfilled? If those who defied the will of their master, not to mention his murderers, were declared not guilty, then obedience would be disrupted, the domestic contract would be destroyed, the chaos inherent in primordial societies would recur. Agriculture would die out, its tools would be destroyed, cultivated fields would be barren and be overgrown with unproductive weed; villagers, unencumbered by any authority above them, would rove about indolent and slothful and would disperse. Cities would experience the omnipotent hand of destruction. Craft would become alien to city dwellers, manufacture would forfeit application and diligence, trade would dry up at the source, wealth would surrender to miserable poverty, the grandest buildings would become dilapidated, the laws would be eclipsed and grow ineffectual. At that point, the immense organism of society would fall into pieces that, separated from the whole, would atrophy; then the seat of royalty, on which the support, bulwark, and integration of society currently rest, would decay and collapse; then the ruler of nations would become a simple citizen and society would witness its end.' This picture, worthy of a hellish brush, my colleagues endeavored to lay before the gaze of anyone who happened to hear about the case. 'It is natural that the president of our court,' they pontificated, 'is minded to defend a murder committed by peasants. Inquire of him as to his social origins. Unless we are mistaken, he himself walked behind the plow in his youth. It is always these newly minted members of the nobility who have odd ideas about the natural rights of the nobility over the peasants. If this depended on him, he would, we believe, lump us all together as peasants with land[57] in order to level his class origins with our own.' These were the words with which my colleagues thought they could insult me and make me hated by the entire society. But this was not enough for them. They said that I had taken a bribe from the wife of the murdered assessor who did not want to be deprived of the peasants she owned if they were sent off to do labor, and that this was the real reason for strange and harmful views of mine that were broadly offensive to the rights of the entire gentry. Mindless as they were, they thought that their mockery would wound me, that their calumny would humiliate me, that their misrepresentation of my good purpose would alienate me from it! They had no knowledge of my heart. They were ignorant that I would always remain unflinching and staunch before the judgment of my conscience, and that my cheeks had no cause to blush with the crimson flush of conscience.

"My venality they alleged on the grounds that the wife of the assessor did not wish to avenge the death of her husband, but rather, led by her own greed and following the practice of her husband, preferred to spare the peasants punishment in order, as she said, not to forfeit her estate. She also came to see me with a request along these lines. I agreed with her about forgiving the murder of her husband, but our motivations differed. She assured me that she would punish them quite enough, whereas I tried to persuade her that in acquitting her husband's murderers it was important not to submit them to the same extreme punishment so that they wouldn't again become evildoers—as they were wrongly called.

"The governor-general was soon informed of my view on this matter, learned that I had tried to win over my colleagues to my thoughts, and that they were beginning to waiver in their reasoning—wherein it was not the firmness and persuasiveness of my arguments that proved conducive but rather the money of the assessor's wife. Being himself a product of the rules of unlimited power over the peasants, he does not agree with my judgments and, indignant on seeing this reasoning, begins to prevail in the deliberation of this affair albeit for other reasons. He sends for my colleagues, admonishes them, asserting the deplorable nature of such views as injurious to noble society, injurious to supreme power because they violate legal statutes; he promises reward to all those who fulfilled the law, threatening with sanction anyone who does not obey it; and he soon brings round to their previous views weak judges lacking principles in their reflections or firmness of spirit. I was not surprised to note the change, since their previous reversal caused me no surprise. It is natural for weak, timid, and base souls to shudder at the menace of power and to embrace its acceptance.

"Our governor-general, having reversed the opinions of my colleagues, perhaps planned, and flattered himself on this, to change mine, too. He had this goal in mind when he summoned me on the morning of what happened to be a holiday. He was obliged to summon me, since I was not in the habit of attending those mindless audiences that pride regards as the duty of subordinates, flattery regards as necessary, but the wise man regards as loathsome and offensive to humanity. He deliberately chose a day of celebration when a large number of people attended his gathering; he deliberately chose a public gathering for his speech, reckoning that this would convince me more conclusively. He counted on discovering in me either a timorous soul or mental weakness. He took aim at both of these in his speech. But I consider it unnecessary to paraphrase for you all that his arrogance, sense of power, and overweening confidence in his astuteness and learning imparted to his eloquence. To his arrogance I replied with indifference and calm; to his power—with firmness, matching logical argument for argument, and I spoke for a long time with icy control. But in the end a shaken heart spilled out its surplus of feeling. The clearer the audience's acquiescence became, the more emotional my speech. In a firm voice and ringing enunciation I finally cried out: 'Each person is born into this world the equal of any other. We all have similar limbs, we all have reason and will. Man considered, therefore, outside society is a being dependent on nobody else for his own deeds. But he puts a limit on these, consents not to subordinate himself to his own will alone, and becomes obedient to the commands of other human beings, in a word becomes a citizen. For the sake of what cause does he restrain his desires? For what purpose does he set a power over himself? Unlimited in the exercise of his willpower, why does he limit it through obedience?—For his own sake,—says reason.—For his own sake,—says an inner voice.—For his own sake,—says wise legislation. It follows that where it is not in his interest to be a citizen there is no citizen. It follows, therefore, that whoever wants to deprive him of the advantage of being a citizen is his enemy. He seeks in the law defense and retribution against his enemy. If the law either does not have the power to defend him or does not wish to do so, or lacks the power to help him immediately in his present woe, then the citizen uses his natural right of defense, preservation, welfare. For the citizen, insofar as he has become a citizen, does not cease to be a person whose first duty, stemming from his organism, is preservation, defense, welfare. The assessor murdered by the peasants violated with his bestial actions their rights as citizens. At that moment when he condoned the violence of his sons, when to the heartache of the betrothed he added rape, when he threatened punishment because they resisted his hellish domination, at that moment the law intended to protect the citizen was remote and its efficacity was negligible. That was when the law of nature awakened and the insulted citizen's power, which positive law does not take away when he is injured, came into force. The peasants who killed the bestial assessor are innocent before the law. Based on the conclusions of reason, my heart acquits them; and the death of the assessor, while violent, was just. Let no one conceive of basing political decisions on prudence, basing the condemnation of the murder of the assessor who gasped his last breath in such malice on the desire for social calm. No matter the station of life into which he was fated to have been born, the citizen is and always will be a person, and for as long as he is a person, the law of nature as the abundant source of benefits will never dry up in him. And one who dares to damage what is in him a natural and indestructible property is a criminal. Woe unto him if the civil law does not punish him. He will be tainted, marked out as despicable among his fellow citizens and every person of adequate strength should avenge the injury done by him.' I fell silent. The governor-general did not address a word to me. Now and again he raised toward me sullen looks charged with the rage of impotence and malignancy of revenge. Everyone remained silent, expecting that I would be taken into custody for offending against all privileges. Now and again from the lips of the servile, one heard a rumbling of indignation. Everyone averted their eyes from me. Terror, it seems, gripped those standing near me. They imperceptibly withdrew as though from someone afflicted with a fatal plague. Fed up with the spectacle of such a mixture of arrogance and the most craven baseness, I departed from this assembly of lickspittles.

"Having failed to find a way to save the innocent murderers whom my heart absolved, I did not want to be complicit in their punishment or be its witness. I petitioned for retirement, received it, and here I am now journeying to lament the pathetic state of the peasants' station, and to alleviate my distress by associating with friends." We parted on this note, and each headed off in his direction.—

My trip that day was not a success. The horses were bad and had to be changed over and over; and finally as we went down a small hill the axle of the carriage splintered and I was unable to advance.—I am accustomed to walking. Seizing my staff, off I marched to the postal station. But for a resident of St. Petersburg a walk along the highway is not very pleasant and bears no resemblance to a stroll in the Summer Garden or the Baba.[58] I got worn out quite quickly and needed to sit down.

While I sat on a stone and drew figures of one kind or another in the sand, sometimes irregular and not at right angles, and thought about this and that, a carriage raced past me. The passenger spotted me and ordered the coach to stop. In him I recognized my acquaintance. "What are you doing?" he asked me. "I am having a think. There is more than enough time for reflection. An axle splintered. What's new?" "Same old rubbish. The weather changes with the wind, now sleet, now fair weather. Ah! . . . There is something new. Duryndin has got married." "That can't be true—he's about eighty." "That's right. Look, here is a letter for you. . . . Read it at your leisure, but I have to be getting on. Bye—," and we parted.

The letter was from my friend. Avid for all sorts of news items, he promised to supply me with them during my absence and kept his word. In the meanwhile they had fitted to my carriage a new axle, fortunately kept as a spare. As I rode I read:

Petersburg

My dear!

Recently a marriage has taken place here between a seventy-eight-year-old young chap and a sixty-two-year-old missy. The reason for so antique a coupling will be a tad hard to guess if I don't tell it. Open your ears, my friend, and you shall hear.—Mrs. Sh . . ., sixty-two years old, widowed from the age of twenty-five, is a hero of a kind and not the least of them. She was married to a merchant who had not been a success in business. She had a pretty face. Left a poor orphan after the death of her husband, and well aware of how hard-hearted her husband's mates were, she declined to have recourse to asking for charity from the haughty but deemed it proper to feed herself through her own efforts. As long as the beauty of youth stayed on her face, she remained in constant work, and received handsome remuneration from her admirers. But as soon as she got a first inkling that her beauty was beginning to fade, and that amorous dalliances were yielding their place to tedious isolation, she gathered her wits and, not finding any more buyers for her faded charms, she began to trade in the charms of others which, while not always possessed of the distinction of beauty, nonetheless had the merit of novelty. This way she amassed several thousands, honorably detached herself from the society of despicable procuresses, and engaged in usury, lending capital accumulated through her own (and others') shamelessness. In the fullness of time, her previous occupation was forgotten, and the former procuress became an indispensable creature in the company of spendthrifts. Having lived sixty-two years in peace, an evil spirit induced her to wed. All her acquaintances are amazed by this. Her close friend N . . . came to see her. "There is a rumor going around, my soul," she says to the hoary bride, "that you are planning to get married. I think this must be false. Some sort of joker has invented a fable."

Sh. "It is the complete truth. Tomorrow will be the engagement party, do come join our celebration."

N. "You are out of your mind. Is it possible that old blood is playing up? Is it possible that some sort of frisky youth has contrived to be taken under your wing?"

Sh. "Oy, mamma! Do you really take me for some young airhead? The husband I am taking is someone suitable. . . ."

N. "Well, yes, I know he is suitable. But recall that they cannot love us anymore unless it be for money."

Sh. "I am not taking the kind who can be unfaithful to me. My groom is older than I am by sixteen years."

N. "You jest!"

Sh. "Honest truth. Baron Duryndin."

N. "This cannot be happening."

Sh. "Come tomorrow evening and see for yourself that I do not like to lie."

N. "Well, even so, still, it is not you he is marrying but rather your money."

Sh. "And who will give that to him? I shall not get so carried away on the first night as to give away my entire estate. The time for that sort of thing is long past. There's the gold snuff-box, silver buckles, and other rubbish that had been pawned and couldn't be dumped. This is all the gain to which my little groomling is entitled. And if he is a noisy sleeper, then I'll banish him from the bed."

N. "At least a snuffbox could come his way, but what is in it for you?"

Sh. "What do you mean, mamma? Leaving aside the fact that in our times it is no bad thing to possess a good rank, so they will call me Your High Ancestry and, if someone is a bit stupider, Your Excellency,[59] and this way there will be someone with whom to play a game of pickup sticks in those long winter evenings. But right now it's sit, and sit some more on my own. At present I haven't even got the pleasure when I sneeze that someone says 'Bless you.' If one has one's own husband then no matter how severe a cold I have, I shall always hear, 'God bless, my light, God bless, my little soul. . . .' "

H. "Good-bye, little mother."

Sh. "Tomorrow is the engagement party and the wedding will be in a week."

N. leaves

Sh. Sneezes. "Looks like she'll not be coming back. How much better to have a husband!"

Do not be surprised, my friend, for it is on a wheel that everything in this world goes round. Today intelligence is in fashion, tomorrow stupidity. I hope that you, too, will see your fair share of Duryndins. If they don't differentiate themselves by marriage then it's by something else. Yet without these Duryndins the world would not last three days.

KRESTTSY

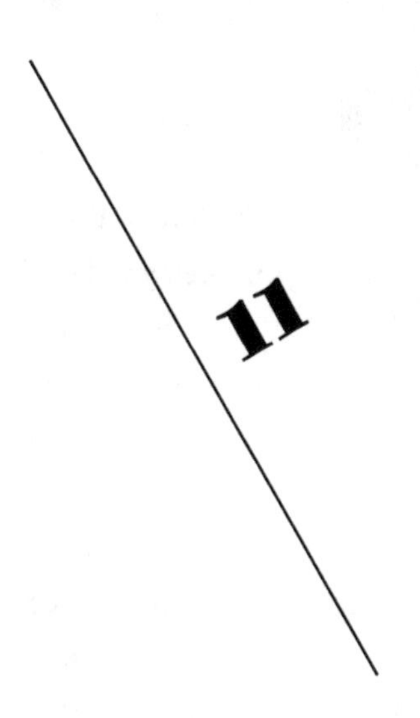

At Kresttsy, I was witness to a parting between father and children that touched me all the more emotionally because I am myself a father and soon, perhaps, shall part from my children. An unfortunate prejudice in the noble rank compels them to enter service. The name alone of service produces an uncommon disturbance in my blood! It is possible to maintain a thousand to one that out of a hundred young squires entering service ninety-eight will become rakes, while two when near old age—or to put it more accurately when they are in their decrepit, if not exactly old, years—will become good people. The rest progress through the ranks, squander or amass an estate and so on. . . .—When I sometimes look upon my older son and think that soon he will enter service or, to put it in other words, that the bird will fly the coop, my hairs stand on end. Not because service in itself corrupts morals, but because it would be fitting for one to begin service with a mature character.—Someone will say, "But who is giving it in the neck to these milquetoasts?" Who? I will follow the general example. A staff officer is seventeen years of age; the colonel is twenty; the general twenty; the chamberlain, senator, governor, commander of the forces. What father would not wish his children, although still in their youth, to be in the distinguished ranks which wealth, honor, and reason follow in due course.—In looking upon my son I imagine: he has begun to serve, made the acquaintance of flibbertigibbets, the debauched, gamblers, fops. He has learned how to dress impeccably, to play cards, to maintain himself by card playing, to talk about everything thoughtlessly, to frequent whores, or to tell nonsensical lies to gentlewomen. Fortune, spinning on its chicken leg, has somehow favored him; and my little, still beardless son has become a distinguished boyar.[60] He has conceived a fancy that he is smarter than everyone else in the world. What good could one possibly expect from such a commander or town governor?—Tell me in truth, child-loving father, tell me, O authentic citizen! Would you not prefer to strangle your little son than let him be in service? Is your heart not pained that your sonny-boy, a grand boyar gentleman, despises the merits and qualities that move slowly along the path to promotion because they do not want to be crafty? You will weep, won't you, to see your dear son, wearing a charming smile, confiscate property, honor; to see him poison and slaughter people not always with his own gentlemanly hands but by means of his minions' paws.

The gentleman from Kresttsy was, I thought, about fifty years old. Scant streaks of gray scarcely appeared in his blond head of hair. His regular facial features signified the tranquility of a soul immune to passions. A gentle smile of unflappable satisfaction, born from kindness, burrowed in his cheeks the dimples that are so fetching on women; when I entered the room where he was seated his gaze was fixed on his two sons. His eyes, the eyes of benevolent reason, seemed draped in a light veil of sorrow; but the veil was shot through with flashes of firmness and hope. Before him stood two youths, nearly equal in age; they differed from one another by one year in time of birth but not in the progress of their mind and heart. For in the younger, the zeal of the father had hastened the opening up of his mind, and brotherly love had tempered the elder's success in learning. They understood matters equally, they knew the rules of life equally, but nature had planted in each a different sharpness of mind and responsiveness of the heart. The gaze of the elder was strong, the features of face were steady, they exhibited the beginnings of a decisive soul and a steadfastness in undertakings. The gaze of the younger was sharp, his face was mobile and changeable. But their smooth motion was the infallible sign of his father's good guidance.—They looked upon their father with a timidity uncharacteristic for them that arose from grief over their pending separation rather than from a sense of power or control over them.—Sparse teardrops flowed from their eyes. "My friends!" said the father, "today we will part," and hugging them as they sobbed, he clasped them to his breast. I had already been witnessing this scene standing still by the doors for several minutes when the father turned to me: "Be a witness, sensitive traveler, be a witness before the world to how heavily it weighs on my heart to satisfy the powerful force of custom. In removing my children from the vigilant paternal eye, the only incentive I have in this regard is that they acquire experience, that they understand man from his actions, and that, once they have grown tired of the clatter of worldly life, they might happily leave it behind. But may they have respite from persecution and daily bread in hardship. This is why I remain in my own cultivated field. Do not allow, Lord Almighty! do not allow them to roam after the charity of grandees and acquire in them a comforter! May their heart be their consoler; may their reason be creator of benefit for them.—Sit down and pay heed to my speech as something that ought to remain in the depth of your souls.—I repeat to you again: today we shall part.—It is with ineffable joy that I behold the tears that sprinkle your cheeks. May the agitation of your soul cause my advice to penetrate to its inner sanctum so that in recalling me it will be shaken—and so that even when absent, I shall be to you as a bulwark from evils and griefs.

"Since taking you into my embrace even from the maternal womb, I never wanted anyone else as your guardian to execute things concerning you. Never did a hired caretaker touch your body and never did a hired tutor touch your heart and reason. The vigilant eye of my zeal kept watch over you day and night lest injury draw close to you; and I call myself a blessed man because I led you to the point of separation from me. But do not imagine that I would wish to wrench from your lips gratitude for the care I showed you or acknowledgment, however weak, of what had been done for you by me. Led by the stimulus of self-interest, what was undertaken for your benefit always kept in view my own delight. And so banish from your thoughts that you both are under my power. You are in no way obligated to me. Not in reason, and even less in law, do I wish to locate the strengths of our bond. It is founded in your heart. Woe unto you if you should forget it! My image, pursuing the destroyer of the union of our friendship, will follow him in his hiding and inflict on him unbearable punishment until he returns to our bond. I repeat again to you: you are in no way obligated to me. Consider me as though I were a vagrant and stranger, and if your heart should feel some tender inclination for me, then let us live in friendship, in that greatest prosperity to be found on earth.—If it should be without any sensation—then let us be oblivious of one another as if we had never been born. All-merciful God, grant that I never see this and that I return to your bosom before it happens. You owe me nothing for your feeding, education, and least of all for your birth.—For birth?—Were you participants in it? Were you asked whether to be born? Whether being born was for your good or ill? In giving birth to their son, do a father and mother know whether in life he will be blessed or miserable? Who can say that in entering into matrimony he thought about lineage and descendants; and if he had such an intention, whether it was for the welfare of the children that he wished to beget them or for the preservation of his name? How can I wish well to someone I do not know, and what would it be? Is it possible to call an undefined wish, instigated by the unknown, a good?—The desire for matrimony also indicates the cause of birth. Attracted more by the spiritual goodness of your mother than the beauty of her face, I employed a reliable method in our mutual ardor—sincere love. I obtained your mother as a spouse. But what was the motive for our love? Mutual pleasure, a pleasure of the flesh and spirit. In partaking of a joy mandated by nature we did not think of you. Your birth was pleasant for us but not for you. Reproducing oneself flattered one's vanity, your birth was a new sensual union, so to speak, a union confirming the union of hearts. It is the source of the primal passion of parents for their sons; it is strengthened by habit, by the sense of one's power, by the reflection on the father in praise for his sons.—Your mother shared my opinion that you owed no meaningful debt for your birth. She made no show of pride before you because she bore you in her womb, demanded no recognition for nurturing you with her blood, did not demand respect in exchange for the pain of birth nor for the tediousness of nourishing you from her own teats. She attempted to give you, as she herself possessed, a worthy soul and she wished to plant there friendship but not a sense of obligation, not duty, or servile submissiveness. Fate did not permit her to see the fruits of her cultivations. She left us, and while her spirit was firm she did not wish for her end, seeing your infancy and my devotion. In becoming like her, we do not forfeit her entirely. She will live with us until we depart to join her. You know that the most pleasant conversation with you is conversing about she who bore you. That is when it seems that her soul converses with us: then she herself is present to us, then she appears in us, then she is still alive." And speaking, he wiped drops of tears pent up in his soul.—

"For your keep, you owe me as little as you owe for your birth. When I offer hospitality to a visitor, when I feed feathered chicks, when I give food to a dog who licks my hand, do I do this for them?—In this I find my own joy, pleasure, and benefit. The same impulse brings about the feeding of children. Born into this world, you have become citizens of the society in which you live. My duty was to nourish you, since I would have been a murderer if I had allowed a premature death to affect you. If I was more thoughtful about your nourishment than many others happen to be, I followed the sensation of my heart. It was in my power to take up your nourishment or neglect it; to preserve your days or be their squanderer; to keep you alive or allow you to die prematurely: this is clear proof that you do not owe me for the fact that you are alive. Had you perished because of neglect by me, as many do, legal retribution would not have pursued me.—But it will be said that you owe me for your tuition and education.—Was it not my own advantage I sought in your being worthy? The praises accorded your good conduct, intelligence, learning, culture, in encompassing you reflected on me like solar rays from a mirror. Those praising you praise me. What would I have gained if you had given in to vice, shunned learning, were stupid in your thoughts, nasty, base, and devoid of sensibility? Not only would I have suffered with you in your crooked behavior, but I would have been a victim, perhaps, of your brutality. But now I remain calm in weaning you from myself. Your capacity to reason is upright, your heart stout, and I live in it. O my friends! Sons of my heart, by giving birth to you I had many duties in regard to you. But you owe me nothing; I seek your friendship and love. If you will grant them to me, I shall depart, blissful, to the beginning of life and when I die shall not rebel over leaving you forever, since I shall live on in your memory.

"But if I have fulfilled my duty in your education, I am obliged to tell you the reason why I raised you in this way rather than another, and wherefore I taught you this rather than something else; and, therefore, you will hear the tale of your education and learn the reason of all my actions upon you.

"From the time of your infancy you have felt no compulsion. Although in your activities you have been led by my hand, you all the same never felt its guidance. Your actions were foreknown and forestalled; I did not want the heavy hand of obedience or submission to leave the least trace upon you. And this is why your spirit, hostile to baseless orders, is pliant to the council of friendship. But if, while you were children, I found that you, compelled by a random force, were deviating from the path I had determined, I then stopped your advance; or, better yet, imperceptibly guided you back onto previous path like a stream that overflowing its embankment is returned to its banks through a skillful hand.

"Diffident tenderness was not a trait of mine when I gave the appearance of neglecting to preserve you from the hostility of the elements and the weather. I preferred your body to have been injured briefly by transient pain to its growing feeble when you were of a mature age. And this is why you often went about barefoot, your heads uncovered; in the dust, in the dirt you stretched out to rest, on benches or on rocks. I made no less an effort to keep you from harmful food or drink. Our efforts were the best spice in our midday meal. Remember the pleasure we took in dining in an unfamiliar village after we lost our way home. How delicious we then found the rye bread and village kvass!

"Do not begrudge me if you sometimes find yourselves mocked because you lack a comely gait, because your posture stands comfortably rather than as custom or fashion dictate; that you dress tastelessly, that your hair is curled by the hand of nature rather than a hairdresser. Do not begrudge me if you are overlooked at assemblies, and particularly by women, because you do not know how to praise their beauty. Recall, however, that you run quickly, that you swim tirelessly, that you can lift weights without strain, that you are able to use a plow, dig a furrow, can use a scythe and axe, a plane and chisel, are able to ride horseback, to shoot. Do not feel sad because you are not able to leap like jugglers. Know that the best dancing contains nothing majestic; and if you should be moved by its appearance, the root of it will be salaciousness, everything else is ancillary to this. But you are able to draw animals and *nature morte,* to draw the features of the king of nature, man. In painting, you shall find genuine satisfaction not only of the senses but of reason as well.—I taught you music so that a string quivering in harmony with your nerves would arouse your slumbering heart; for music, by setting inwardness into motion, makes a habit of tenderheartedness in us.—I taught you the barbaric art of fencing, too. But may this art remain dormant in you until self-preservation requires it. It will not, I reckon, make you arrogant; since you are firm of spirit and will not take offence if an ass kicks you with its hoof or a pig grazes you with its stinking snout.—Do not fear telling anyone that you are able to milk a cow, that you can braise cabbage and porridge, or that a piece of meat roasted by you will be tasty. A person who is able to do something himself will be in a position to make another do it and will be forgiving of mistakes because he knows all the difficulties of performance.

"In your infancy and adolescence, I did not burden your reason with readied reflections or alien thoughts, did not burden your memory with too many topics. But having offered you the path to knowledge, since that time you have begun to sense the power of your own reason, you stride by yourselves along the way that is open to you. Your knowledge is better founded because you acquired it not through repetition, as the proverbial saying goes, like parroting birds. In accordance with this rule, for as long as your powers of reason were inactive, I did not present you concepts about the Almighty Being and even less about Revelation. For what you learned before you acquired reason would have been prejudice in you and hindered reasoning. When I then observed that in your ratiocinations you were led by the mind, that was when I suggested to you the connection of concepts that lead to the awareness of God. I am convinced in the depth of my heart that it is more pleasant for the all-munificent Father to behold two unspoiled souls in whom the lamp of learning is not ignited by prejudice, but of their own accord rise aloft to the primal fire to be kindled. That was when I made a proposition to you about the law of Revelation without hiding from you everything that had been said by many in refutation of it. Because I wanted you to be able to discriminate between milk and bile, and joyously saw that you accepted this vessel of comfort boldly.

"In giving you instruction in the sciences, I did not neglect to acquaint you with various peoples, having taught you foreign languages. But above all my duty was that you should know your own language so that you would be able in it to express your thoughts orally and in writing and so that your style would be unforced and not cause a drop of sweat to form on your face. I tried to give you greater familiarity with the English language,[61] as well as Latin, than with others. For the resilience of the spirit of freedom, when transmuted into the signification of language, also trains reason in the concrete concepts essential to all governments.

"But if I allowed your reason to guide your steps on the paths of learning, I endeavored to be all the more vigilant in your moral education. I tried to moderate in you momentary anger, subjecting to reason the anger that is extended and leads to retribution. Retribution! . . . Your soul abhors it. Of this natural inclination of creatures endowed with sensitivity you have only by defying the urge to repay violence kept the defensiveness of your organism.

"The time has now arrived when your feelings, after reaching an apogee of agitation still short of a complete understanding about what has been stimulated, begin to be alarmed by every external stimulus and to produce a dangerous tremor within you. Now you have reached the time when, as it is said, reason becomes the determinant of your activity and inactivity; or better to say when feelings, earlier sustained by the fluidity of infancy, begin to feel disturbance, or when vital juices, having filled the vessel of youth, begin to overflow its brim in search of a path that suits their current. I preserved you inviolable until now from corrupt disturbances of feelings, but did not hide from you, by using the cloak of ignorance, the fatal consequences of being diverted from the path of moderation in sensual satisfaction. You were witnesses of how awful an excess of sensual satisfaction is and abhorred it; you were witnesses of the terrible tumult of passions that overflowed the banks of their natural course, recognized their fateful devastation and recoiled. My expertise, watching over you like a new Aegis, protected you from pointless pains. Now you shall be your own pilots, and while my advice will always be a lamp for your own initiatives, since your heart and soul are open to me, but like a light that grows dimmer as it grows distant from the object, so shall you, at a distance from my presence, feel the weak warmth of my friendship. And this is why I shall teach you the rules of private life and civic life so that you shall feel no disgust at activities done in a passionate state once they have subsided, and shall not know the meaning of remorse.

"The rules of private life, insofar as this pertains to you, must relate to your body and morality. Never forget to use your physical powers and your feelings. Their moderate exercise will strengthen but not exhaust them, and will serve to benefit your health and longevity. And for that reason practice in the arts, crafts, and skills that you know. Mastery in them might sometimes be required. The future is unknown to us. Should inimical fortune strip you of everything it has given you, you will be rich in the moderation of your desires, sustained by the work of your hands. But if you neglect to practice in days of happiness, it will be late to think about this during sad times. Luxury, indolence, and the immoderate satisfaction of senses destroy both the body and spirit. For one who exhausts the body through lack of restraint exhausts the strength of the spirit. But use of your strength will reinforce the body and with it the spirit. If you feel an aversion to foodstuffs and illness comes knocking at the door, leap up then from your bed on which you indulge your senses, engage your sleeping limbs in action with exercise, and you will feel an immediate renewal of your strength. Restrain yourself from the food needed when you are healthy and hunger will make sweet the food that tasted bitter when you were full. Remember always that to put hunger to rest, all that is needed is a morsel of bread and ladle of water. If sleep, the beneficial deprivation of external sensations, should depart from the head of your bed and you are unable to renew your mental and physical powers—flee from your halls and once you have wearied your limbs to the point of exhaustion, lie down on your bed and you will fall asleep for the sake of health.

"Be fastidious in your attire, keep your body clean since cleanliness conduces to health while negligence and fetidness of the body open an insidious path to vile vices. But in this too be not immoderate. Do not shirk from helping to raise up a cart stuck in the mud in a ditch and to help someone who has fallen: get your hands, legs, and body dirty but enlighten your heart. Enter the cabins of degradation, comfort one suffering from poverty, taste his victuals, and your heart will be assuaged through giving joy to the sufferer.

"You have reached now, I repeat, that terrible time and hour when the passions begin to awaken, but when reason is still a weak curb on them. For on the scales of will, the tray of reason without experience will rise up but the tray of passions instantaneously drops very low. There is, therefore, no other way to approach equilibrium except by dint of effort. Put your body to work, your passions will not experience so strong a disturbance; put your heart to work by practicing goodness, sensibility, compassion, generosity, forgiveness, and your passions will find a happy issue. Put your reason to work, laboring at reading, reflections, the search for truth and facts, and reason will guide your will and your passions. But do not have the presumption in a fit of reason that you are able to eliminate the roots of the passions and that you can be completely dispassionate. The root of the passions is good and founded by nature on our sensibility. When our senses, external and internal, weaken and become dulled the passions, too, weaken. They produce in man a beneficial disquiet without which he would fall asleep in inertness. An absolutely dispassionate person is a dolt and ludicrous dummy equally incapable of good and evil. There is no merit in holding back from bad designs if you are unable to carry them out. A man missing an arm is unable to wound anyone but nor can he give aid to a drowning man or restrain a man on the shore who falls into the abyss of the sea.—Therefore moderation in passion is a good; progress on the middle path is secure. Excess in passion is fatal, dispassion is moral death. Like the wayfarer who, wandering away from the middle of the path, risks the danger of falling into this or that ditch, so, too, is the pathway for morality. But should your passions be directed toward a positive goal by experience, reason, and the heart, throw off from them the reins of wearying prudence, do not stymie their flight; grandeur will always be their goal, and there only can they come to rest.

"But if I encourage you not to be dispassionate, more important than anything is moderation of erotic passion in your youth. It has been planted in our heart by nature for our pleasure. Hence a mistake can arise in the lack of moderation and the object but never in its coming to life. Take care, therefore not to be mistaken in the object of your love and not to mistake a semblance for mutual ardor. If the object of love is good, you will not know the immoderateness of passion. As we are talking about love, it would be natural to speak as well about marriage, about this holy social union whose rules nature did not outline in the heart, but whose sanctity flows from the fundamental condition of society. To your reason, scarcely embarked on this path, this would not be clear; to your heart, as yet not having experienced in society the egotistical passion of love, a story about it would be imperceptible to you, and therefore useless. If you should wish to have an idea about marriage, recall her who gave birth to you. Remember me with her and with you, revive in your hearing our words and mutual kisses, and clasp this picture to your heart. You will then feel in it some sort of pleasant shudder. What is it? With time you will recognize, but for now be contented with its sensation.

"Let us now briefly consider the rules of civic life. They cannot be prescribed accurately since their arrangement often takes shape according to momentary circumstances. But to avoid mistakes as much as possible, interrogate your heart in every initiative; it is good and can in no way betray you. What it tells you that is what you should do. By following your heart in youth you will not be mistaken if you have a good heart. But anyone is truly a madman who thinks he can follow reason even before they have hairs on their chin signifying experience.

"The rules of civic society relate to the fulfilment of customs and popular mores, or to the fulfilment of the law, or to the performance of virtue. If in society mores and customs are not contrary to the law, if the law does not present obstacles to virtue on its path, then adherence to the rules of civil society is easy. But where does a society of this type exist? All those known to us are full of many contradictions in mores and customs, the laws and virtues. This is why the fulfilment of one's duty as a human being and citizen becomes difficult, since they frequently occur in complete contradiction.

"Inasmuch as virtue is the acme of human actions, its accomplishment, therefore, must not be hindered in any way. Disregard the mores and customs, disregard civil and sacred law, things held in such respect in society, when their accomplishment separates you from virtue. Do not attempt, above all, to cover up the failure of virtue with cowardly prudence. Without virtue you will be superficially fortunate but never blessed.

"In following what customs and mores require of us, we acquire the goodwill of those with whom we live. By implementing the prescription of the law, we may acquire the name of an honest person. By observing virtue, we acquire general trust, respect, and admiration even among those who otherwise have no wish to feel these in their soul. When giving a cup of poison to Socrates, the treacherous Athenian Senate trembled inwardly before his virtue.

"Never dare to observe customs contrary to the law. The law, however bad, is the connecting principle of society. And even if the ruler himself were to bid you to violate the law do not obey him, since he is mistaken to his own detriment and that of society. Should he abolish the law whose violation he orders, then obey it since the ruler is the source of laws in Russia.

"But if the law, or ruler, or some other earthly power incited you to a lie and the ruin of virtue, remain steadfast. Fear not mockery nor torment nor illness nor prison nor even death. Remain resolute in your soul like a stone surrounded by rioting but powerless waves. The fury of your tormentors will be smashed on your firmness; and if you are consigned to death they will be mocked, while you will live on in the memory of noble souls to the end of time. Be careful in advance about calling weakness in affairs prudence: weakness is the first enemy of virtue. Today you will infringe virtue for some sort of deference, tomorrow its ruin will seem to be virtue itself; and thus it is that vice will come to reign in your heart and distort the features of innocence in your soul and on your face.

"The virtues are private or civil. Motivations for the first are a good heart, gentleness, compassion, and their roots are always good. Motivations for civic virtues often have their origin in vanity and ambition. But one should not stop in their implementation. The purpose that moves them gives them importance. In the figure of Curtius who saved his fatherland from a fatal plague nobody sees a person who was vain or gloomy or desperate but rather a hero. If, however, the motivations to our civil virtues have their origin in a philanthropic firmness of soul, then their brilliance will be that much the greater. Always test yourself in the private virtues in order to be worthy of the implementation of the civic virtues.

"I shall propound to you also several rules of life to follow.—More than anything try in all your actions to earn your self-respect so that when in moments of solitude you turn your gaze inward you shall not only have nothing to regret in what you have done but will look upon yourself with reverence.

"Consistent with this rule, stay aloof insofar as possible from even the appearance of obsequiousness. When you enter the world, you will quickly learn that there is custom in society. The custom of visiting important figures in the mornings on celebratory days is miserable, meaningless, displaying in the visitors the spirit of timidity and in the visited a spirit of arrogance and feeble reason. The Romans had a similar practice, which they called ambition, that is 'aspiration' or 'cultivation,' which is why the love of honor is called ambition since the young through their visits to distinguished people sought for a path for themselves to ranks and distinctions. The same also happens now. But if the custom of the Romans was introduced so that young people could learn through their courting of experienced individuals, I doubt that the goal of this custom has always been preserved uncorrupted. In our times, in visiting distinguished lords nobody has education rather than the attainment of favor as a goal. And thus may your foot never cross the boundary separating obsequiousness from the discharging of a duty. Never visit the antechamber of an important lord if it is not in the performance of your duty. Then even the one whom the contemptible crowd adulates with servility will, in the depths of his soul, not confuse you with the rest, even if he does so with umbrage.

"If it should happen that death truncates my days before you are firmly established on the good path, and the passions lure you off the path of reason while you are still young—do not despair when you see your sometimes misguided course. In your error, in your obliviousness to yourself, love the good. A debauched life, limitless ambition, arrogance, and all the vices of youth leave intact a hope for correction since they glide on the surface of the heart, not wounding it. I would prefer that you be debauched in your young years, spendthrift, arrogant, than tightfisted or even excessively frugal, foppish, more concerned with your appearance than anything else. A disposition we might call systematic to foppishness always indicates a closed mind. If it is recounted that Julius Caesar was a fop then his foppishness had a goal. A passion for women in his youth was the stimulus to this. But from a fop he would have clad himself in a flash in the vilest rag if that had facilitated the attainment of his desires.

"In a young person not only is passing foppishness forgivable, but so is practically every kind of foolishness. If, however, you are going to camouflage treachery, mendacity, perfidy, avarice, pride, vengefulness, beastliness with dazzling actions then while you will blind your contemporaries with the brilliance of your shiny appearance (although you will find nobody who loves you sufficiently to hold up the mirror of truth to you) do not think, however, that it will dull the gaze of perspicacity.—It will penetrate the shiny raiment of cunning, and virtue will expose the blackness of your soul. Your heart will start to hate virtue, and like a sensitive plant will wither at your touch, its arrows will wound and torment you not immediately, but from afar.

"Farewell, my dear ones, farewell, friends of my soul. Today, helped by a fair wind cast your boat off from shores of someone else's experience, course along the waves of human life so you may learn to govern yourselves. Blessed you will be if, having avoided disaster, you reach the berth we crave. Have a happy voyage, that is my sincere wish. My vital forces, exhausted by activity and life, will grow weak and will peter out. I shall leave you for evermore. But this now is my testament to you. If inimical fate exhausts all its arrows on you, if your virtue no longer can find a refuge on earth, if pushed to the last extreme you have no protection from oppression, remember then that you are a person, recall your majesty, seize the crown of beatitude though others attempt to filch it from you.—Die.—I bequeath you the words of the dying Cato.—But if you know how to die in virtue, then know how to die in vice as well, and be, one might say, virtuous in evil itself.—If you hasten after bad deeds, having forgotten my prescriptions, your soul accustomed to virtue will be alarmed, and I shall appear to you in a dream.—Rise, then, from your bedstead, follow in your soul my apparition.—If a tear flows from your eyes, you go back to sleep, you will wake up ready for improvement. But if amidst your bad initiatives, your soul remains unmoved and your eye remains dry. . . . Here is the steel, here is the poison.—Spare me the grief, spare the earth this shameful burden.—Remain, still, my son.—Die for virtue."

While the old man was speaking, a youthful blush covered his wrinkled cheeks; his glance emitted rays of hopeful rejoicing, the features of his face shone with a supernatural substance.—He kissed his children and, conducting them to the carriage, remained firm to the final farewell. But scarcely had the ring of the little postal bell announced to him that they had begun to withdraw from him, this resolute soul softened. Tears filled his eyes, his breast heaved; he reached out his arms for the departing and seemingly wanted to stop the horses in their rush. The youths, spotting from afar that their progenitor was in such a state of sorrow, began to sob so loudly that the breeze carried their pitiful groan to our hearing. They likewise stretched out their arms to their father and seemingly called him to them. The old man was unable to bear the spectacle, his strength waned, and he fell into my embrace. In the meanwhile a hillock screened the youths as they departed from our sight, and once the old man revived, he stood on his knees and raised his arms and eyes to the sky. "Lord," he cried out, "I beseech You to strengthen them in the ways of virtue, pray that they will be blessed. Thou knowest, munificent Father, that I have never bothered You with a pointless supplication. I am certain in my soul how good and just You are. In us what is dearest to You is virtue; the actions of a pure heart are for You the best sacrifice. . . . Today I have separated my sons from myself. . . . Lord, may Your will be done upon them." Troubled but resolved in his hope, he left for his home.

The speech of the nobleman from Kresttsy would not leave my head. His arguments on the futility of the power of parents over children seemed incontestable to me. Even if in a well-policed society the young must respect the old, and the inexperienced must respect perfection, there is no apparent necessity for parental power to be unlimited. If the bond between father and son is not established on tender sentiments of the heart, it is of course not firm, and it will remain not firm despite all the legislation. If the father sees in his son his slave and searches the legislation for power, if the son respects the father for the sake of an inheritance, what good is this to society? Either just another slave in addition to many others, or a serpent at one's breast. . . . A father is obliged to nourish and educate a son and ought to be punished for the son's misdeeds until he has entered his maturity, and a son should find his duties in his heart. If he doesn't feel anything, then the father is guilty because he has not planted anything in him. The son has truly the right to demand a helping hand from the father for as long as he is helpless and immature, but once of age this inherent and natural link lapses. The chick does not seek the aid of the birds who produced it once it begins to find food on its own. The male and female forget their chicks when these have become mature. This is the law of nature. If the civil laws become estranged from it they always produce a freak. The child loves his father, mother, or teacher for as long as his love has not turned to another object. May your heart not be insulted by this, child-loving father, nature requires this. The sole comfort you will have lies in remembering that even your son's son will love his father only to a mature age. Whereupon it will be up to you to attract his zeal to yourself. If you succeed in this, you will be blessed and deserving of respect.—These were my thoughts as I arrived at the post station.

YAZHELBITSY

It was determined by fate that this day was to be a test for me. I am a father, I have a tender heart toward my children. This was why the speech of the nobleman from Kresttsy so moved me. But while it shook me to my inner being, it poured out some soothing hopeful sensation that our bliss on account of our children depends in large part on ourselves. But in Yazhelbitsy it was my lot to be a witness of a spectacle that planted in my soul a deep root of sadness, and there is no hope it will be uprooted. O youth! Listen to my tale, learn your error, refrain from a voluntary disaster, and block the way to future repentance.

I was riding past a cemetery. The extraordinary wail of a man who was tearing out his hair compelled me to stop. Getting closer, I saw that a funeral was taking place there. The moment had already come to lower the coffin into the grave. The man I had seen from afar tearing his hair out threw himself onto the coffin and by clutching at it with considerable strength hindered its descent into the earth. It was with great difficulty that he was deflected from the coffin, and they hastily lowered it into the grave and buried it. At that moment the sufferer addressed those present: "Why have you deprived me of him, why did you not bury me alive with him and not put an end to my sorrow and remorse? Know, know that I am the murderer of my beloved son, the dead one you consigned to the ground. Feel no surprise at this. I shortened his life neither by sword nor poison. No, I did worse. His death I had prepared before his birth by giving to him a life already poisoned. I am a murderer—there are many such—but I am a far crueler murderer than the others. A murderer of a son, my son, before his birth. I, I alone shortened his days by pouring insidious poison into his inception. It prevented his body from growing strong. During his entire lifetime not for a single day did he enjoy health; the diffusion of the poison interrupted the course of life of one who was dwindling in vitality. Nobody, nobody will punish me for my evil deed!" Despair was emblazoned on his face and he was carried from the spot practically lifeless.—

A startling chill poured through my veins. I froze. I thought I had heard my condemnation. I recollected the dissolute days of my youth. I brought to mind all the instances when, thrown into tumult by feelings, my soul pursued their satisfaction, considering the mercenary partner in my amorous pleasure as a true object of ardor. I recollected that the lack of restraint in fornication visited a fetid disease on my body. Oh, if only its root had not penetrated so deeply! Oh, if only the satisfaction of fornication had put an end to it! Receiving this poison in our merriment not only we do incubate it in our loins, but we bequeath it as an inheritance to our descendants.—O my dear friends, O children of my soul! You do not know how badly I have sinned before you. Your pale brow is my condemnation. I dread informing you about the sickness you sometimes feel. You will, perhaps, hate me and you will be justified in your hatred. Who can reassure us, you and myself, that you do not bear in your blood the hidden sting destined to prematurely end your life span? Having contracted this fetid poison in my body at a mature age, the firmness of my limbs has resisted its spread and fights with its lethalness. But you, having contracted it at birth, carry it within you as integral part of your organism: how will you resist its destructive combustion? All your maladies are the results of this toxicity. O my dear ones! Weep over the error of my youth, invoke in aid the art of medicine, and, if you can, do not hate me.

But it is now that the full extent of this voluptuous crime opens before my eyes. I sinned before myself by incurring when still youthful an untimely old age and decrepitude. I sinned before you by having poisoned your life juices before you were born and thereby predetermined your feeble health and, perhaps, a premature death. I sinned—and may this be a punishment to me—I sinned in my amorous ardor when I took your mother in marriage. Who can guarantee to me that I was not the cause of her extinction? A death-dealing poison, diffused in pleasure, was transferred to her chaste body and corrupted her innocent limbs. Its lethalness was all the greater by being more hidden. A false primness had prevented me from warning her; however, she was not wary of her poisoner in her passion for him. The inflammation that beset her was, perhaps, the fruit of the poison that I had given her. . . . O my dear ones, how greatly you must hate me!

But who is the reason that this fetid illness produces in all kingdoms such devastation, mowing down not only the current generation but also shortening the span of future generations? Who is the cause if not the government? By sanctioning remunerated debauchery, it not only opens up the path to many vices but poisons the life of citizens. Public women find defenders, and in some countries come under the protection of the authorities. If the release of amorous passion for pay were prohibited then, some maintain, the shocks felt not infrequently in society would be powerful. Amorous passion would be the cause of not infrequent abductions, rapes, and murder. They might even shake the very foundations of societies.—And you would rather have quiet and the fatigue and sorrow that go with it than the health and bravery that go with disquiet. Keep silent, revolting teachers, you who are the mercenaries of tyranny, which, by always preaching peace and quiet, ensnares in chains those who have been lulled by flattery. Tyranny fears even peripheral disturbance. It would prefer thought to agree with it everywhere so that it can be reliably cossetted in grandeur and wallow in fornication. . . . I am not surprised by your words. It is proper that slaves want to see everyone in chains. A uniformity of fates eases their lot, while anyone's superiority oppresses their reason and spirit.

VALDAI

The story goes that this little town was settled by Poles taken into captivity during the reign of Tsar Alexei Mikhailovich. This little town is remembered for the erotic inclinations of its residents, and most especially its unmarried women.

Who has not been to Valdai, who is not familiar with the pretzels of Valdai and Valdai's rouged-up wenches? The brazen wenches of Valdai, their shame cast aside, impede every voyager and attempt to inflame the traveler's concupiscence in order to profit from his generosity at the expense of their chastity. Comparing the morals of the inhabitants of this village, raised to the status of a city, with the morals of other Russian cities, you would take the former to be the most ancient, its corrupt morals are the sole vestige of its ancient founding. But as it is only a little more than a hundred years since it was settled, one can conclude how debauched even its first residents must have been.

The baths were, and still are, a place for amorous festivities. Once the terms of his visit with an accommodating old lady or a lad have been agreed, the traveler takes up temporary residence where he intends to make his sacrifice to Lada,[62] the universally worshipped. Night has fallen. The bath is already prepared for him. The traveler undresses, enters the bath where the hostess, if she is young, greets him—or her daughter, or relations, or neighbors. They rub down his tired limbs, they wash off his dirt. They do this having shed their clothing, they ignite in him an erotic fire, and he spends the night here, losing money, health, and precious travel time. The story goes that in the past, in order to appropriate his property, these lascivious monsters would consign to death the incautious traveler, subdued by his erotic conquests and wine. I do not know whether this is true, but it is true that the brazenness of these Valdai wenches has diminished. And while they do not even now refuse to satisfy the desires of a traveler, their previous brazenness is no longer apparent.

Lake Valdai, on which this city is built, will still be remembered in tales about the monk who sacrificed his life for the sake of his lover. One and a half *versts** from the city, on an island in the middle of the lake, is situated the Iversk Monastery, built by the famous Patriarch Nikon. One of the monks of this monastery, when visiting Valdai, fell in love with the daughter of a resident of Valdai. The love soon became mutual, soon they hurtled towards its consummation. Once they had tasted its delight, they no longer had the strength to resist its compulsion. But the position of each created a barrier to this. The lover could not often be absent from his monastery; his mistress could not visit the cell of her lover. But their passion overcame all: out of the besotted monk it made a fearless man and endowed him with practically supernatural strength. Scarcely had

* one mile—Trans.

the night covered everything visible in its black mantle, when this new Leander,[63] in order to take his pleasure daily in the arms of his mistress, quietly emerged from his cell, and, taking off his cassock, swam across the lake to the opposite bank where he was welcomed into his beloved's embraces. A bath and its amorous delights were already prepared for him and he would forget the danger and difficulty of the crossing, as well as fear that his absence could be discovered. He returned to his cell several hours before sunrise. He thus spent a long time in these dangerous traversals, compensating with nocturnal pleasure for the boredom of his daily confinement. But fate put an end to his amorous triumphs. On one of the nights when the intrepid lover set off across the waves to behold his dear one, a biting headwind suddenly rose up halfway through his trip. All his efforts to overcome the furious waters were futile. In vain did he exhaust himself by straining every muscle; in vain did he raise his voice to be heard in the moment of danger. When he saw the impossibility of reaching the shore, he conceived the idea to return to his monastery. With the wind behind him, it would be easier to reach that bank. But no sooner had he reversed his course when the waves, overpowering his tired muscles, plunged him into their yawning depths. On the morn, his body was found on a distant shore. If I had been writing an epic poem about this, I would have represented to my reader his mistress in anguish. But that would be excessive here. Everyone knows that at least for an initial moment a mistress despairs to learn the death of her dear one. But I do not even know whether our new Hero[64] threw herself into the lake or perhaps on the next night yet again prepared a bath for a traveler. The chronicle of love relates that the beauties of Valdai did not die of love . . . except perhaps only in the hospital.

The mores of Valdai have also encroached upon the closest postal station, Zimnogorye. Here the same sort of reception is readied for the traveler that he has in Valdai. The first thing to meet their gaze will be rouged-up girls and their pretzels. But since my youthful years had already passed, I hastily parted company with the painted sirens of Valdai and Zimnogorye.

EDROVO

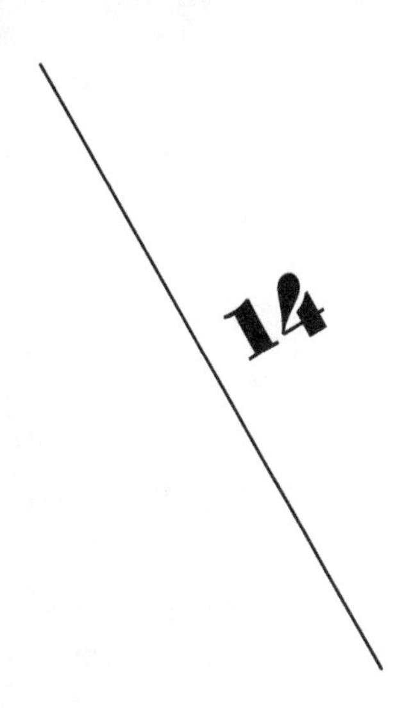

Having arrived at at a settlement, I got out of the carriage. Not far from the road, over the water, stood many women and young girls. The lust that had my entire life dominated me, though by now dimmed, took its usual course and directed my steps to the throng of these rustic beauties. This crowd consisted of more than thirty women. They were all in their holiday clothing, their necks exposed, feet bare, elbows uncovered, each dress tucked up in front under the girdle at the waist, white undershirts, cheerful glances, health written on their cheeks. Although coarsened by heat and cold, these attractions were no less charming for the lack of artifice: the beauty of youth in its full brilliance, a smile on the lips or a hearty laugh from which a row of teeth whiter than the purest ivory became visible. Teeth that would drive fashionable dressers out of their minds. Come hither, dear Muscovite and Petersburg young ladies, look at their teeth, learn from them how to keep them pure. They have no dentist. They do not daily rub the shine off their teeth with brushes and powder. Stand next to any of them as you please, mouth to mouth. None will infect your lung with their breath. But your own breath, your own might, perhaps, in them deposit the basis of . . . disease . . . which one I fear to say; while you might not blush, you would be angry.—Am I telling a lie?—One of you, your husband goes about with all the trashy wenches. Having contracted the disease, he drinks, eats, and, why, sleeps with you, while another woman deigns to have lovers by the year, month, week, or, God forbid, day. Having made his acquaintance in a day and fulfilled her desire, the next day she does not know him; indeed, sometimes she does not even know that she has already become infected through a mere kiss of his.—And you, my little dove, a fifteen-year-old maiden, perhaps you are still innocent; but I can see on your brow that your blood has been thoroughly poisoned. Your father of blessed memory hardly left the care of doctors, but to set you on her own pious path your good lady and mother has found you a bridegroom, a worthy elderly general, and only rushes to give you away in marriage in order not to make a visit to the orphanage with you. No bad thing it is to be married to a codger, complete freedom to do as you please. The main thing is to be wedded, all the children are his. Should he be jealous, so much the better: there is more pleasure to be had in frolics snatched secretly; from the first night, it should be possible to train him not to follow the stupid old custom of sleeping in one bed with his wife.—

I was not keeping track how long you, my dear city in-laws, aunties, sisters, nieces, and so on, detained me. To tell the truth, you don't deserve it. You have rouge on your cheek, rouge on your heart, rouge on your conscience, and on your sincerity you have . . . soot. It's all the same whether it is rouge or soot. I would flee from you at full pelt to my country beauties. It is true that some among them resemble you, but there are others unheard of and never seen in cities. Look how round, stout, straight, and sound the limbs of my beauties are. You are amused that their feet are five or even six *vershok*[*] long. Well, then, my dear niece, with a foot size of three *vershok*[†], stand next to them and launch into a race. Who will reach the tall birch at the end of the meadow faster? Tut-tut, that's not your business.—And you, my dear little dove, dear sister, whose waist is three-quarters of an *arshin*[‡], you deign to laugh that my country sprite's belly is uncorseted. Hold on, my dear dove, I shall laugh a bit at you too. Here we are, more than nine months since marriage and your three-quarter *arshin* figure is already ruined. And when you get as far as childbirth, then you'll sing a different tune. May God grant that be no more than a laughing matter. My dear brother-in-law goes around feeling blue. He has already thrown into the fire all your corset laces. He has removed the stays from your dresses but it's too late—no way can he straighten those limbs of yours that grew crooked.—Grieve, my dear brother-in-law, grieve. Heeding the deplorable fashion known for causing the death of women in childbirth, for you our mother has laid up grief for many years to come, illness for her daughter, a weak constitution for your children. Illness now brandishes over her head the fatal knife and if it does not touch your spouse's life, thank chance; and if you believe that Divine Providence is concerned with the matter, then thank Providence if you like.—But I haven't yet finished with these city ladies.—This is what habit does; no wish to have done with them. And, honestly, I'd not have parted from you if I could have

---

[*] nine or ten inches—Trans.

[†] five inches—Trans.

[‡] twenty-one inches—Trans.

persuaded you not to disguise with rouge your faces and sincerity. And now, goodbye. —

While I gazed at the rustic nymphs washing dresses, my carriage left without me. I intended to follow it on foot when one wench who looked about twenty and was, of course, no more than seventeen, laying her wet laundry on the carrying pole, took the same road as I. Drawing level with her, I began a conversation with her. "Do you not find it hard to carry such a heavy load, my dear (what your name is I do not know)?" "My name is Anna, and my load is not heavy.[65] And even if it were heavy, I would not have asked you, Master, to aid me." "Why be so stern Annushka, my soul, I wish you no harm." "Thank you, thanks. We often see rakes like you. Please, be on your way." "Anyutushka, honestly, I am not how I seem to you and am not like those about whom you speak. They, I venture, do not initiate their conversation with village girls as I have, but always begin with a kiss; but even if I were to kiss you then it would only be, of course, as though you were my very own sister." "Do not sidle up too close, please. I have heard stories of this kind; and if you intend no harm, what do you want from me?" "Annushka, my soul, I would like to know whether you have a mother and father, how you live, richly or scantily, or cheerfully, and whether you have a bridegroom." "And what's it to you, Master? This is the first time in my life I hear such speeches." "From which you may judge, Anyuta, that I am not a villain, do not wish to bully or dishonor you. I love women because their constitution is made in a way that suits my capacity for tenderness; and I love country or peasant women even more because they are still ignorant of dissembling, do not assume the cover of feigned love, but when they love they love with all their heart and sincerely. . . ." All this time the girl looked at me, her eyes popping with astonishment. And it could only be this way, since who does not know how impudently the nobleman's bold hand grasps after tricks indecent and offensive to the chastity of country girls? In the eyes of old and young members of the nobility, these creatures were made for their delectation. They behave as you'd expect, especially with the unfortunate subjected to their commands. During the recent Pugachev disturbance, when all servitors took up arms against their masters, some peasants (this story is not untrue) tied up their master and were taking him to certain execution. What was the reason for this? He had been in every respect a good and humane master, but a husband was insecure concerning his wife and a father concerning his daughter. Every night the master's scouts fetched for him a woman he had chosen that day to be sacrificed in dishonor. It was known in the village that he had defiled sixty girls, violating their virginity. When it arrived, a detachment of soldiers rescued this barbarian from the hands of his angry peasants. Stupid peasants, you sought justice from a Pretender![66] Why did you not inform your legal authorities about this? They would have condemned your master to civil death and you would have remained innocent. Now, however, the villain has been saved. Blessed is he if the immediate sight of death has changed his way of thinking and altered the flow of his vital juices.—But we said that the peasant is dead in the eyes of the law. . . . No, no, he is alive, he will be alive, if he wants it. . . .

"If, Sir, you are not jesting," said Anyuta, "then this is what I will tell you. I have no father, he died about two years ago. I have a mother and younger sister. Dad left us five horses and three cows. We have enough small livestock and poultry, but we do not have a worker at home. They wanted to arrange my marriage into a wealthy household to a ten-year-old lad, but I did not want this. What do I want with such a child: I will not love him. And by the time he grows up I will be old and he will start to chase after others. They also say that family's father-in-law himself sleeps with the young daughters-in-law while the sons are growing up. That is why I had no wish to join his family. I would like someone my own age. My husband will be the one I love, and he will also love me, I have no doubt about that. I do not like going out with young men, but wish to get married, Master. And do you know why?" said Anyuta, lowering her eyes. "My dear, tell me, Anyutushka, do not be ashamed. On the lips of innocence all words are blameless." "Here is what I will tell you. Last summer, a year ago, the son of our neighbor married my friend with whom I always used to attend gatherings. Her husband loves her, and she loves him so much that she bore him a son in the tenth month after their marriage. Every evening she goes out to fuss over him at the gates. She cannot look at him enough. It seems that the little boy, too, already loves his mother. She says 'goo goo' and he laughs aloud. I am on the verge of tears daily. I so much would love myself to have a little boy like that. . . ." I was unable to contain myself and embraced Anyuta and kissed her with all my heart. "Look here, Master, what a sham you are, you are already dallying with me. Sir, off you go, stay away from me, leave a poor orphan," said Anyuta bursting into tears. "If my father were alive and saw this then he would have given you quite a hiding, despite the fact that you are a master." "Do not be offended, my dear Anyutushka, do not be offended, my kiss will not defile your innocence. In my eyes, it is sacred. My kiss is a sign of the respect I bear you and was wrenched by rapture from a deeply moved soul. Do not fear me, dear Anyuta, I am not akin to a beast of prey like our young lordlings who consider the violation of virginity as a mere trifle. Had I known that my kiss was going to offend you,

I swear to you before God that I would never have dared." "Consider for yourself, Master, how could I not get cross about a kiss when they are all already promised to another? They have already been given in advance and I have no power over them." "You delight me. You already know how to love.[67] You have found another heart suited to your own. You will be blessed. Nothing will debase your union. You will not be surrounded by spies trying to ensnare you in their web of perdition. The friend-of-your-heart's hearing will not be ensnared by a seductive voice tempting him to the destruction of his fidelity to you. But why then, my dear Anyuta, are you deprived of the satisfaction of enjoying happiness in the embraces of your sweet friend?" "Ah, Master, because they will not permit him to move to our house. They want one hundred rubles. And my mother will not give me up: I am her only worker." "Does he love you?" "And how can he not! In the evenings, he comes to our house and together we look at my girlfriend's little boy. . . . He would like such a little one of his own. I will be sad, but shall have to put up with it. My Vanyukha[68] wants to go to Piter[69] on the barges to work and not come back until he has earned a hundred rubles toward buying his freedom." "Do not let him, dear Anyutushka, do not let him go; he is going to his doom. There, he will learn to get drunk, to be profligate, to be a glutton, learn to stop loving fieldwork—and the worst of it is that he will stop loving you." "Ah, Master, do not scare me," said Anyuta, nearly crying. "It will be all the sooner, Anyuta, if he happens to serve in the nobleman's house. The example of the master infects the upper servants, the lower ones catch it from the upper servants, and from them the infection of debauchery reaches as far as the countryside. An example is a true plague: to see something is to do it." "Then what should we do? So I will never be married to him. It is, indeed, time for him to wed. He doesn't chase after others; since I am not allowed to marry him and go live in his house they will plight his troth to another girl, and I, poor me, will die from grief. . . ." She said this, weeping bitter tears. "No, my dear Anyutushka, tomorrow you will be married to him. Lead me to your mother." "Here's where we live," she said as she stopped. "Walk past, my mamma will see me and think ill. And even though she does not beat me, her word alone is worse than any blows." "No, my Anyuta, I'll go with you . . ." and, without waiting for her answer, I entered the gates and went straight up the steps to the hut. Anyuta shouted after me, "Stop, Master, stop." But I paid no need. In the hut, I found Anyuta's mother who was mixing dough; next to her, on the bench sat her future son-in-law. Without further hemming and hawing, I told her that I wanted her daughter to marry Ivan and to that end I had brought her what was needed to eliminate an impediment to that business. "Thank you, Master, "said the old lady, "there is no need for this anymore. Vanyukha has just now come to say that his father gives him leave to come to my home. So we will have the wedding on Sunday." "Then let what I have promised be Anyuta's dowry." "And for that thank you. Boyars do not give dowries to maidens for no reason. If you have wronged my Anyuta, and that is why you are giving her a dowry, then God will punish you for your bad conduct; but I shall not take your money. If you are a good person and do not abuse the poor, bad people will think who knows what if I take your money." There was no end to my surprise in finding so much nobility in the manner of thought of these rustic dwellers. In the meantime, Anyuta entered the hut and showered praise on me to her mother. I again attempted to give them money, giving it to Ivan for the establishment of their home. But he said to me, "I have, Master, two hands, and with them I shall establish my household." Noting that my presence was not very pleasant for them I left them and returned to my carriage.

While I was leaving Edrovo, Anyuta did not quit my thoughts. Her innocent sincerity pleased me infinitely. The noble action of her mother captivated me. I compared this venerable mother, her sleeves rolled up over the dough or with a milking pail next to a cow, with city mothers. The peasant woman did not want to take my untainted, well-intended hundred rubles, which in proportion to wealth would be like ten, fifteen, or more thousand for the wife of a colonel, state councillor, major, or general; indeed, if to a madam colonel, major, state councillor . . . (in accordance with my promise to the widow of the Edrovo carriage driver) whose daughter has a not bad-looking face, or is at least innocent, which would itself be sufficient, a distinguished gentleman of a seventy-year or, God forbid, seventy-two-year vintage, would offer five, ten, fifteen thousand or a fine dowry of an undetermined amount, or would find a high-ranking groom, or would get for her a maid-of-honor position at court—if that were so I ask you, city mothers, would your heart not skip a beat? Would you not want to see your daughter covered in diamonds in a gilded carriage drawn by four horses instead of walking on foot; or see her transported by a train of horses rather than the two famished nags that drag her? I agree with you on the point that you would observe ceremony and propriety and that you would not surrender readily, as stage actresses do. No, my little doves, I give you a month or two but not more. But if you should compel a grandee lover to sigh away for a longer time pointlessly, then he, preoccupied as he is with affairs of state, will leave you in order not to waste valuable time with you that he could better spend for the good of society.—A thousand voices rise up against me, they curse me with all the possible foul names: rogue, thief, rasc . . . , dev . . . , and so on and so on.—My little doves, calm down, I am not besmirching your honor. Are all of you like this? Take a good look in this mirror. If any of you recognizes yourself in it then curse me without mercy. I shall not make a complaint about her, I shall not take her to court over this.

Anyuta, Anyuta, you have turned my head! Why did I not meet you fifteen years ago? Your sincere innocence, impervious to the lascivious daring of a seducer, would have taught me to stay on the path of chastity. Why was the first kiss of my life not the one I planted on your cheek in a state of spiritual rapture? The reflection of your liveliness would have penetrated to the depths of my heart, and I would have avoided the nastiness that has filled my existence. I would have kept my distance from putrid women hired for lust, respected the marital bed, not disturbed the bond of family with my fleshly insatiety; virginity would have been to me the holy of holies and I would not have dared to touch it. O my Anyutushka! Remain always seated by the village gate and be an example through your uninhibited innocence. I am certain that you will turn to the path of good behavior one who has begun to stray from it and will reinforce one inclined to stray. Do not be alarmed if someone rooted in corruption, having grown grey in the embraces of shamelessness, walks past you and despises you. Do not attempt in vain to hinder his progress with the pleasure of your conversation. His heart is already stone, his soul has a carapace of diamond. The beneficial prod of innocent virtue is incapable of leaving on him a deep trace. Its tip will skate over the surface of his smoothly hardened vice. Take care lest your stinger is blunted against it. But do not let pass the youth deceived by the dangerous delights of beauty, catch him in your net. He seems proud, arrogant, impulsive, insolent, bold, insulting, wounding. But his heart will give way to the impression you make and open up to receive your positive example.—Anyuta, I cannot take my leave of you although already I spot the twentieth milestone from you.—

What is this custom about which Anyuta was telling me? They wanted to give her in marriage to a ten-year-old child. Who could allow such a union? Why does the hand guarding the laws not act for the extirpation of such an abuse? In Christian law marriage is a sacrament, in civil law an agreement or contract. What kind of hierophant could bless such an unequal marriage, or what sort of judge could record it in his journal? Where ages are not equivalent there can be no marriage. The laws of nature prohibit this sort of thing as something that is useless for humanity; it should be prohibited by civil law as harmful to society. A man and wife in society are two citizens who make an agreement confirmed by law binding them to give one another reciprocal sensual pleasure (may nobody dare to contest this most elementary law of cohabitation and a foundation of marital concord, the basis of untainted love, and the firm foundation stone of spousal harmony), undertake to live together, to share a common property, to cultivate the fruits of their passion, and so as to live peacefully not to harm one another. Given the disparity in years, is it possible to keep the terms of such an agreement? If the husband is ten years old and the wife twenty-five, as often happens among the peasantry; or the husband is fifty and the wife is fifteen or twenty, as happens among the nobility, can there be any reciprocal pleasure of the senses? You tell me, oldster husbands, but speak in conscience, do you deserve the name of a husband? You are only able to ignite an amorous fire but not to extinguish it. One of the primary laws of nature is violated by the inequality of years. Can, then, a fundamental law be secure if it does not have a basis in nature? Let us be clear: it does not even exist.—To cultivate the fruits of mutual passion.—But can there be reciprocity in this instance when, on the one hand, you have a flame and, on the other, insensateness? Can there be a fruit here if the tree that has been planted is deprived of the benefit of rain and nourishing moisture? And if a fruit should result then it will be scrawny, ugly, and doomed to speedy decay.—Not to harm one another.—This rule is eternal and reliable: if the feelings of the couple are equally satisfied through a felicitous sympathy, then the marital union will be fortunate; small domestic tribulations soon quiet down at the onset of joy. And when the chill of old age will shroud erotic joy in an unbreachable carapace, then the recollection of former joys will calm a sullen antiquity of years.—Only one condition of the marital contract can be fulfilled in inequality: to live together.—But will it have reciprocity?—One will be a despotic ruler, holding power in his hands, the other will be a weak subject and a complete slave, able only to fulfill the bidding of the lord.—These, Anyuta, are the good thoughts you inspired in me. Farewell, my dear Anyutushka, your lessons will forever be engraved in my heart and the sons of my sons will inherit them.

The Khotilov postal station was already visible yet I continued to reflect on the Edrovo wench and in a burst of ecstasy exclaimed loudly from my spirit: “O Anyuta! Anyuta!” The road was not smooth, the horses advanced at a walk; the coach driver listened in to my speech turning round: “It is clear, Master,” he said to me with a smile and righting his hat, “that you have taken a fancy to our Anyutka. That’s some girl! You are not the only one she’s run rings round. . . . She’s got it all. . . . There are lots of fetching girls at our postal station but by comparison with her the rest are nothing to speak of. What a mistress she is of dancing! She will outdo everyone, no matter who. . . . And when she goes out to harvest in the field . . . what a fine spectacle. Well . . . my brother Vanka is happy." "Ivan is your brother?" "My cousin. There's a fellow! Three lads began to court Anyutka. Ivan sent them all packing. They pleaded this and that, but she was having none of it. And Vanyukha immediately reeled her in. . . . (We were already driving through the village gate. . . .) That's the way it is, Master. Anyone can dance—but not everyone can dance like a juggler." And he drove up to the station courtyard.

"Anyone can dance—but not everyone can dance like a juggler," I repeated as I got down from the carriage. . . . "Anyone can dance—but not everyone can dance like a juggler," I repeated, bending down and, after picking up, unfolding. . . .

15

KHOTILOV

Project for the Future

By having gradually led our beloved fatherland to the flourishing state which it presently enjoys, we see the sciences, arts, and crafts elevated to the highest level of perfection that man is permitted to achieve; we see in our lands that human reason, freely extending its wings, everywhere rises unchecked and unerringly to greatness and has now become the reliable guardian of the laws of society. Under its mighty aegis, our heart is also able to say freely and with ineffable joy in prayers wafted to the Supreme Creator that our fatherland is a pleasant abode for the divinity, since its constitution is based not on prejudices and superstitions, but on our interior sensation of the munificence of the Father of All. The enmities that so often divide people because of their confession are unknown to us, just as coercion of conscience therein is unknown to us. Born into this freedom, we genuinely consider one another as brothers, belonging to one family, having one Father, God.

The beacon of knowledge overseeing our law code now distinguishes it from that of many of the world's other legal systems. A balance of powers, equality of property ownership, cuts off at the root civic disputes. Moderation in punishments obliges one to respect the laws of the higher powers and is like the instructions of tender parents to their offspring, preempting even unpremeditated crimes. The clarity of rules about the acquisition and preservation of estates prevents family feuds from recurring. The boundaries separating a citizen on his domain from his neighbor are clear, obvious to all, and respected by all as sacred. Private offenses between us are rare and get resolved amicably. Public education has made it a concern that we should be mild-tempered, that we should be peaceful as citizens, and above all, that we should be human beings.

As we revel in our domestic peace, having no enemies, taking society to the higher blessing of citizenly cohabitation, could we possibly remain such strangers to a feeling of humanity, strangers to feelings of pity, strangers to the tenderness of noble hearts, strangers to fraternal love, and abandon to our eternal discredit, to the disapproval of furthest posterity, an entire third of our fellows, our equal citizens, our brothers adored in nature, placed in the heavy shackles of slavery and captivity before our very eyes? The bestial custom of enslaving one's fellow man, a custom that originated in the torrid regions of Asia, a custom suited to savage nations, a custom signifying a petrified heart and complete absence of soul, spread across the face of the earth, quickly, far, and wide. And we, the sons of glory, we, glorious by name and deeds among the peoples of the earth,[70] stunned by the benightedness of ignorance, have adopted this practice; and have maintained it intact even to the present day to our shame, to the shame of past centuries, to the shame of this Age of Reason.

You know from the deeds of your fathers, everyone knows from our chronicles, that the wise rulers of our people, incited by a genuine philanthropy and from having understood the natural tie of the social contract, attempted to place a limit on this hydra-headed evil. But their sovereign triumphs were then rendered useless by the hereditary nobility. Now being retrograde and sunk into scorn, they were known at the time for their arrogant privileges in the rank-based order of our government. Despite the might of the scepter's power, our sovereign ancestors were powerless to destroy the chains of civic bondage. Far from realizing their good intentions—indeed, ensnared by the aforementioned rank-based order—they were induced to accept rules that were against their heart and mind. Our fathers viewed these wreckers with tears, perhaps heartfelt tears, as they tightened the bonds and weighed down the shackles of society's most useful members. To the present day, landworkers are slaves among us; we do not acknowledge them as fellow citizens equal to us, have forgotten the human in them. O fellow citizens beloved of us! O true sons of the fatherland! Look around you and recognize your error. The servants of the eternal Divine One strove for the benefit of society and the benefaction of man following ideas similar to ours, explained to you in their sermons that were preached in the name of the all-beneficent God about how it contravened His wisdom and love to rule arbitrarily over one's neighbor. They attempted through arguments drawn from nature and our heart to demonstrate to you your cruelty, falsehood, and sin. In the temples of the living God, their voice triumphantly continues to cry out loudly: "Come to your senses, misguided ones; relent, hard-hearted ones. Shatter the shackles of your brothers, open the dungeon of captivity, and grant your fellow humans to partake of the sweetness of communal life for which they have been readied by the Munificent One, just like you. On a par with you, they rejoice in the beneficial rays of the sun, their limbs and feelings are the same as yours, and their right to use them should be the same."

But if the servants of the Divine represented to your gaze the injustice of human enslavement, we consider it our duty to reveal to you its damage to society and the unfairness to the citizen. It would seem superfluous, at a time long marked by the philosophical spirit, to furnish or renew arguments about the essential equality of men and, therefore, of citizens. To one who grew up under the protection of freedom, filled with noble feeling rather than prejudices, the proofs of the primacy of equality are the ordinary motions of one's heart. But here is the misfortune of mortal life on this earth: to blunder in the light and not to see what stands before one's own eyes.

When you were young, you were taught in school the foundations of natural law and civil law. Natural law showed you men conceived outside society, endowed with the same organism by nature and thereby possessing the same rights; consequently, equal in everything to one another and individually, not subordinated one to another. Civil law showed you men having exchanged unlimited freedom for a peaceful use of it. However, if everyone imposed a limit on their freedom and a rule to their own actions, since they are equal from the maternal womb in respect of natural freedom, they should then be equal in respect of its limitation. It follows, therefore, that here, too, the individual is not subservient to another. In society, the first sovereign is the law, since it is the same for all. But what was the motivation to enter into a social bond and fix arbitrary limits to actions? Reason will say: self-interest. The heart will say: self-interest. The uncorrupted civil law will say: self-interest. We live in a society that has already spanned many stages of improvement, and we have, therefore, forgotten its original state. But consider all young peoples and all societies in a state of nature (if one can put it that way). First, slavery is a crime;

second, only the criminal or enemy experiences there the oppression of captivity. By looking at these attitudes, we recognize how far we have strayed from the goal of society, how far we still stand from the summit of social welfare. Everything said by us is familiar to you, and rules like these you have sucked with your mother's milk. Only a momentary prejudice, only greed (may you not be stung by our utterances), only greed blinds us so we become akin to people going mad in the dark.

But who among us wears chains, who feels the weight of servitude? The landworker! the nourisher of our wants, the feeder of our hunger, he who gives us health and sustains our life has not the right to utilize what he cultivates or what he produces. Who has the tightest claim to the field if not its cultivator? Let us imagine in our minds men who have arrived in the wilderness in order to set up a society. In considering their subsistence, they divide the land overgrown by grass. Who in the division receives a parcel of land? Is it not he who is able to plow, is it not he who has sufficient strength and desire? A land grant would be useless for a youngster or an old man, for the weak, infirm, and lazy. The land would remain fallow and the wind would not rustle its corn. If it is useless to its cultivator it will be just as pointless to society: its cultivator will have no surplus to give to society since he will not have enough for himself. This is why at the origin of society the person able to work the field had a right to own it and had exclusive use by means of that work. But how far have we strayed from that primordial position of society in respect of ownership! With us, not only is the person who has a natural right to ownership completely excluded but, while cultivating someone else's land, he sees his subsistence depend on the power of another! To your enlightened minds, these verities cannot be unfathomable;

however, your actions in the implementation of these truths, as we already said, have been impeded by prejudices and greed. Can it be that your hearts, full of love for mankind, prefer greed to the sensations that delight your heart? What gain is there in this for you? Can a state in which two-thirds of the citizens are deprived of civic status and are in part dead in the eyes of the law be called blessed? Can the civic condition of the peasant in Russia be called blessed? Only the insatiably bloodthirsty would say that the peasant is blessed since he has no idea of a better situation.

We shall try now to refute these beastly rulers' regulations, just as once upon a time our forerunners in their own actions sought unsuccessfully to refute them.

Civic welfare can appear in various forms. Blessed is the state, they say, when peace and order reign. Blessed it seems when its fields are not barren and when in its cities proud buildings soar. Blessed they call it when the power of its arms extends far and it reigns beyond itself not only through force but also through the power of the word over the opinions of others. But all these forms of welfare can be called superficial, momentary, ephemeral, partial, and theoretical.

Let us gaze upon the valley that spreads out before our eyes. What do we see? A vast military camp. Everywhere peace reigns there. All the warriors stand in their place. The greatest possible order is beheld in their ranks. A single command, a single wave of the hand of their leader, moves the entire camp and moves it harmoniously. But can we call the soldiers blessed? Turned into puppets by the accuracy of their martial regimentation, they forfeit even the freedom to move that is intrinsic to living matter. They know only the command of the leader, think only as he wishes, and move headlong where he directs. Such is the omnipotence of the scepter over the mightiest force of the state. Together they achieve all things. When divided and on their own, they graze like cattle where the shepherd bids. Order at the expense of freedom is as contrary to our welfare as are very chains.—A hundred prisoners, fixed to the benches of their ships, moved on its course by their oars, live in peace and order. But look into their heart and soul. Torment, grief, despair. Often would they want to exchange life for death; but even this they are refused. The end of suffering is bliss for them; but bliss and bondage are incompatible, and so they live. Let us then not be blinded by the superficial calm and order of the state and for these reasons alone consider it to be fortunate. Always look into the hearts of fellow citizens. If you find in them calm and peace then will you be able to say in truth: they are blessed.

The Europeans, having pillaged America, her fields fattened with the blood of her native inhabitants, ended their murders when there was a new form of gain. The barren fields of this hemisphere, renewed by strong shocks of nature, felt the plow tear up its entrails. Grass that grew on the rich meadows and dried out fruitlessly felt its stalks cut short by the blade of the scythe. Proud woods topple down on the hills whose heights they had shaded from time immemorial. Barren forests and bitter thickets develop into productive fields and grow covered by hundreds of crops unique to America or successfully transplanted there. Rich meadows are trampled on by many cattle destined for food and labor for man. Everywhere can be seen the creative hand of the maker, everywhere there is the appearance of prosperity and the outward sign of harmony. But who with a hand so mighty nudges scanty, lazy nature to yield its fruit in such abundance? Having slaughtered in one go the Indians, the enraged Europeans, those proponents of peace in the name of the True God, teachers of meekness and philanthropy, graft onto the root of furious murder the practice of the cold-blooded murder that is slavery through the purchase of captives. These unfortunate victims from the torrid banks of the Niger and Senegal, torn from their homes and families, transported to lands unknown to them, under the crushing scepter of orderliness within society, churn up the fertile lands of the America that despises their labor. And will we say of this land of devastation that it is blessed because its fields are not overgrown with weed and its tilled fields abound in various crops? How can we call a land blessed in which a hundred proud citizens wallow in luxury while thousands lack secure provision and their own shelter from heat and frost? Oh, if only these abundant lands could once again become desolate! If only weed and thistle, sinking deep their roots, could destroy all the expensive products of America! Tremble, my beloved ones, lest it be said of you: "Change your name and the story talks about you."[71]

Even now we are amazed by the scale of Egyptian buildings. The incomparable pyramids will for a long time demonstrate the bold architectural design of the Egyptians. But for what were these piles of ludicrous stones prepared? For the burial of the arrogant pharaohs. These haughty potentates, avid of immortality, wished even after death to be set apart in appearance from their people. And, thus, the colossal mass of socially useless buildings gives clear proof of the servitude of the latter. In the debris of lost cities, where the general welfare formerly settled, we find the ruins of schools, hospitals, hotels, aqueducts, theaters, and similar buildings; in those cities where an "I" rather than "we" was more famous, we find the debris of magnificent royal palaces, vast stables, the homes of beasts. Compare one and the other: our choice will not be hard to make.

But what do we find in the very fame of conquests? Din, thunder, pomposity, and depletion. I compare this kind of fame to the balloons invented in the eighteenth century. Pieced together from silk, they rapidly fill with hot air and fly off at the speed of sound to the lofty heights of the ether. But the thing that comprises their force constantly seeps out from within through the finest chinks: the weight that was spinning upward takes the natural path of gravity downward; so that something whose fabrication took entire months of labor, effort, and expense affords the glances of spectators delight for barely a few hours.

Inquire, then, what the conqueror craves, what he seeks, when devastating populated lands or by subjugating the deserts to his power? An answer is given to us by the most ferocious among them, Alexander, called the Great—but he, in truth, was great not in his deeds but in the force of his spirit and in the havoc he caused. "O Athenians!" he proclaimed, "how dear has your praise cost me." Thoughtless one, gaze upon your path. In rampaging through your territory, the impetuous whirlwind of your ascent pulls the inhabitants into its vortex and, dragging the power of the state in its precipitancy, leaves behind it desert and dead space. You do not understand, O raging wild boar, that by laying waste victoriously to the land you conquer you will acquire nothing to give you pleasure after the conquest. If you acquire a desert, it will serve as a grave in which your citizens will disappear; if you populate a new desert, you will render abundant land infertile. What gain is there in turning deserts into villages if you empty other settlements to do so? If the land you acquired is inhabited, count up your murders and be horrified. You need to eliminate all the hearts that have learned to hate you for your thunder bearing, since you could not possibly think that they could love someone they have been forced to fear. After the extermination of brave citizens, timid souls will remain and be subjected to you, ready to accept the yoke of slavery; however, in them, too, hatred of your crushing victory will take root. The fruit of your conquest will be—do not flatter yourself—murder and hatred. You will remain in the memory of descendants as a scourge; you will be punished knowing that your new slaves revile you and seek from you your own death.

Stooping to closer considerations about the condition of landworkers, how harmful we find it is to society. It is harmful to the increase of plants and people, it is harmful by way of example, and it is dangerous because of the insecurity it creates. Man, motivated in his initiatives by self-interest, undertakes what is of benefit to him, near or distant, and retreats from that in which he finds no immediate or future use. Following this natural instinct, everything we undertake for ourselves, everything that we do unforced, we do with dedication, care, well. Conversely, everything we do unwillingly, everything that we complete not for our good, we do shoddily, lazily, higgledy-piggledy. Landworkers in our state are this way. Their field is not their own, its produce does not belong to them. And this is why they cultivate it so lazily and are not concerned if it goes empty under their care. Compare this field with the one granted by an arrogant owner for the meagre subsistence of its cultivator. He does not stint on the effort he undertakes for it. Nothing distracts him from its cultivation. He overcomes shortage of time by not sleeping; hours set aside for rest he spends at work; on days designated for amusement, he shuns it. This is because he takes care of himself, works for himself, does everything for himself, and thus the field will give him an exceptional harvest; and this is how all the fruits of the labors of landworkers die or do not grow back; and yet they would have grown and survived to nourish citizens if the cultivation of the field were done carefully, if it were free.

But because compulsory work gives a smaller yield, the earth's productivity falls short of its goal, hindering population growth by the same amount. Where there is nothing to eat there will be no one since even if there were someone they would die of starvation. By not yielding a full harvest, serf cultivation kills off the citizens to whom surplus was allocated by nature. Is this, however, the only way in which slavery stymies high productivity? To the inadequate supply of subsistence food and clothing has been added an exhausting workload. Compound this with offenses of arrogance and abuses of power, which affect even the tenderest sensibilities of man, and then you will see with horror the incipient destructiveness of slavery, differing from victories and conquests only in that it does not allow to come about what victory will cut down in the first place. But serfdom is more pernicious. Everyone can see easily that the one devastates randomly and instantaneously; the other destroys for the long term and always. The one, when it has run its course, terminates its ferocity; the other only begins where the former leaves off and cannot change except perhaps only by the collapse, always dangerous, of its entire internal structure.

But nothing is more damaging than having the objects of slavery always in view. On the one hand, arrogance is born; on the other, timidity. Between them there can be no connection except force. Concentrated within a small sphere, it ponderously exercises its oppressive power everywhere. The champions of slavery are not only those who hold power and a weapon in their hands, its most fanatical advocates can be those imprisoned in chains. It seems that the spirit of freedom becomes so atrophied in slaves that not only do they not wish to see their own suffering end, but they find it unbearable to watch others being free. They have come to love their chains if it is possible for a human being to love his destruction. I believe we see in them the serpent that brought about the fall of the first man.—Examples of power wielding are contagious. We our very selves, we must admit, armed with the cudgel of bravery and of nature to attack the hydra-headed monster that sucks dry the communal nourishment prepared for the sustenance of citizens—we have, perhaps, succumbed to the temptation to act tyrannically, and although our intentions have always been good and directed toward the general welfare, our imperious conduct cannot be justified by its usefulness. And we now implore you thus to pardon our unpremeditated audacity.

But do you know, our dear fellow citizens, how great the destruction is before us, how great the peril in which we find ourselves? All the coarsened sentiments of a slave, which even by a wave of the happy wand of freedom are not moved to action, will only intensify and lead this internal sensation to fulfilment. A stream, blocked in its course, becomes stronger the harder the resistance it finds. Once it breaks through the dam, nothing can oppose its overflow. Such are our brothers held in chains. They await chance and the moment. The bell sounds. And then ferocious destructiveness rapidly overflows. We will see ourselves surrounded by the sword and torch. Death and fire will be recompense for our harshness and inhumanity. And the slower and more stubborn we will have been in the dissolving of their bonds, the swifter they will be in their revenge. Remember for yourself recent history. Enticement incited even slaves to such violence directed at the destruction of their masters! Lured by some rude pretender, they streamed in his wake and want nothing more than to free themselves from the yoke of their overlords; in their ignorance they devised no better means for this than their murder.[72] They spared neither sex nor age. They sought more the joy of revenge than the usefulness of the shaking off their shackles.

This is what awaits us, this is what we must expect. Destruction gradually mounts and danger already hovers over our heads. Having already raised its scythe, time waits for the convenient moment, and the first flatterer or lover of mankind, arisen to stir the unfortunate, will hasten his blow. Beware.

But if the horror of destruction and the threat of the forfeiture of property can move the weak among you, can we not be so brave as to suppress our prejudices and combat our greed; can we not free our brethren from the chains of slavery and resurrect the natural equality of all? Understanding the disposition of your hearts, I know that it is more pleasant for them to be reassured by arguments found in the human heart rather than in the enumeration of egotistical reasons and even less still in fear of danger. Go, my dear ones, go into the homes of your brethren, announce to them the change to their fate. Announce it with heartfelt feeling: "Moved to pity by your fate, empathizing with our peers, fathoming your equality with us, and convinced by the common good, we have come to kiss our brethren. We have forsaken the proud distinction that has for so long separated us from you, we have forgotten the inequality that used to exist between us. Now let us rejoice in our victory and this day on which the chains of our fellow dear citizens have crumbled, may this day remain as the most famous in our chronicles. Forget our former crime against you and let us love one another sincerely."

This will be your speech, this is already audible in the inner chambers of your hearts. Do not tarry, my beloved ones. Time flies, our days pass in inaction. Let us not finish our life having only arrived at a good idea and unable to implement it. May posterity not take the opportunity to remove our laurels and say of us disdainfully: they had their moment.

This is what I read on the mud-spattered paper that I picked up in front of the postal station when I got down from my carriage.

Having entered the station, I asked which travelers had arrived shortly before me. "The last of the travelers passing through," said the station master, "was a man of about fifty. He was traveling on a post-horse voucher to Petersburg. He left behind here a bundle of papers that I shall now send after him." I asked the postman to give me these papers to look at and from unbundling them learned that the paper I found belonged to that set. I persuaded him to hand over these papers by giving him a gratuity. On looking through them, I learned that they belonged to my true friend, and for that reason did not consider their acquisition to be theft. As of now, he has not asked them back from me and has left me to do as I wished with them.

Meanwhile as they were harnessing afresh my horses, I grew curious as I examined the papers that I had acquired. I found many similar to the sheet I had already read. I consistently encountered the character of a philanthropic heart, consistently saw the citizen of future times. More than anything it was clear that my friend had been stunned by the inequality of civilian rankings. A large bundle of papers and legal sketches concerned the abolition of slavery in Russia. But my friend, knowing that the supreme power in Russia lacked sufficient strength to change opinion immediately, had sketched a way forward for incremental legislation toward the gradual emancipation of landworkers in Russia. I shall here demonstrate his train of thought. His first regulation concerns the distinction between rural serfdom and domestic serfdom. The latter is abolished first, and nobles are forbidden to take into their homes all rural dwellers and anyone registered in the census. Should a landowner take a landworker into his home as a servant or laborer then the landworker becomes free. Serfs should be permitted to enter into marriage without requiring the agreement of their master. A bride-price should not change hands in the process. The second regulation relates to property and the defense of landworkers. They should own as their property the parcel of land they cultivate since they pay their own poll tax. Property acquired by a peasant should belong to him; let no one deprive him of it on a whim. The landworker should be restored in the status of citizen. It is appropriate that he will be tried by his equals, in peasant courts, for which the jury selection be made from serfs as well. The peasant is to be permitted to acquire fixed property, that is to buy land. He will be permitted the unrestricted acquisition of freedom by paying the master an agreed sum for manumission. Arbitrary punishment without trial is to be forbidden. "Disappear barbaric custom, perish power of tigers!" proclaims our legislator. . . . The complete abolition of slavery follows this.

Among the many decrees relating to the restoration, insofar as possible, of equality of citizens I found the Table of Ranks.[73] How anachronistic it is in the present day, and inadequate, each can imagine himself. But presently the bell on the tracing rein of the middle horse rings and summons me for departure; and for that reason I decided that it would be better to think about what is more suitable for the traveler by coach: that his horses proceed at a trot or amble; or what is more suitable for the postal nag, whether to be an ambler or charger—better this than to get caught up in what does not exist.

16

VYSHNY VOLOCHOK

I have never driven past this new city without going to see the locks here. The first person who conceived the idea of imitating nature in its positive actions and to create an artificial river in order to establish a better nexus connecting all the ends of the region deserves a monument for most distant posterity. When for natural and moral reasons current powers collapse, when their gilded fields become overgrown by brambles, and grass snakes, serpents, and toads hide in the ruins of the magnificent palaces of their proud rulers, then the curious traveler will find eloquent remains of their magnificence in commerce. The Romans built great roads, aqueducts whose durability amazes to this day and rightly so. But they had no concept of the interconnected waterways that currently exist in Europe. Our roads will never be the like those of the Romans. Our long winter and the hard frosts prevent it, but even without lining canals will take a long time to disappear.

More than a little delight was afforded me by the sight of the canal at Vyshny Volochok full of vessels loaded with grain and other merchandise being prepared to pass through the locks for their sailing onward to Petersburg. Here we could see the true abundance of the land and the surpluses of the landworker. Here, plain and visible in all its brilliance, was the powerful stimulus to human actions: the profit motive. But if at first glance my mind was pleased by the sight of prosperity, my rejoicing soon dissipated on the breaking down of my thoughts into parts. For I recalled that many landworkers in Russia do not work for themselves; and therefore in many regions of Russia the productivity of land demonstrates the oppressed lot of its inhabitants. My pleasure changed into indignation comparable to my feelings when in the summertime I walk on the pier at the customs station, gazing on the ships that transport to us America's surpluses and her expensive products, like sugar, coffee, pigments, and other items in which the sweat, tears, and blood drenching them during their production have yet to dry out.

"Imagine," my friend said to me once, "that the coffee poured into your cup, and the sugar dissolved in it, deprived someone just like you of rest, that they caused him to make exertions beyond his strength, caused his tears, groans, punishment, and abuse. Hard-hearted one, go on, dare to slake your throat." The look of disapproval accompanying this speech shook me to my inner core. My hand began to tremble and the coffee spilled.

And you, O residents of Petersburg, who feed on the surpluses of the productive regions of our fatherland at magnificent feasts or at a friendly dinner, or on your own, when your hand picks up the first piece of bread designated for your satiety, stop and think. Might I not tell you the same thing that my friend told me about products of America? Might it not be through sweat, tears, and groaning that the fields on which it grew have been fattened? Blessed are you if the piece of bread you hunger after derives from grains originating in a field classified as state property; or at least in a field that pays quitrent to the landowner. But woe unto you if its dough is from grain collected in a granary belonging to a nobleman. Woe and despair resided there; it was branded with the curse of the Almighty who once in his wrath uttered: "Cursed is the ground in its needs."[74] Take care lest you be poisoned by the food you desire. The bitter tear of a pauper lies heavy on it. Cast it from your lips. Keep the fast, fasting can be true and useful.

A tale about a certain landowner will show that man forgets about the humanity of his fellow men due to his greed and that for an example of hard-heartedness we have no need to go to distant lands nor to search for wonders at the end of the world. They are being perpetrated in our realm before our eyes.

Mr. Someone, having not found in his government service what is commonly called happiness or not wishing to stoop to finding the like, left the capital, acquired a small estate, with, say, one hundred or two hundred souls, and decided to make his income in agriculture. He did not assign himself to the plow but intended in the most practical way conceivable to make all possible use of the natural vitality of his peasants and apply them to the cultivation of the land. He determined that the most reliable way to do this was to create out of his peasants instruments devoid of will and initiative; and he genuinely fashioned out of them in certain respects soldiers of a contemporary kind directed as a cohort—as a cohort racing headlong to war—who individually had no significance at all. To achieve his goal, he withdrew from them the small portion of plowland and meadows that noblemen normally give them for their essential subsistence in return for all the compulsory labors they require from their peasants. In a word, this landowner, Mr. Someone, forced all his peasants, their wives, and their children, to work all the days of the year for him. And lest they die of hunger he allocated them a fixed amount of bread known by the name of the monthly allocation.[75] Those who did not have families did not receive the monthly allocation but, in the fashion of the Lacedaemonians, dined together in the manor house, for the maintenance of their digestion using cabbage soup without meat on meat days and on fast days bread and kvass. Reliable breakings of a fast used to take place probably during Easter week.[76]

For peasants maintained this way, clothing was produced that was proper and suited their situation. They made their own footwear for winter, that is baste shoes; foot wraps they received from their master while in the summer they went barefoot. Consequently, such prisoners had neither a cow nor horse nor ewe nor ram. They were deprived by their master not of permission to keep them but of the means to do so. Anyone who was a bit more prosperous, anyone who was moderate in their food consumption, kept some poultry, which sometimes the master would take for himself, paying whatever price he felt like.

Given this sort of arrangement, it is not surprising that tillage in Mr. Someone's village was in a flourishing state. When everyone else had a poor harvest, his grain was four times more; when others had a good harvest his came to ten times or more. Within a short time, in addition to the two hundred souls he already possessed, he bought a further two hundred victims of his greed, and by treating them exactly as he had the first lot, he increased his property year by year, augmenting the number of people groaning in his fields. By now he counts them in the thousands and is famed as a land manager.

Barbarian, you are unworthy of the name of citizen! What good is it to the state to have several thousand more units of grain generated if those who produce it are treated on a par with the ox assigned to plow a difficult furrow? Or do we think that the welfare of citizens consists in the granaries being full of grain while stomachs are empty so that a single person rather than thousands blesses the government? The wealth of this bloodsucker does not belong to him. It has been accumulated through robbery and by law deserves severe punishment. There are, indeed, people who when gazing upon the opulent fields of this executioner make out of him an example of advancement in tillage. And you would like to be known as lenient bearers of the name of the guardians of general prosperity. Instead of encouraging coercion of this kind, which is what you consider the source of the state's wealth, visit upon this villain of society a philanthropic vengeance. Destroy his agricultural equipment, burn his haycocks, barns, granaries, and scatter the ashes in the fields where his brutality took place, brand him as a common thief so that everyone who sees him will not only feel revulsion but shall avoid his approach in order not to be contaminated by his example.

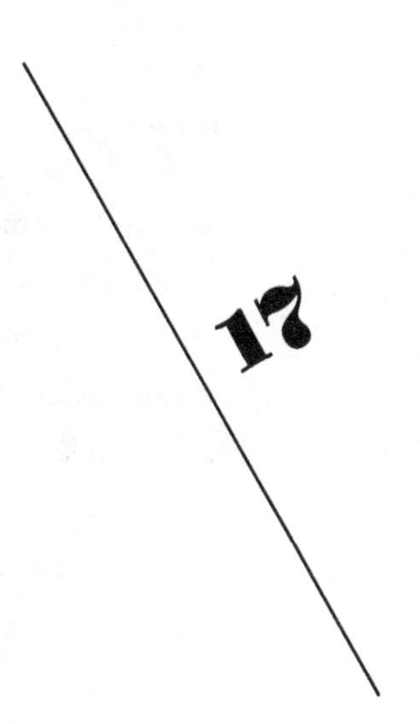

VYDROPUSK

Here I resumed looking at the papers of my friend. I happened upon the sketch of a proposal for the abolition of court ranks.

Project for the Future

When introducing gradually once again the natural and civic equality that had been destroyed in society, our ancestors considered the reduction of the privileges of the nobility to be not the least means thereto. Originally useful to the government owing to its personal merits, the nobility grew weak in its accomplishments due to its inherited status: sweet when first planted, its root at the end bore bitter fruit. Instead of bravery, arrogance and self-love set in; instead of nobility of the soul and generosity, servility and lack of self-confidence took root, genuine impediments to greatness. By living among these small souls, moved to perform petty deeds due to flattery of hereditary virtues and merits, many monarchs assumed that they were gods and that everything they touched would become blessed and luminous. This should be what our deeds are like but only for the public good. Such was their fantasy about the greatness of their power that Tsars imagined that their slaves and servants, by constantly coming before their gaze, assimilated their radiance; that royal splendor by being refracted, so to speak, in these new reflections, appears multiplied and more sparkling. Such was their deluded idea that Tsars erected idols of the court, who like little god-lings of theater, obey a whistle or a rattle. Let us review the degrees of court ranks and let us with a pitying smile avert our gaze from those who are proud of their service; but let us weep when seeing them preferred over merit. My steward, stable boy, and even groom and driver, cook, waiter, bird catcher and the hunters supervised by him, my room servants, the man who shaves me, the man who combs the hair on my head, he who cleans the dust and dirt from my shoes, not to mention many others, are deemed equal or superior to those who serve the fatherland with their spiritual and physical strength and for the fatherland spare neither their well-being nor blood, loving even death for the sake of the glory of their state. What good is it to you that cleanliness and tidiness reign in my home? Will you be fed heartily if my meal is prepared better than yours and if wine from all parts of the world is in my goblets? Will you be protected in your travels from inclement weather if my chariot is gilded and my horses are fat? Will a field produce for you better fruit, will your meadows be greener if they are trampled upon when animals are hunted for the sake of my enjoyment? You will smile with a feeling of pity. But the person will not be rare who in righteous indignation says to us: he who cares for the condition of your palaces; he who warms them; he who combines the fiery spice of equatorial plants and cold stickiness of northern animal fat for the delight of your weakened digestion and jaded palate; he who makes the sweet juice of the African grape foam in your glass; he who lubricates the round part of your carriage wheel, feeds and waters your horses; he who in your name wages a bloody war against the beasts of the forest and birds of the sky—all these parasites, all these panderers to your arrogance, like many others, are superior to me who shed streams of blood on the battlefield; who lost the most essential limbs of my body when defending your cities and palaces in which your timidity was veiled by a curtain of pomposity disguised as bravery; who pass my days of joy, youth, and delights in the saving of the smallest mite to lighten insofar as possible the general burden of taxes; who did not take care of my estate, working day and night in the quest for means to achieve general welfare; who trample kinship, friendship, the union of heart and blood, by declaring in court the truth in your name so that you will be loved. Our hair turns white amid our exploits, our forces are exhausted in the labors we have undertaken, and on the brink of the grave we scarcely earn your approval, whereas all those calves fattened on the teats of leniencies and vice, those illegitimate sons of the fatherland, will inherit our property.

This and even more, in fairness, is how many of you speak out. What shall we, holders of power, answer in return? Let us disguise our humiliation in indifference, but an enraged fury in our eyes will glare at those uttering in this manner. Often these are our answers to declarations of truth. And may no one be surprised when the best of us dares this sort of thing. He lives among flatterers, talks with flatterers, sleeps with flattery, walks in flattery. And flattery and toadying have made him deaf, blind, and dull.

May such a reproach not fall on us. Having conceived a hatred for flattery from youth, we safeguarded our heart from its poisonous sweetness even to the present day; and now a new effort in our love and loyalty toward you shall be manifest. Today we are eliminating the parity between court-based service and the military and civil service. Let the practice, to our shame having survived for so many years, be eliminated in our lifetime. May genuine merits and qualities, concern for the general good, receive a reward for their labors and be the only ones to be distinguished.

Having cast from our heart so unbearable a burden, long oppressing us, we shall reveal to you our reasons for the elimination of ranks so offensive to merit and worth.—The assertion is made to you, and our ancestors were of the same views, that the Tsar's throne, the strength of which resides in the opinions of citizens, ought to be distinguished by its external brilliance in order that the idea of its majesty remain always perfect and unassailable. From this stems the opulent appearance of the rulers of nations, from this stems the troop of slaves surrounding them. Everyone must agree that external trappings may dazzle narrow minds and small souls. But the more enlightened a people, that is the more individuals it has who are enlightened, the less effect external appearance has. Numa was able to convince the still uncouth Romans that the nymph Egeria[77] guided him in establishing the laws. The weak Peruvians willingly believed Manco Cápac[78] that he was the scion of the sun and that his law descended from the heavens. Mohammed was able to entice the nomadic Arabs with his ravings. They all used trappings, even Moses took up the tablets of the commandments on the mount amidst the flashing of lightning. But now should anyone wish to entice, it is not a brilliant exterior he will need but the appearance of arguments, if one may put it that way, the semblance of persuasions. If anyone now should want to affirm his message from above, he would sooner use the semblance of utility and everybody will be moved by this. But we who are focusing all our energies on what is good for all and for each, what does brilliance of external appearance matter to us? Is it not the usefulness of our resolutions, directed toward the good of the state, that makes our countenance resplendent? Each person considering us will see our good intention, will see his own benefit in our action and for that reason will bow to us not as to one walking in terror but as to one enthroned in goodness. If the ancient Persians had always been ruled generously then they would not have imagined the existence of Ahriman, or the hated origin of evil. But if opulent trappings are of no use to us, how dangerous their upholders are in the state. If in service their only duty is to indulge us how resourceful they will be in all that can please us. Our inclination will be anticipated; not only will no inclination be allowed to be born in us, but not even a thought since its satisfaction will already have been prepared. Look with terror on the effect of these sorts of indulgences. The firmest soul will falter in its principles, will lend an ear to flattering mellifluousness, will fall asleep. And these delicious charms will work round reason and the heart. Others' despair and injury will scarcely make an impression on us as passing afflictions; to feel grief about them we will consider either unbecoming or repugnant, and we shall forbid even complaining about them. The most biting sorrows and wounds, and even death, will look like the inevitable results of the course of things; and since they appear to us from behind an opaque screen, they can hardly produce in us even the ephemeral effects that theatrical performances produce in us. For it is not in us that the piercing arrow of illness or the prod of evil shudder.

This is a pale picture of all the detrimental consequences of the conceited actions of kings. Are we not be blessed if we have been able to hide from the perversion of our good intentions? Are we not blessed also if we have put a limit to the contagion of example? Assured of our good-heartedness, assured that there will not be corruption from without, assured of the moderation of our desires, we will flourish again and shall be an example to the most distant posterity of how power and freedom should be conjoined for the common good.

TORZHOK

Here in the postal yard I was greeted by a man heading to Petersburg on a quest to submit a petition. This petition was to attain permission to establish in this city a free press. I told him that permission was not needed for this, since freedom has already been granted to all in this regard. But he wanted freedom from censorship and here are his thoughts on the matter:

"We all have permission to possess printing establishments, and the time when it was feared to grant this to private individuals has already passed; the reason whereby at the time they refrained from introducing a general good and useful institution was that they feared forged passes could be printed on private presses. Now everyone is free to maintain printing tools but what can be printed remains under regulation. Censorship has become a nanny to reason, wit, imagination, all that is grand and exquisite. But where there are nannies it follows that there will be children; they go about in a harness, as a result often their legs are crooked; where there are guardians, it follows that there are young, immature minds unable to control themselves. If nannies and guardians carry on forever, then the child will long go about in a harness and at maturity be a complete cripple. This minor will always be a Mitrofanushka,[79] unable to take a step without his tutor, unable to manage his inheritance without a guardian. These are the sorts of things that everywhere are the consequences of routine censorship, and the stricter it is the more damaging the consequences. Let us listen to Herder.[80]

> The very best way to encourage the good is nonhindrance, license, freedom in thought. An inquisition is damaging in the kingdom of knowledge: it thickens the air and hampers breathing. A book that passes through ten censors before it comes into the world is not a book but the product of the Holy Inquisition, a prisoner often disfigured, beaten with rods and a muzzle in its mouth, and always a slave.... In the spheres of truth, in the kingdom of thought and spirit, no kind of earthly power can give permissions nor should it; the government cannot do this, even less the censor whether wearing a *klobuk* or a lanyard.[81] In the kingdom of truth, the censor is not the judge but the defendant, so too the writer. Improvement can only occur through enlightenment; without a head and brain neither a hand nor leg will stir.... The more principled a state is in its rules, the more ordered, brighter, and firmer it is in itself, the less it can falter and be buffeted by the gust of every opinion, each piece of ridicule from an angry writer; and the more a government exercises benevolence in freedom of thought and freedom of writing, the gain therefrom will be in the end, of course, to truth. Wreckers are suspicious; secret villains are timid. A bold man, one doing right and firm in his principles, will permit any word to be said about him. He walks in the light and turns the calumny of his enemies to his own advantage. Monopolies of opinion are dangerous.... Let the ruler of the state be objective in his views so that he might apprehend the opinions of all

and in his kingdom permit, enlighten, and dispose them to the good:
here you have why truly great rulers are so rare.

"Convinced of the usefulness of publishing, the government granted permission to all; but convinced even more that curbs on thoughts would invalidate the good intention of the freedom to publish, it entrusted censorship, or the supervision of editions, to the Department of Public Morals. In this respect, its duty can only be to ban the sale of offensive works. However, even such censorship is superfluous. It only takes one stupid police official to do the greatest harm to enlightenment and for many years bring to a halt the progress of reason: he can forbid a useful invention, a new idea, and deprive all of something great. There is an example in a small thing. A translation of a novel was submitted for approval to the police. Following the author, when speaking about love, the translator dubbed it 'a crafty god.' The censor in uniform, imbued with the spirit of piety, blacked out this expression saying 'it is improper to call a Deity crafty.' If you don't understand something then stay right out of it. If you want wholesome air, then place the smokery at a distance from yourself; if you want light, then cast aside obscurity; if you want a child not to be cowed, then banish the birch from school. In the house where whips and cudgels are in use servants are drunkards, thieves, and even worse.*

---

* It is said that a censor of this kind did not give permission to print compositions in which God was mentioned, saying "I have nothing to do with Him." If in any sort of composition the customs of the people of one or another state were faulted he considered this to be unacceptable, saying that Russia had a friendship treaty with them. If there was a mention in a work of a prince or count he did not allow this to be printed, saying: this is a personal affront since we have princes and counts among our people of quality.

"Let everyone print whatever comes into their mind. Anyone who finds himself insulted in print should be granted a trial as per the regulation. I am not speaking in jest. Words are not always acts nor are thoughts crimes. These are the rules of the Instruction about the new law code.[82] But an insult in speech remains an insult in print as well. It is not permitted by law to insult anyone, and everyone has freedom to make a complaint. But if someone tells the truth about another, whether this should be considered libel or not is not in the law. What harm can there be if there are books in print without the police seal? Not only is there no harm, but there is advantage, advantage from the first to the last, from the smallest person to the greatest, from the Tsar to the last of citizens.

"The usual rules of censorship are: to underline, black out, forbid, shred, burn everything contrary to natural religion and revelation, everything contrary to government, every personal affront; anything antithetical to morality, order, and public peace. Let us review this in detail. If a madman in his raving, not only to himself in his heart, but in a loud voice says: 'There is no God,' in the mouths of all madmen a loud and hasty echo will resound: 'There is no God, there is no God.' Well, what of it? An echo is a sound; it will strike the air, cause it to vibrate, and disappear. In the mind it will rarely leave a trace, and a weak one at that; but in the heart, never. God will always be God, sensed even by those who do not believe in Him. But if you think that the Almighty will be offended by blasphemy, how can a clerk in the office of the police be a plaintiff on His behalf? The Almighty does not place His confidence in one who brandishes a rattle or strikes the tocsin to sound an alarm. He who wields thunder and lightning, to whom all the elements obey; He who dwells beyond the boundaries of the universe and shakes all hearts, abhors it if revenge is taken for His sake even if this is by the Tsar himself, who fancies himself His deputy on earth.—Who, indeed, can be the judge of an offence to the Eternal Father?—He gives offence who thinks: I am able to judge about His insult. He will answer to this before Him.

"The apostates of revealed religion have done more harm to this day in Russia than the deniers of the existence of God, atheists. Of the latter, we have few since there are still few among us who think about metaphysics. The atheist loses his way in metaphysics, but a Schismatic becomes deluded in the matter of three fingers.[83] We call Schismatics all Russians who depart in any manner from the general teaching of the Greek church. Of these there are many in Russia, which is why their liturgy is permitted. But is there any reason to prohibit the manifestation of any error? The more apparent it is the sooner it will crumble. Persecutions used to make martyrs, cruelty was a prop of the very Christian religion. Schisms can sometimes have dangerous effects. Prohibit them. They spread by example. Destroy the example. It is not because of a printed book that a Schismatics will immolate themselves, but because of a sly example. To forbid foolishness is tantamount to encouraging it. Give it free rein, everyone will see what is stupid and what is smart. What is forbidden is wanted. We are all the children of Eve.

"But in banning freedom to publish, timorous governments do not fear blasphemy, they fear having critics. Anyone who in hours of madness does not spare God will in hours of lucidity and reason not spare unlawful power. The one who does not fear the Almighty's thunderbolts laughs at the gallows. This is why liberty of thought is terrifying to governments. Shaken to his very core, the freethinker will reach out to the idol of power a bold but powerful and unwavering hand, tear off its mask and cloak, and expose its build. Each will see its feet of clay, each will retract the support he granted it, power will return to its source, the idol will fall. But if power does not rest upon a fog of opinions, if its throne stands on a sincere love of the general good, will it not be strengthened by the divulgement of its principles? Will not he who loves sincerely not then be loved? Reciprocity is a feeling from nature, and this urge resides in nature. To a strong and firm building its own foundation should be sufficient: it has no need for supports and buttresses. Only if it totters from dilapidation will it require support. Let the government be truthful, its leaders not hypocritical: then all its spittle, then all its vomitings will throw back their fetidness on their belcher, while truth will forever be pure and fair to see. Whoever stirs things up with speech (so as to please power this is how we name all firm thoughts based in truth that contradict power) is just as mad as one who blasphemes against God. If power should travel on its rightful path, then it will not be troubled by the empty sound of calumny, just as the Lord of Hosts is not rattled by blaspheming. But woe unto power if out of avidity it violates the truth. Then even a sole firm thought troubles it, the word of truth will destroy it, a virile deed will scatter it.

"A personal attack, if it is damaging, is an offense. A personal attack that is truthful is as permissible as truth itself. If a biased judge rules in favor of a lie and the defender of innocence exposes his ruling to the world as crooked, if he exposes his trickery and falsehood, this is a personal attack but can be condoned. If he should call the judge 'hired,' 'false,' 'stupid,' this personal affront can be condoned. However, if he should take to calling him by the foul nicknames and curse words, as used in markets, this personal affront is malicious and unacceptable. It is not the role of the government, however, to defend a judge even when he has been disparaged for being right. It is not him as judge, but the offended man who will be the plaintiff in this matter. As for the judge, let his deeds alone vindicate him in the eyes of the world and those who named him a judge.* This is how one should think about a personal attack. It deserves punishment, but if it is printed will do more good than harm. When everything is in order, when verdicts always conform to law, when the law is founded on truth and oppression is contained, then and only then, perhaps, can a personal attack corrupt morals. Let us say something about good conduct and to what extent words can damage it.

"Obscene writings, full of lewd descriptions, breathing debauchery, whose every page and line gape with a titillating nudity, are harmful for the young and those of immature feeling. In fanning an already inflamed imagination, stirring the sleeping feelings and stimulating a heart that was quiet, they instill a precocious maturity, deceiving youthful senses about their resilience and laying the groundwork for their infirmity. Writings of this kind can be harmful; but they are not the root of corruption. If by reading them young men develop a taste for the ultimate satisfaction of amorous passion, they would be able to do nothing about it were it not for those who hawk their beauty. In Russia, such writings are still not

* Mr. Dickinson, who took part in the recent American Revolution and thereby earned a reputation, did not shirk when he became president of Pennsylvania from taking on his detractors. The most violent libels were published against him. The preeminent governor of the region descended into the arena, had his defense published, justified himself, refuted the allegations of his enemies, and covered them in shame. . . . Here is an example to follow in the way to take revenge when one is attacked in writing in public. If published lines render someone furious they give reason to think that what has been published is true and that the person taking revenge is just as they have been depicted in print.

in print, yet on every street in both capitals we see harlots garishly made-up. Action more than language corrupts, and example most of all. Itinerant harlots, granting their hearts at a public auction to the bidder, will infect a thousand youths with venereal disease and all this thousand's progeny. But a book has not yet produced illness. Let the censure of female hustlers stand; it has no bearing on the works of the mind, even if debauched.

"I shall close with this: censorship of print matter belongs to society. Society will award a laurel crown to the author or will use his sheets for wrapping paper. This is just like the approval the public, rather than the director of the theater gives to a work for theater. Similarly, the censor awards neither fame nor infamy to a work that has seen the light. The curtain has risen, the gazes of all are riveted on the action; it pleases—they applaud, it does not please—they stamp and jeer. Leave stupidity to the discretion of public judgment: it will find a thousand censors. The most severe police are no match for a disgruntled public when it comes to stymying the dregs of ideas. They will listen to these ideas one time, then these ideas will die never to be resurrected. But if we acknowledge the uselessness of censorship and, moreover, its harmfulness in the kingdom of knowledge, then let us recognize the widespread and unlimited benefit of freedom of the press.

It seems proof of this is not needed. If everyone is free to think and to express his thoughts unhindered, then it is natural that everything that is conceived, invented, should be known; what is great will remain great, the truth will not be hidden. The rulers of nations will not dare to stray from the path of truth and will fear lest their conduct, malice, and cunning be exposed. On signing an unjust sentence, the judge will begin to tremble and will tear it up.

Anyone who has power will be ashamed to use it for the satisfaction only of his whims. Theft that is hidden will be called theft, murder that is covered up will be called murder. The wicked, all of them, will take fright at the severe gaze of truth. Tranquility will be genuine in the absence of a grain of fermentation. At present, only the surface appears smooth, but the silt lying at the bottom stirs up and obscures the clarity of the waters."

When saying goodbye to me, the critic of censorship gave me a small notebook. If, reader, you are not prone to boredom, read, then, what lies before you. If, however, it should happen that you yourself belong to the censorship committee, then turn down the corner of the page and skip past.

A Short Account of the Origins of Censorship[84]

If we say and confirm with evident proofs that censorship and the Inquisition have one and the same root; that the founders of the Inquisition invented censorship, that is, the mandatory examination of books before they see the light of day, then, while this will be saying nothing new, it does allow us to extract from the obscurity of past times, adding to the many others, clear proof that priests were always the inventors of the chains whereby human reason has at various times been weighed down; and that priests always clipped the wings of reason to hinder its flight toward majesty and freedom.

As we traverse epochs and centuries that have passed, we everywhere encounter features of power that torment; everywhere see force rising up against truth, sometimes superstition taking arms against superstition. The Athenian people, incited by hierophants, outlawed the writings of Protagoras,[85] ordered that all copies be confiscated and burned. Was it not the same people that in its madness consigned to death, to its indelible shame, the very personification of truth, Socrates? In Rome we find more examples of such ferocity. Titus Livy recounts that the writings found in the grave of Numa were burned by order of the Senate. At different epochs it happened that books of augury were ordered surrendered to the Praetor. Suetonius recounts that Caesar Augustus ordered that close to two thousand such books be burned. Yet one more example of the incongruity of human reason! Can it be that in prohibiting superstitious writings these rulers thought that superstition would be destroyed? Each person individually found himself banned from having recourse to divination, which was used not infrequently to assuage a pang of grief; permission remained only for the state predictions of auguries and haruspices. But if in time of enlightenment they had got it into their heads to prohibit or burn books teaching divination or propagating superstition, would it not be amusing if truth itself took up the scepter of persecution against superstition? And that truth sought, for the vanquishing of error, the support of power and the sword, even though the sight of truth alone is the harshest scourge of error?

But Caesar Augustus visited his persecutions not on divination alone: he ordered the books of Titus Labienus to be burned. "His persecutors," says the rhetorician Seneca, "devised for him a new type of punishment. It is unheard of, most unusual, to derive an execution from learning. But to the state's good fortune this rational ferocity was discovered after Cicero. What might have happened if the Triumvirate had decided that it was good to condemn the mind of Cicero?" But the tyrant soon took revenge on the person who demanded the burning of Labienus's works.[86] During his own lifetime he saw his own works condemned to the pyre.*[87] "It was not some evil example that was followed but his own," says Seneca.†[88] May heaven permit that villainy always rebound on its inventor and that anyone mounting persecution of thought would always see his own thoughts mocked and condemned to vilification and destruction. If there is an act of revenge that can ever be excused, then perhaps this is it.

During periods of plebeian rule in Rome, persecution of such a kind was only visited on superstition, but during the Empire it extended to all firm convictions. In his *History,* Cremutius Cordus[89] named Cassius for having dared to mock the tyranny Augustus exercised against the works of Labienus, the last Roman. The Roman Senate, groveling before Tiberius, to please him ordered Cremutius's book burned. But many copies survived. "All the more reason," says Tacitus, "one can mock the care of those who dream that in their omnipotence they are able to annihilate the memory of the next generation. Although power might well unleash furious punishment upon reason, its ferocity has caused shame and disgrace for itself, but glory for them."

Jewish books did not escape burning during the reign of Antiochus Epiphanes, the Syrian king.[90] Similar fates were meted out to Christian writings. The Emperor Diocletian ordered books of Holy

---

* The works of Arias Montano, who printed in the Netherlands the first inventory of forbidden books, were entered into the same inventory.

† Cassius Severus, the friend of Labienus, on seeing the writings of the latter devoured by the fire said: "Now you will have to burn me since I know them by heart." This was the occasion for the law of libelous writings under Augustus, which due to the human tendency to ape one another, was adopted in England and also in other countries.

Scripture to be placed in the fire.[91] But the Christian dogma, having achieved a victory over persecution, subdued its very torturers and now remains as true testimony that the harassment of ideas and opinions not only lacks the force to destroy them but rather implants and propagates them. Arnobius[92] rightly protests against such persecution and martyrdom. "Some declare," he says, "that it is useful for the state that the Senate ordered the writings serving as proof of the Christian confession, which refute the significance of ancient religion, to be destroyed. But to prohibit writing and to wish to destroy what is promulgated is not to defend the gods, rather it is to fear the testimonials of truth." Nevertheless, after the spread of the Christian confession, its priests displayed just as much hostility to writings that opposed them or were of no benefit to them. Not long before had they criticized this severity among the pagans, not long before had they considered it a sign of mistrust regarding what they defended; yet they themselves were soon armed with omnipotence. The Greek emperors, more occupied by ecclesiastical debates than matters of state, and for that reason ruled by priests, mounted persecution against all those whose understanding of the deeds and teachings of Jesus differed from their own. Such persecution also extended to the product of mind and reason. Already the tormentor Constantine, called the Great, following the decision of the Council of Nicaea relegating Arius's teaching to anathema, banned his books, condemned them to be burned, and anyone who possessed these books was sentenced to be executed.[93] Emperor Theodosius II ordered the condemned books of Nestorios to be collected and consigned to the fire.[94] At the Council of Chalcedon, the very same resolution was adopted for the writings of Eutychus.[95] In the Pandects of Justinian are preserved a number of similar resolutions.[96] Senseless people! They were unaware that by destroying a corrupt or foolish interpretation of Christian teaching and prohibiting reason to labor in the investigation of opinions of any kind, they were stopping its progress; they deprived truth of a strong support, variety of opinions, debate, and the unmenaced statement of thoughts. Who can guarantee that Nestorios, Arius, Eutychus, and other heretics might not have been the predecessors of Luther, and that had it not been for these ecumenical councils' being convoked Descartes might have been born ten centuries earlier? What a backward step was made toward darkness and ignorance!

After the destruction of the Roman Empire monks in Europe were the guardians of learning and science. But nobody disputed their freedom to write what they wished. In 768 Ambrosius Opert, a Benedictine monk, sending his interpretation of the Book of the Apocalypse to Pope Stephan III and seeking permission to continue his work and to publish it, says that he was the first of writers to seek such permission. "But let freedom of writing," he continues, "not vanish because abasement was proffered voluntarily." The Council of Sens in 1140 condemned the views of Abelard, and the Pope ordered the burning of his compositions.[97]

But neither in Greece nor in Rome do we anywhere find an example that a judge of thought was appointed that he brazenly say: "Seek permission from me if you wish to open your lips for eloquence; reason, science, and enlightenment are stamped for approval by us, and everything that has seen the light without our seal of approval we denounce in advance as stupid, vile, unworthy." Such a shameful invention was reserved for the Christian clergy, and censorship was contemporary with the Inquisition.

Rather often in reviewing history we find that reason goes with superstition and the most useful inventions stand alongside the coarsest ignorance. At the moment when cowardly mistrust of the object of an affirmation incited monks to establish censorship and to destroy an idea at its birth, at that very time Columbus dared to set off into the unknowability of the seas in pursuit of America; Keppler anticipated the existence of gravitational force in nature, proven by Newton; at that same moment Copernicus, who charted the path in space of the heavenly bodies, was born. But concerning a greater regret about the fate of human reasoning, we shall say that a great idea sometimes gave birth to ignorance. Printing gave birth to censorship; philosophical reason in the eighteenth century produced the Illuminati.

In the year 1479 we find the oldest hitherto known permission to print a book. At the end of the book titled *Know Thyself*, printed in 1480, the following was added: "We, Maffeo Ghirardi,[98] by the grace of God Patriarch of Venice, primate of Dalmatia, after the reading of the above-named gentlemen who bear witness to the composition described above, and after its conclusion and authorization being added, we bear witness that this book is Orthodox and pious." A most ancient monument to censorship though not the most ancient to madness!

The oldest legislation on censorship known hitherto we find in 1486, published in the same city where printing was invented. The monastic authorities were prescient that it would be the agent of the destruction of their power, that it would hasten the opening up of reason in general, and that power based on opinion rather than on the common interest would find its demise in printing. May we be permitted here to add a historic document, at present still extant as a detriment to thought and to the disgrace of the Enlightenment. A decree on the prohibition to publish Greek, Latin, and other books in the vernacular without the prior approval of scholars, 1486.*[99]

"Berthold, archbishop by divine grace of the holy precinct of Mainz, archchancellor and Prince-Elector in Germany. Although the divine art of printing makes it possible in the acquisition of human learning to obtain books pertaining to various sciences more bountifully and more freely, it has nonetheless come to our attention that certain people, induced by the wish for vain fame or wealth, abuse this art and what was bestowed for education in human life they turn into ruin and slander.

"We have seen books concerning sacred duties and the rituals of our confession translated from Latin into the German language circulate, as is inappropriate for the sacred law, in the hands of simple folk. And what, then, is to be said about the sacred prescriptions of rules and laws? Although they were written carefully and intelligently by people expert in legal study, the wisest and most intelligent possible, the science is in itself so difficult that the entire life of a most eloquent and learned person would scarcely be sufficient.

"Some stupid, brazen, and ignorant people take it upon themselves to translate into the vernacular these sorts of books. Many learned people on reading these translations admit that owing to their considerable improper and poor use of words they are more obscure than the originals. What would we say about works in other fields in which they often mix the false, introduce mistaken appellations and for which more buyers are found the more they attribute their own ideas to famous writers.

* *Codex diplomaticus*, published by Gudenus, volume IV.

"Let these translators—if they love the truth—no matter the intention with which they have acted, good or bad, let them tell us whether the German language is suitable for transposing into it what the most elegant Greek and Latin writers have written exquisitely and intelligently on the loftiest considerations of the Christian faith and about other sciences? One is obliged to admit that owing to its poverty our language is barely sufficient, and for that reason they have to devise in their heads unknown names for things; and even if they use the old ones it will be by corrupting their true meaning, the thing we fear most in Holy Scripture given their importance. For who will reveal the true meaning to the uncouth and ignorant people and the female sex into whose hands the books of sacred scripture fall? When the text of Holy Gospel or the Epistles of the Apostle Paul are read, every intelligent person will admit that there are in them many scribal additions and corrections.

"What has been said by us is well known. What should we think about what is found in the writings of the Catholic church that depends on the strictest scrutiny? We can give many examples but for our purpose the aforesaid is already sufficient.

"Given that the origin of this art, to speak the truth, appeared miraculously in our famous city of Mainz, and presently continues in it, corrected and enhanced, it is right that we take its dignity under our protection. For our duty is to preserve the Holy Scriptures in a state of uncorrupted purity. Having discussed in this manner the errors and presumption of brazen and wicked people, and desiring as much as we can, with the help of God, of Whom this is about, to warn them and to put a halt to each and every one them, clerical and civilian subject of our region and on those who trade outside its boundaries, no matter their rank and station, herewith we order all that no work in any science, art, or branch of learning, being translated from the Greek, Latin, or another language into German, or already existing in translation with a change only of title or anything else, may be distributed or sold, openly or clandestinely, forthrightly or in a secret manner, if it does not possess before printing or after printing before publication, clear permission to be printed or published as granted by our most esteemed, exalted, and noble doctors and masters of the university, that is: in our city of Mainz permission from Johannes Bertram von Naumburg in the matter of theology; from Alexander Diethrich in jurisprudence; from Theoderich von Meschede in the medical sciences; and from Andreas Oehler in letters, those doctors and masters selected for this purpose in our city of Erfurt. [We declare that no work] . . . can be distributed or sold . . . also in the city of Frankfurt if these books published for sale have not been vetted and confirmed by an esteemed and dear to us master of theology and one or two doctors and licentiates, who have been maintained on an annual salary by the Council of the same city.[100]

"If anyone should scorn this, our curatorial decree, or give advice, help, or support against our order in person or through another, he will thereby subject himself not only to excommunication but also to having confiscated these books and will pay one hundred gold gilders in fine into our treasury. And let no one without special decree dare to infringe this resolution. Granted in the Castle of St. Martin in our city of Mainz with our seal affixed. In the month of January, on the fourth day of the year 1486."

Once again Berthold on the manner in which to discharge censorship: In the year 1486 Berthold etc. To the most honored, learned, and in Christ dear to us J. Bertram (Doctor of Theology), A. Diethrich

(Doctor of Law), F. de Meschede (Doctor of Medicine), and A. Oehler (Master of Letters) we bid greeting and attention to the attached below.

"Being informed of deceptions and forgeries having been perpetrated by some translators and printers of scholarship, and being anxious to preempt them and willing if possible to head them off, we decree that nobody in our diocese and region shall dare to translate books into the German language, print or distribute printed matter, until such compositions or books have been inspected by you in our city of Mainz and, concerning the subject matter itself, they will not appear until confirmed by you in translation and for sale in accordance with the aforenoted decree.

"Firmly trusting in your reasonableness and prudence, we entrust to you that: when compositions or books designated for translation, printing, or sale shall be brought to you, you will review their contents and should it prove not easy to perceive their true meaning, or if they are able to engender mistakes and temptations or to offend against purity of morals, then reject them; while those you freely release will have to be signed at the end in your own hand, namely, by two of you that it will thereby be clear that these books were reviewed and approved by you. You render to our Lord and state valuable and useful service. Granted in the Palace of St. Martin. 10 January 1486."

While reviewing this law, new at the time, we find that it favored prohibition so that few books were published in the German language. Put differently, the people remained perpetually in ignorance. Censorship, it seems, did not extend to compositions written in Latin. For those already knowledgeable in the Latin language, it seemed, were already protected from error, impermeable to it, and what they read they understood clearly and accurately.* And thus the clergy wanted that only their allies in power were to be enlightened, so that the people would consider learning to be of divine origin beyond their comprehension and would not dare touch it. And so what was devised to confine the truth and enlightenment within the strictest boundaries, devised by a mistrusting power for its own might, devised for the continuation of ignorance and benightedness, now in days of science and philosophy, when reason has shaken off the shackles of superstition alien to it, when truth gleams in a hundred guises stronger and stronger, when the source of learning flows through the furthest branches of society, when the efforts of governments expedite the destruction of error and the opening of paths for reason to reach the truth unimpeded, this shameful monastic invention emanating from a trembling power is now accepted everywhere, has taken root, and is considered a good bulwark against error. Raving ones! look around, you strive to prop up truth with falsehood, you wish to enlighten nations with falsehood. But beware lest benightedness be restored. What is the use to you of ruling over ignoramuses, all the more uncouth because they remained ignorant not due to a lack of the means to enlightenment or due to their natural simplicity, but rather, having taken a step toward enlightenment, they were stopped in their progress and turned back, driven into darkness? What use is it to you to fight with yourself and rip out with your left hand what your right hand planted? Regard the clergy as they rejoice in this. You already are of service to them. Scatter

* One can compare this with the permission to possess foreign books of any type and the ban on the very same books in the vernacular language.

benightedness and feel the chains that are on you: if they are not always the chains of ecclesiastical superstition, they are of political superstition, less ridiculous albeit equally destructive.

However, it is to the good fortune of society that printing has not been banished from your countries. As a tree planted in an eternal spring does not lose its greenery, so the instruments of printing can be stopped in their action but not destroyed.

Having understood the danger that freedom of the press could pose to their dominion, the popes were not slow to pass laws about censorship, and this regulation acquired the force of a general law at the council that took place shortly thereafter in Rome. Holy Tiberius, Pope Alexander VI, was the first of the popes to pass a law about censorship in 1501. Weighed down himself by all his evildoings, he had no shame in showing concern for the purity of the Christian faith. But whenever has power blushed! He begins his papal bull with a complaint against the devil who sows corn cockles among the wheat and says: "Having learned that by means of the aforementioned art* many books and compositions printed in various parts of the world, particularly in Cologne, Mainz, Trier, Magdeburg, contain various errors and damaging teachings inimical to the Christian faith, and even now are still printed in some places, wishing without delay to preempt this odious ulcer, for each and every printer of the aforementioned art and for all those belonging to it and for all who are active in the business of printing in the places mentioned above, under pain of anathema and a fine to be determined and collected for the benefit of the Apostolic Camera by our honorable brethren the archbishops of Cologne, Mainz, Trier, and Magdeburg, or their

* "Aforementioned art" here and below refers to printing.—Trans.

vicars in their regions, we forbid by virtue of our apostolic power to print or to submit for printing books, treatises, or writings unless they have been referred to the aforementioned archbishops or vicars and unless they have been granted authorization that has specifically been without personal compensation; we charge them on their conscience so that, before they grant authorization of this kind, they will consider carefully the writings designated for print or have them examined by the scholarly and truly religious; and that they maintain the utmost vigilance that nothing be published that is contrary to the true faith and capable of giving rise to impiety and temptation." And so that books already in existence cause no further harm it was decreed that all inventories of books and all printed books be inspected and that those whose contents in any part opposed the Catholic confession be burned.

O! you who establish censorship, remember that you may be compared to Pope Alexander VI and may shame overcome you![101]

In 1515, the Lateran Council passed a decree on censorship that no book could be printed without the permission of the clergy.

From the preceding, we have seen that censorship was invented by the clergy and that it was adopted exclusively by them. Accompanied by anathema and a fine, censorship could at the time seem like a terrible thing to the violator of the rules published about it. But the rejection by Luther of pontifical authority, the breach of various rites from the Roman church, disputes among different powers during the Thirty Years War, gave rise to many books published without the usual seal of approval from the censor. Everywhere, however, the clergy arrogated to itself the right to exercise censorship on publications and when in 1650 secular censorship was established in France, the Faculty of Theology of the University of Paris protested against this new ordinance by arguing that it had in fact for two centuries enjoyed this right.

It was shortly after the introduction of printing in England* that censorship was established.[102] The Star Chamber, no less terrible in its time for England than the Inquisition in Spain or the Secret Chancery[103] for Russia, decided on the number of printers and printing presses and established the office of the vetter of print matter without whose authorization one would not dare print anything at all. The excesses of the Star Chamber against those who wrote about the government were endless and its history abounds in this kind. If, therefore, in England clerical superstition was incapable of imposing on reason the heavy curb of censorship, it was imposed by political superstition. But each of these made it their business to preserve power intact, that the orbs of enlightenment be veiled by the fog of enchantment, and that coercion dominate at the expense of reason.

It was the death of the Earl of Strafford that precipitated the demise of the Star Chamber;[104] but neither the liquidation of the latter nor the trial and execution of Charles I were able to confirm the freedom of the press in England. The Long Parliament restored the old regulations established against it. They were again restored during the reigns of Charles II and James I. Even in 1692 at the conclusion of the Glorious Revolution this legislation was confirmed although only for two years. When the two years were over in 1694,

---

* In England, William Caxton, a London merchant, established a printing press in the reign of Edward IV in 1474. The first book printed in the English language was *A Treatise on Chess,* translated from the French. The second was the *Collection of Sayings and Speeches of Philosophers,* translated by Lord Rivers.

liberty to print was fully restored and after a final gasp censorship gave up the ghost.*

The American states adopted freedom to publish among the very first laws establishing civil liberties. In chapter 1 of its constitution, in article 12 of the preamble concerning the rights of its residents, Pennsylvania says: "The people have the right to express, write, and publish their opinions; it follows that freedom to publish must never be subject to restriction." In chapter 2, paragraph 35, respecting the mode of government: "Let freedom of the press be guaranteed to all who wish to inspect the work of the legislative assembly or any other branch of government." In the draft relating to the type of government for the state of Pennsylvania, printed in July 1776 in order that the residents be able to share their comments, at paragraph 35: "Let freedom to print be guaranteed to all those who desire to study the legislative body, and the general assembly may not in any circumstances limit it. No publisher may be brought before a tribunal because he published remarks, evaluations, observations bearing on the works of the general assembly, the various branches of government, public affairs, or the conduct of government servants insofar as it relates to the jobs they do." The State of Delaware, in the declaration made of its rights, says in article 23: "Let the freedom to print be maintained in its inviolability." The State of Maryland uses the same terms in article 38. Virginia expresses itself in these words in article 14: "Freedom of the press is for the State the best bulwark of the freedom."[105]

---

* In Denmark freedom to print books was brief. The verses of Voltaire addressed to the King of Denmark on this occasion are proof that one should not hasten to praise a law, however wise it was.

The press, before the revolution of 1789 that took place in France, was nowhere so constrained as in this state. A hundred-eyed Argos, a hundred-handed Briareus, the police of Paris raged against writings and writers. In the dungeons of the Bastille wasted away the unfortunate who had the audacity to denounce the greed and depravity of ministers. Had the French language not enjoyed such universal use in Europe, France, which suffered under the lash of censorship, would not have attained that grandeur of thought to which so large a number of its writers offers proof. But the widespread use of French gave a reason to establish presses in Holland, England, Switzerland, and in the German lands, and everything you could not dare to be published in France was published freely in other places. So in this way power, flaunting its muscles, was derided and was not frightful; so it was that the maws foaming with fury remained empty, and firm speech slipped out of them unscathed.

How not to marvel at the incongruity of the human mind! Now when in France all are breathless about liberty, when brazenness and anarchy have reached the limit of possibility, censorship in France has not been abolished. And while everything can be published there now with impunity, it is clandestine. Not long ago we read—and may the French weep for their fate and with them all of humanity—we read not long ago that the Assemblée Nationale, acting as autocratically as the monarch had done hitherto, seized by force a book and put its author on trial for having dared to write against the Assemblée Nationale. Lafayette was the perpetrator of the sentence. O France! You continue to skirt the abyss of the Bastille.

With their equipment hidden from the authorities, the proliferation of printing presses in the German lands deprives them of the capacity to rage against reason and enlightenment. The smaller German governments, even though they are trying to impose a limit on freedom to publish, have been unsuccessful. Even though Wekhrlin was put under arrest by a vengeful government, the *Gray Monstrosity* remained in everyone's hands.[106] The late Frederick II, the Prussian king, in his lands all but established freedom to print: he did it not through the promulgation of any legislation, but only by tacit permission and the example of his own ideas. Why be surprised that he did not abolish censorship? He was an absolute monarch whose cherished passion was omnipotence. Contain your laughter.—He learned that someone was planning to assemble and publish his decrees. He assigned to them two censors—or perhaps it would be more appropriate to say inspectors. O domination! O omnipotence! you do not trust your own physical strength! You fear the accusation you make of yourself, you fear lest your tongue betray you and lest your own hand box your ears!—But what good could they do, these tyrannical censors? Far from doing good, they only could do harm. They secreted from the scrutiny of posterity some absurd law that power was ashamed to submit to future judgment, a law that once published could be a bridle on power so that it dares not to realize monstrous deeds. The Emperor Joseph II[107] removed in part an obstacle that barred the path to enlightenment and oppressed reason in the Austrian lands during the reign of Maria Theresa. But he was unable to shake off the burden of prejudices and published a very long memorandum on censorship. If he can be praised for not having banned criticism of his decisions, any complaint about his behavior, and the like, from being published in the press, still we will reproach him for leaving this curb on the freedom of expression of ideas. How easy it is to use this for bad ends! . . .* Why feel any surprise? We say now what we said earlier: he was an emperor. Tell me, then, where can there be more incongruities than in a royal head?

In Russia. . . . What happened in Russia with censorship you will learn another time. And now, without imposing censorship on the postal horses, I set off on my journey in haste.

---

* We read in the most recent news that the successor of Joseph II intends to renew the censorship committee abolished by his predecessor.

MEDNOE

"In a field a birch tree stood / in a field it curly stood / oi lyuli-lyuli-lyuli-lyuli." A round dance of young womenfolk and maidens—they dance. "Let us draw closer," said I to myself while unfolding the found papers of my acquaintance.—But I read the following. I was unable to walk up to the round dance. My ears were blocked with sadness and the joyous voice of plain cheerfulness failed to penetrate my heart. O my friend! Wherever you are, harken and judge.

Twice weekly the entire Russian Empire gets the news that N.N. or B.B. either cannot or does not want to pay what he borrowed or took, or the sum demanded of him. The borrowed sum is gambled away, spent on travel, used up, eaten up, drunk up, . . . up or given away, lost in fire or water, or through some other set of circumstances either N.N. or B.B. has gone into debt or repossession. Both reasons are printed by newspapers.—As printed: "On this day . . . at 10 o'clock in the morning, on the remand of the district court or the city magistrate, at a public auction will be sold the real estate, house, located in . . . quarter, at number . . . and with it six souls male and female, of the retired captain G; the sale will be held at the said house. All those interested may view in advance."

A bargain always has many seekers. The day and hour of the sale arrives. The purchasers are gathering. Those who have been condemned to sale stand motionless in the room where it is being conducted. An old man of about seventy-five, leaning on an elm club, craves to guess which pair of hands fate will give him to, who will close his eyes. He was with his master's father in the Crimean campaign in the time of Field Marshal Münnich;[108] at the battle of Frankfurt, he carried his wounded master on his shoulders from the front line. On return home, he was serf tutor to his young master. He saved him in his childhood from drowning, plunging into the river where the other had fallen during his crossing on a ferry and at danger to his own life saved him. In his youth, he bailed his master from the prison to which he had been sentenced because of debts incurred during his time as a junior officer in the guards.—An old woman of eighty years, his wife, was wet nurse to the young master's mother, was his nanny, and had oversight of the house until the very hour when she was brought to this auction. For the entire period of her service, she never lost anything of her masters', never coveted anything, never lied, and if she irritated them in any way then it was only perhaps through her truthfulness.—A woman of forty years, a widow, the wet nurse of her young master. Even now she still feels for him a measure of tenderness. Her blood runs in his veins. She is a second mother to him, and he owes his life to her more than to his natural mother. She who conceived him in pleasure gave no thought to his childhood. His wet nurse and nanny raised him. They part from him like a son.—A young woman of eighteen, her daughter and the granddaughter of the old people. Vicious beast, monster, fiend! Look at her, look at her crimson cheeks, tears flowing from her delightful eyes. Is it not you who, when unable to capture her innocence by means of seduction and promises, nor to intimidate with threats and punishment her constancy, finally used deception by marrying her to a collaborator in your vileness and in this guise take the pleasure that she abhorred to share with you? She discovered your deception. Her husband was never allowed to touch her bed again and you, deprived of your toy, used rape. Four villains, the instruments of your will, hold her hands and legs . . . but we shall not complete this. On her brow is grief, in her eyes despair. She holds the babe, the dolorous fruit of deceit or rape, but the living copy of his adulterous father. After giving birth to him, she forgot the father's beastliness and her heart began to feel tenderness toward him. She fears that she might fall into the hands of someone similar to the father.—The infant. . . . Your son, barbarian, your blood. Or do you think that where a church rite has not taken place there is no obligation then? Or do you think that the blessing given on your order by the hired performer of the divine word confirmed their union? Or do you think that a forced marriage in God's temple can be called a union? The Almighty reviles compulsion, He revels in heartfelt desires. Only they are pure. Oh, between us how many acts of adultery and defilement are committed in the name of the father of joys and the comforter of ills in the presence of witnesses unworthy of their stature.—A lad of twenty-five, her lawful husband, is the companion and confidant of her master. Brutality and vengeance can be seen in his eyes. He repents of his craven acts for his master. A knife is in his pocket; he grabbed hold of it fiercely, his plan not hard to work out. . . . Your zeal is fruitless. You will be given over to another owner. The hand of your owner, held constantly over the head of his slave, will bend your neck into compliance. Hunger, cold, heat, punishment, everything will be against you. Your mind is alien to noble thoughts. You do not know how to die. You will submit and will be a slave in spirit as much as in station. And if you were to want to resist you would die a slow death in chains. There is no judge to come between you. Your tormentor would not want to punish you personally. He will be your accuser. He will give you over to the municipal justice system.—The justice system!—where the accused scarcely has the power to defend himself.—Let us walk past the other unfortunate people put up for auction.

Scarcely had the terror-inducing hammer emitted its dull sound and unfortunates learned their fate—then tears, sobbing, groaning penetrated the ears of the entire assembly. Even the most callous were moved. Hardened hearts! What is the point of fruitless empathy? O Quakers! if we had your soul, we would have clubbed together, bought these wretches, gifted them freedom.—After living in harmony for many years, these victims of abusive sale will feel the pain of separation. But if the law—or, to put it better, barbaric custom since this is not written—permits such a mockery of humanity, what right do you have to sell this infant? He is illegitimate. The law frees him. Stop, I shall be the denouncer, I shall redeem him. If only I were able to save others with him! O Fortune! why have you stinted so miserably on my portion? I presently yearn to taste your enchanting gaze, for the first time I began to feel a passion for wealth.—My heart was so constrained that I bounded out of the meeting and fled after emptying my purse of my last ten kopecks to the victims. On the staircase I met a foreigner, a friend of mine. "What has happened to you? You are weeping!" "Turn back," I told him, "do not be a witness to this shameful spectacle. You once cursed the barbaric custom of selling black slaves in the distant settlements of your country; turn back," I repeated, "do not be a witness to our decline and may you not carry back our shame to your fellow citizens by conversing with them about our mores." "I cannot believe this," my friend said to me, "it is impossible that in a place where everyone is permitted to think and worship as they wish such a shameful custom exists." "Do not be surprised," I said to him, "the establishment of freedom of religion offends only priests and monks, and even they would sooner wish to acquire for themselves a sheep than a sheep for their Christian flock. But the freedom of rural dwellers will damage what they call the right of ownership. And all those who could champion freedom, all are the great landowners, and it is not from their councils that one should expect freedom, but from the burden of enslavement itself."

TVER

"The art of writing poetry in Russia," my dinner companion at the inn was saying, "understood in its various senses, is still far from greatness. Poetry had nearly awakened, but now once again slumbers; whereas versification had taken one step and then came to a standstill.[109]

"Lomonosov, having perceived what was ridiculous in the Polish cladding of our verses, stripped from them their foreign doublet. After giving good examples of new verses, he fitted on his followers a great model that turned out to be a bridle, and nobody has yet dared to move a step away from it. It was unfortunate that Sumarokov happened to live at the same time and he was an excellent versifier. He practiced verse on the model of Lomonosov, and now all those who follow them cannot imagine that there could be meters other than iambics as practiced by these two famous men. Although both these versifiers taught the rules for other meters, and Sumarokov left behind examples of all types, they were too insignificant to merit from anyone imitation. If Lomonosov had adapted Job or the psalmodist in dactyls; or if Sumarokov had written *Semiramis* or *Dimitry* in trochees, then Kheraskov, too, would have thought it possible to write in meters other than iambs and would have attracted greater fame in his eight-year endeavor by having described the siege of Kazan in a meter suited to epic.[110] I am not surprised that the ancient three-cornered hat fitted to Virgil was cut in the style of Lomonosov, but I would have preferred Homer to appear among us not in iambs but in feet similar to his hexameters; and Kostrov, albeit a translator rather than a poet, would have inaugurated an epoch in the history of our prosody, since he would have advanced the progress of poetry itself by an entire generation.[111]

"But Lomonosov and Sumarokov were not the only ones to halt Russian versification. Trediakovsky, that tireless workhorse, contributed not a little to it with his *Tilemakhida*. It is very difficult at present to give an example of new versification, since models of good and bad prosody have put down deep roots. Parnassus is surrounded by iambs, and rhymes stand guard everywhere. If anyone took it into his head to write in dactyls, Trediakovsky was immediately assigned as mentor, and the most beautiful child long remained ugly in appearance until such time as a Milton, Shakespeare, or Voltaire were born. That is when Trediakovsky will be dug out from a grave overgrown with the moss of neglect, and good lines will be found in *Tilemakhida* and set as an example.[112]

"An ear that has grown accustomed to rhyme will for a long time be an impediment to a beneficial change in verse form. After a long time hearing concordant endings in verse lines, unrhyming will seem crude, rough, and dissonant. So shall it be for as long the French language is in greater use in Russia than other languages. Our senses, like a soft and young tree, can be cultivated to be straight or crooked, as one wishes. Moreover, in a poem, as in all things, a fashion can dominate and if there is at least something natural, then that will be accepted without contradiction. But everything fashionable is ephemeral, especially in poetry. An external shine can become rusty, while genuine beauty will never fade. Homer, Virgil, Milton, Racine, Voltaire, Shakespeare, Tasso, and many others will be read for as long as the human race has not been destroyed.

"I consider it unnecessary to converse with you about the different verse forms natural to the Russian language. What the iamb, trochee, dactyl, or anapest are everyone knows who has even the slightest understanding of the rules of versification. But what would not be superfluous is if I were to give sufficient examples of the different types. But my ability and insight are limited. If my advice were able to do anything then I would say that Russian, indeed even the Russian language, would be greatly enriched if translations in verse were not always into iambs. It would be considerably more suitable to the epic poem if a translation of the *Henriade* were not in iambs, and unrhymed iambs are worse than prose."[113]

All of the above my feasting companion uttered in one breath and so fluently that I did not have a chance to voice any objections although I had to say quite a lot of something or other in defense of iambs and all those who wrote in them.

"I myself," he continued, "followed the infectious example and composed verse in iambs, but they were odes. Here is a remaining fragment of one of them, all the others were consigned to burn in a fire; and indeed the very same fate that affected her sisters awaits the remaining bit. In Moscow nobody wanted to publish it for two reasons: the first was that the sense in the verse was unclear and many of the lines were hackwork; the second that the subject of the poem was inapplicable to our country. I am now going to Petersburg to ask about its publication, hoping, like a tender father of his little child, that because of the second reason for which it wasn't published in Moscow, they will look indulgently at the first. If it's no trouble to you to read some stanzas," he said to me as he handed over a sheet.— I unfolded it and read the following: *Liberty . . . Ode . . .* "On account of the title alone they refused me the publication of this poem. But I remember very well that in the *Instruction on the Establishment of a New Law Code,* in speaking about liberty, it is said: 'liberty ought to be called the fact that all must obey the same laws.' It follows that it is appropriate to speak about liberty in our country."[114]

1

O! gift of heaven beneficent,
Originator of all great deeds,
O liberty, liberty, gift munificent,
Allow a slave to hymn as needs.
With ardor fill my heart replete,
The dark of slavery will to light retreat
When by your muscles strong is stirred,
That Tell and Brutus may yet arise
That kings enthroned in power's guise
Will by your voice be perturbèd.

"This stanza has been faulted for two reasons; for the verse 'The dark of slavery will to light retreat.' It is stilted and hard to utter because of the frequent repetition of the letter T and because of the frequent collocation of consonantal letters, *bstva t'mu pretv*—for ten consonants there are three vowels, yet in the Russian language it is just as possible as in Italian to write harmoniously. . . . Agreed . . . although others considered this line to be successful, finding in the roughness of the verse an evocative expression of the difficulty of the very act. And here is another: 'That kings will by your voice be perturbèd.' To wish a Tsar perturbation is the same as wishing him ill; consequently. . . . But I do not want to bore you with all the comments made on my verses. Many of them, I admit, were fair. Allow me to be your reader.

2

I came into the world, and you with me. . . .

Let us go past this stanza. Here is its content: Man is free in every way at birth. . . .

3

What hindrance is there to being free?
Limits to my wishes everywhere I see,
Shared power has arisen in the polity,
A common curb on powers has come to be.
To it society obeys in everything,
Everywhere unanimous agreeing.
The common good has no anxiety.
In the power of all I see my fate,
In the will of all my will partakes,
This is what the law is in society.

4

Amidst a lush and grassy valley,
Among fields bowed with harvest crops,
Where flourishes the tender lily,
Among the peaceful shade of olive groves.
Than Parian marble even whiter,
Than luminous days yet brighter,
A temple stands, its sides diaphanous,
No sacrifice burns there in falsity,
A fiery note hangs there, we see:
"An end to woes of innocence."

5

With branch of olive crowned,
On hardened stone there seated,
Remorseless and cold-blooded,
A deaf divinity. . . . .

and so on—law is portrayed as a divinity in a temple whose guards are truth and justice.

6

He elevates his steely gazes,
Joy and awe about him pouring,
Fairly looks on all the faces,
Neither loving them or hating.

To flattery alien, and deception, withal,
He ancestry, eminence, wealth reviles,
Material sacrifice is nothing fine,
To kinship and attachment blind,
Reward and punishment do not him bind,
For on this earth his image is divine.

7

Behold this monster terrible,
A hydra with its hundred heads,
In tears, insistent to implore,
Rife with poison in his jaws.
It tramples hard on earthly powers
Its head as high as heaven towers,
Proclaims that region as its sphere
Phantoms, darkness, everywhere it sows
To flatter and deceive is the thing it knows,
Obedience from all is what's held dear.

8

With darkness reason dimming,
And spreading widely lowly venom . . .

A depiction of holy superstition depriving man of sensibility, dragging him into the yoke of servitude and error, dressing him in armor:

To fear the truth was commanded . . . .

Power calls this a slander of divinity; reason, a deception.

9

In regions wide we do survey,
Where stands a throne of slavery darkly. . . .

In a period of peace and tranquility, sacred and political superstition, the two reinforcing one another,

Together by them society is hassled.
One takes aim to pin down reason,
T'other strives free will to pinion,
For the common good this is declared.

10

In the shade of servile rest,
Crops will never be their best,
Where hindrance slows down very thought,
Grandeur's bound to come to naught.

And all the evil consequences of slavery, such as: carelessness, indolence, cunning, hunger, and so on.

11

His arrogant brow uplifted,
The Tsar a steely scepter prizes,

Upon a thund'rous throne ensconced
The people like some vermin he despises.
Life and death are within his grasp:
'A villain I can spare,' he spake,
'Power I am able to bequeath,
When I laugh everyone laughs too
When I in menace frown, all feel rue
You will live if I order you to live.'

12

And we harken calmly . . .

how a hungry serpent, reviling all, poisons days of joy and merriment. But, whilst around your throne all kneel—tremble, now an avenger advances, prophesying liberty. . . .

13

The martial host arises, widely bristling,
Hope her arms on all does fasten,
In blood of crowned tormentor glistening,
To wash away one's shame they hasten.
The sword is sharp, I spy it widely gleams,
In many guises death flies down, it seems,
Above the prideful head it holds.
Exalt you nations now in fetters,
By right of nature avenge tormentors
And lead the king up to the scaffold.

14

And now the vail of lying night,
With mighty crash is sorely pierced,
The idol huge of stubborn might,
Of might conceited—it lies trampled;
A giant hundred-armed in chains
Is, like a citizen, dragged back again
To face the throne the people claim:
"You violator of power granted me!
Tell, you villain, crowned by me,
How dare you rebel and inflame?

15

I clothed you in a cloak of porphyry,
Equality in society to oversee,
To keep the widow and the orphan ever free
From woe, their innocence yours to foresee.
To innocence a father, child-loving,
But as avenger implacably unbending
'Gainst falsehood, vice and calumny;
Deeds with honor given to rewarding,
Evil by good planning given to preempting,
Morality preserved in all her purity.

16

I covered the sea in ships. . . .

Gave a means to the acquisition of riches and well-being. I wished the landworker to be not captive in his field and would bless you. . . .

17

In the shedding of blood unstinting,
A thunderous host I mounted,
Canons, huge, of bronze, by casting,
Evildoers from abroad I punished.
Obedience to you was decreed,
Pursuit of glory was our ardent need.
Anything goes for everyone's advancement,
The depths of earth I excavate,
Metal, gleaming, I amalgamate
For your enhancement.

18

The oath you gave me now forgotten,
You forgot that I it was who chose you;
For your pleasure you think the crown begotten,
And who is Lord, who subject, misconstrue.
My statutes with a sword you've smashed,
All rights to silence you've reduced
And ordered truth to feel ashamed.
You've cleared a way for depredations,
Appealed to God, but I was not named,
And treated me like abomination.

19

Procuring by sweat and blood
The fruit for food I planted,
Crumbs were shared for chewing cud,
And effort was not stinted;
But treasures will never you suffice!
Did they really fall so short in price
That off my back you tore my shirt?
Shower with gifts your favorite kiss-ass!
And the lady whose honor suffered mishaps!
Is gold the only God to whom you now revert?
Have you recognized gold as your God?

20

An insignia devised for excellence
You awarded as a badge to arrogance.
A sword sharpened for an enemy's defense
You began to aim against innocence.
Troops as bulwark have been marshaled—
Do you lead them into splendid battle,
Humanity to punish?
You fight in bloody valleys,
So that the drunks in Athens
Shall, yawning, 'A hero!' admonish.

21

Villain, most horrid of all the villains . . .

You conjoined all atrocities and directed your stinger at me. . . .

'Die! Die, you, and a hundredfold!'—

The people declared. . . .

22

O great man, in treachery abounding,
Hypocrite, blasphemer, flunkey!
Alone you give the world so resounding
An example, one for posterity.
A villain, Cromwell, I do you hold
Since with your power bold
Freedom's stronghold you destroyed.
But by the generation from you they learned
How peoples can themselves be avenged:
You Charles, on trial, executed.

23

And this is the voice of liberty resounding to all the ends of the Earth. . . .

To the *veche*[115] the nation flocks;
The cast-iron throne they bring down;

Like Samson of old they shake down
The palace full of nasty plots.
By law is nature's fortress firmed,
How great you are, spirit of freedom,
Of founders, just like God himself!

24

The next eleven stanzas contain the description of the kingdom of freedom and its effects; that is, safety, tranquility, well-being, greatness. . . .

34

But passions, sharpening malice . . .

turn the tranquility of the citizenry into ruin . . .

Turn father against son,
Tear apart marital bonds,

and all the consequences of the limitless desire to exercise power. . . .

35, 36, 37

Description of the fatal consequences of luxury. Internecine strife. Civil war. Marius, Sulla, Augustus. . . .

He sedates anxious liberty.
He wound round the cast-iron scepter with flowers . . .

as a result—enslavement. . . .

38, 39

Such is the law of nature: from torment arises liberty, from liberty slavery. . . .

40

Why one should wonder at this,—and man too is born to

The next eight stanzas contain prophecies of the future fate of the fatherland, which will be divided into parts.[116] The larger it is, the quicker this comes about. But the time has not yet come. Indeed, when it does come then

The door bolts of the awful night will crack.

Resilient power at its extinction will set a guard on speech and will gather all its strength so as with one final blow to crush liberty as it arises. . . .

49

But mankind will howl in chains and, guided by the hope for freedom and the indestructible right of nature, will act. . . . And power will be brought to tremble. At that time the consolidation of all forces, at that time heavy power

> Will be dissipated in a single second.
> O day most sought of all days!

50

> I already hear the voice of nature,
> The primal voice, the voice of divinity.

The gloomy firmament shuddered, and liberty shone forth.

"Here finally is the end," said the newfangled versifier to me.

I was very glad of it and almost wished to utter, perhaps, unpleasant criticism of his poem, but the little bell announced that it was more seemly to hasten on the road on postal nags than to clamber on to Pegasus if it is willful.

GORODNYA

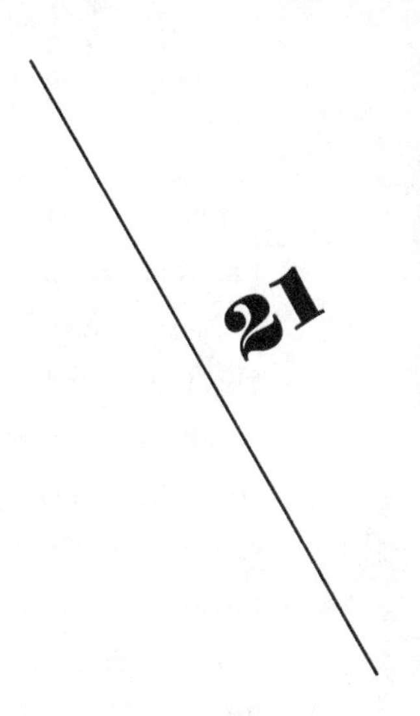

On arriving in this village, it was not singing in verses that struck my hearing but the heart-piercing lamentations of women, children, and elders. Leaving my carriage, I sent it off to the postal yard, curious as I was to learn the cause of the noticeable disturbance from the street.

On drawing close to one gang, I learned that conscription was the cause of the sobbing and tears of the throng. From many hamlets, belonging either to the state or landowners, conscripts had gathered on their way to surrender for conscription.

In one crowd an old woman of about fifty years, holding a twenty-year-old lad by the head, wailed, "My dear little child, for whom are you abandoning me? To whom are you entrusting the parental home? Our fields will be overgrown with grass; our hut, with moss, and I, your poor elderly mother, will be forced to go begging. Who will warm my decrepit body from cold, who will shelter it from the heat? Who will give me to drink and feed me? Well, this does not lie so heavily on the heart but who will close my eyes when I expire? Who will receive my parental blessing? Who will commit my body to our shared mother, the raw earth? Who will come to commemorate me at the grave? Your burning tear will not fall on it, that comfort I shall not have."

Next to the old woman there stood a maiden, already grown up. She, too, wailed: "Farewell, friend of my heart, farewell, my beautiful little sun. For me, your chosen bride, there will no longer be any consolation, any amusement. My girlfriends will not envy me. The sun will not rise over me to bring me joy. You abandon me to grieve though neither as a widow nor as a married wife. If only our elders, inhuman though they are, had allowed us to marry; if you had only, my dear friend, gone to sleep just one night, gone to sleep on my white breast. Perhaps God would have taken pity on me and given me a little boy as a comfort."

The lad said to them, "Stop weeping, stop tearing my heart out. Our ruler summons us to service. My lot was chosen. It is God's will. He will live to whom it is not given to die. Perhaps somehow with the regiment I shall come to see you. Perhaps I shall somehow manage to earn a rank. Do not grieve, my little dear mother. Look after little Praskovya for me." This conscript was rendered from a state settlement.

My ear picked out from the crowd standing nearby words of a completely different type. In their midst I saw a man of about thirty years, average height, standing staunchly and cheerfully gazing upon those standing around.

"The Lord has heard my prayer," he said. "The tears of an unhappy man have reached the comforter of all. Now I shall at least know that my fate will depend on my good or bad behavior. Until now it depended on female caprice. The simple thought that I shall not be punished by the cudgel without a trial consoles me."

Having learned from his speech that he was a house serf, I was curious to learn the reason for his uncommon delight. To my question about this he replied: "If, Sir, on the one side stood the gallows and on the other side was a deep river, and standing between the two perils there was no way to avoid going right or left, into the noose or the water, what would you choose, what would reason and sensibility force you to wish? I think that you and indeed any other person would choose to plunge into the river in the hope that once he swam across to the other bank the danger would have passed. Nobody would agree to test with their own neck whether or not the noose was firm. This was my case. The soldier's life is a hard one, better than the noose, though. And it would be a good thing if all it meant were death rather than perishing from a slow death, under the cudgel, cat-o'-nine-tails, in chains, in a cellar, naked, barefoot, thirsty, hungry, under ceaseless harassment. Dear sir, although you consider serfs your property, often worse than cattle, it is to their bitterest misfortune that they have not been deprived of sensation. You find it surprising, I see, to hear words like these from the mouth of a peasant; but now that you have heard them, why do you not feel surprise at the hard-heartedness of your brethren, the nobility?"

And in truth, I had not anticipated what was said from someone dressed in a rough plain rough caftan with a shaven brow. Yet out of a desire to satisfy my curiosity I asked him to explain to me how, being of such low extraction, he had attained an understanding those wrongly called noble frequently lacked.

"If you will not be bored listening to my tale, then I shall tell you that I was born into slavery, the son of the serf tutor of my former master. What delight it is for me that I shall no longer be called Vanka nor by some abusive appellation nor be summoned by whistling. My old master, a good-hearted man, wise, and virtuous, not rarely aggrieved for the fate of his slaves, wishing to reward me, too, for my father's long-term service, gave me an education equal to his son's. There was hardly any difference between us except that the cloth on the caftan he wore was somewhat finer. What the young gentleman was taught, I was also taught. Our lessons were equal in every way and I can say without boasting that I excelled my young owner in much.

"'Vanyusha,' the old gentleman would say to me, 'your happiness depends entirely on you. You have greater motivation to learning and morality than my son. After my death, he will be rich and will know no need, whereas you have known it from birth. So then, try to be worthy of the care I have taken of you.' When my young master was in his seventeenth year, he and I were sent to foreign lands with a tutor who was instructed to consider me a companion rather than a servant. As he saw me off, my old master said to me, 'I hope that you will return for my own peace of mind and that of your parents. Within the borders of this state you are a slave, but outside them you are free. When you return, the shackles that were laid on you at birth will not be restored.' We were away five years and were on the way back to Russia. My young master was in a state of joy to see his parent, while I, I admit, felt hopeful about using the promise I'd been made. My heart trembled as I crossed again the borders of my fatherland. And in truth, the heart's foreboding was not wrong. In Riga, my young master received the news of his father's death. He was moved by it, I was brought to despair. For all my efforts to earn the friendship and trust of my young master had always been futile. Not only did he not love me but hated me, perhaps because of the envy typical of small souls.

"Seeing the dismay the news of his father's death caused me, he told me that he would not forget the promise made to me provided

I were deserving. It was the first time he dared to mention this, since after attaining his independence after the death of his father, he immediately dismissed his tutor in Riga, after paying him generously for his labors. One has to be fair to my former master since he has many good qualities but they are overshadowed by a timidity of spirit and flightiness.

"A week after our return to Moscow my former master fell in love with a young woman, fine of countenance. But she joined to her physical beauty the most vile spirit and a cruel and severe heart. Brought up in the arrogance of her pedigree, she regarded only appearance, nobility, wealth as distinctions. In two months, she became the spouse of my master and my mistress. Until that time, I felt no change in my condition and lived in the home of my owner as a companion. Although he did not give me orders, I sometimes anticipated his wishes, aware of his power and my lot. Scarcely had the young mistress crossed the threshold of the home in which she was determined to be in charge than I sensed the hardship of my fate. On the first evening after the wedding and the next day, when I was introduced to her by her spouse as his companion, she was occupied by the usual concerns of a new marriage. But in the evening, when in the presence of the bustling assembly everyone came to the table and sat down to the newlyweds' first supper, I, as was customary, took my place at the lower end. The new mistress told her husband fairly loudly that if he wanted her to sit at the table with the guests, he should not allow serfs to sit there. After a look at me, prompted now by her, he sent to tell me to leave the table and take supper in my room. Imagine how strongly I felt this humiliation. I, however, hid the tears welling up in my eyes and withdrew. On the next day I did not dare to show up. Not inquiring about me, they brought me my dinner and supper. It was the same on subsequent days. One day in the afternoon, a week after the wedding, the new mistress, inspecting the house and assigning duties and lodgings to all the servants, entered my rooms. They had been allocated to me by my old master. I was not at home. I will not repeat what she said while in my rooms by way of mockery, but when I returned, I was informed that she had ordered me to be assigned a corner on the ground floor, together with unmarried domestics where my bed, the trunk with clothing and linen, were already placed. Everything else she left in my rooms, where she installed her maids.

"What took place in my soul on hearing this is easier to feel than describe, if anyone could. But in order not to detain you with perhaps excessive storytelling: my mistress, having assumed the management of the house and not finding in me a fitness for service, designated me a lackey and dressed me in livery. The slightest imagined infringement in my work incurred slaps in the face, cudgels, and cat-o'-nine-tails. O my good sir, it would be better not to have been born! How many times did I resent my deceased benefactor for giving me a sensitive soul. Would that I had grown up in ignorance, unaware that as a man I was the equal of everyone else. Long, long ago, would I have deprived myself of my hateful life, if an interdiction by the Supreme Judge of all did not stop me. I resolved myself to endure my fate patiently. And I endured not only bodily wounds but also the wounds she inflicted on my soul. But I came close to violating my pledge and taking away the lamentable remnants of my life after there occurred a new wound to my soul.

"My mistress's nephew, a lad of eighteen years, a sergeant of the Guards, brought up in the fashion of Moscow fops, fell in love with his aunt's chambermaid and, having prevailed because of her shrewd ardor, made her a mother. Resolute though he was in his amorous affairs, he became somewhat embarrassed by the outcome since his auntie, when she learned about this, banned her chambermaid from her presence and gently scolded her nephew. In the manner of merciful masters, she intended to punish her former favorite and to give her in marriage to a stable hand. But since they were all married, and a pregnant woman needed a husband for the honor of the house, she could find no one worse than me among all her servants. And of the 'special favor' my mistress informed me in the presence of her husband. I could no longer endure the abuse. 'Inhuman woman! You have the power to torment me and to mutilate my body: you say that the laws give you this right over us. This I scarcely believe. What I do know for sure is that nobody can be forced to enter into marriage.' These words effected beastly silence from her. Turning to her spouse then: 'Ungrateful son of a humane father, you forget his last wishes, forget also your declaration; but do not drive to despair a nobler soul than your own, beware!' I could say no more than that because, on my mistress's order, I was taken to the stables and mercilessly whipped with a cat-o'-nine-tails. The next day I could hardly get out of bed because of the beating; and again I was brought before my mistress. 'I will forgive you your impudence of yesterday,' she said. 'Marry my Mavrushka, she entreats you, and I, fond of her despite her transgression, want to do this for her.' 'Everyone heard my response yesterday,' I told her. 'This is the only answer. I shall only add that I will lodge a complaint against you to the authorities since you have no right to force me to do this.' 'Well, it is time for you to be conscripted,' my mistress shrieked furiously. . . . A traveler who has lost his way in a terrible desert would feel less joy on recovering it than I had when I heard these words. 'Conscripted,' she repeated, and the next day this was carried out.—Foolish woman! She thought that becoming a soldier would be a punishment, as it is for peasants. For me this was joy, and as soon as they shaved my brow, I felt reborn. My strength was renewed. Reason and spirit began to work again. O! hope, sweet sensation of the unfortunate, abide with me." A heavy tear, but not laden with grief and despair, fell from his eyes. I clasped him to my heart. New joy lit up his face. "Not everything is lost; you give strength to my soul," he told me, "against sorrow, giving me the sense that my calamity will not be endless. . . ."

I went across from this unfortunate man to a crowd in which I saw three men shackled with the heaviest chains. "Cause for surprise," I said to myself looking at these captives.—"Now they are dejected, weary, timid, and not only do not they want to be soldiers, but it takes the greatest cruelty to put them in this position. But once they come to grips with performing their difficult calling, they become vigorous, enterprising and even despise their former state." I asked the man nearby who, to judge by his clothes, looked like a government official steward: "Surely, it was out of fear for their escape that they were bound in such heavy chains?" "Your guess is correct. They belonged to a landowner who needed money for a new carriage, and to obtain it he sold them to state peasants as prospective recruits."

I: "My friend, you are mistaken, state peasants cannot buy their own brethren."

He: "It is not done in the form of sale. The owner of these unfortunate men, taking money by agreement, sets them free. They are presumed to be following their own wishes to register as state peasants in the district that paid the money for them, and the district, following a general arrangement, enrolls them as soldiers. They are now being transported, together with their manumission papers, for registration in our district."

Free people who committed no crime are being sold like cattle! O laws! Your wisdom is often contained only in the letter. Is not this a clear mockery? But even more than this, it is a mockery of the sacred name of freedom! Oh! If the slaves oppressed by their heavy shackles in furious despair, using the irons that impede their freedom, shattered our heads, the heads of their inhuman masters, and stained their fields with our blood, what would the state lose because of this? From their midst great men would soon erupt to succeed the massacred tribe. But their view of themselves would be different, and they would give up the oppression of others as their right.—This is not a dream, but my gaze penetrates the thick curtain of time that hides the future from our eyes. I gaze across the entire century.—In indignation I walked away from the crowd.

But the shackled detainees are now free. If they had at least some initiative, they would frustrate the oppressive intentions of their tyrants. . . . Let us return. "My friends," I told the captives in their own fatherland. "Are you aware that if you do not want to join the military nobody can force you to do so?" "Master, stop mocking wretched people. Even without your joke it is painful for one of us to part from his decrepit father; for the other, from his young sisters; for the third, from his young wife. We know that our master sold us for a thousand rubles, to be conscripted." "If until now you did not know this, then know that it is forbidden to sell people to be conscripted; that peasants cannot buy people; that your master manumitted you; and that those who bought you want you to register in their district as if by your accord." "Oh, if this is so, Master, thank you. When they line us up for measurement, we all will say that we do not want to be soldiers and that we are free people." "Add to this that your owner sold you at a time when it was not legal and that you have been conscripted unwillingly."* It is easy to imagine the joy that spread across the faces of these unfortunate people. Bouncing up from their place and vigorously shaking their shackles, it looked as if they were testing their strength to throw them off. But this conversation almost caused me great trouble: when they understood my speech, the recruiting agents were incandescent with anger and accosted me, saying: "Master, you are meddling in others' business, get out of here while still in one piece." And they began to push me so strongly as I resisted that I hastily had to move away from this crowd.

On walking up to the post station, I found another crowd of peasants surrounding a man in torn frock coat, somewhat drunk, it seemed, and making faces at the bystanders who looking at him laughed until they cried. "What wonder do you have here?" I asked one boy. "What are you laughing at?" "This recruit here is a foreigner, cannot utter a peep in Russian." From a few words that he uttered I learned that he was a Frenchman. My curiosity arose even more. I wanted to learn how a foreigner could be given up for conscription by peasants. I asked him in his native tongue: "My friend, by what chance do you find yourself here?"

The Frenchman: "Fate wanted it so. Where it is good, that's where one should live."

I: "But how did you manage to become a recruit?"

Frenchman: "I like the military life, I know it already, I myself wanted it."

---

* It is forbidden to make and complete bills for the sale of peasants at the time of conscription.

I: "But how did it come about that you were taken as a recruit from the village? From villages they usually take to be soldiers only peasants and only Russians. I see that you are neither a peasant nor Russian."

Frenchman: "This is how. In Paris, as a child, I trained to be a hairdresser. I went to Russia with a certain gentleman. In Petersburg, I dressed his hair for an entire year. He did not have money to pay me. I left him and, unable to find a position, nearly died from hunger. Fortunately, I managed to get a place as a sailor on a ship sailing under the Russian flag. Before leaving for sea I was put under oath as a Russian subject, and went to Lübeck. At sea, the captain often beat me with the end of a rope for being idle. Being careless, I fell from the rigging onto the deck and broke three fingers, which made me forever unable to manage a comb. Upon arriving in Lübeck, I ran into Prussian recruiters and served in different regiments. I was beaten with sticks, not infrequently, for idleness and drinking. While drunk I stabbed to death a fellow soldier and left Memel where I was stationed. Recalling that I was bound to Russia by oath, like a faithful son of the fatherland, I set off to Riga with two thalers in my pocket. On the way I fed myself by alms. In Riga, my luck and art served me well: I won about twenty rubles in a tavern and, having bought myself a good caftan for ten, went with a merchant to Kazan' as a lackey. But, passing through Moscow, I met in the street two of my countrymen who advised me to leave my master and look for a position as a teacher in Moscow. I told them I was not good at reading. But they responded: 'You speak French, that is enough.' My master did not notice when I left him on the street. He continued on his way and I stayed in Moscow. Soon my countrymen found me a position as a teacher for a hundred and fifty rubles, a *pood* of sugar, a *pood** of coffee, ten pounds of tea a year, meals, a servant, and the use of carriage. But I had to live in the country. So much the better. There they were unaware for a whole year that I could not write. But one of the in-laws of the gentleman in whose house I lived gave my secret away to him, and they sent me back to Moscow. Unable to find another such fool and unable to practice my skill as a hairdresser because of my broken fingers, afraid to die of hunger, I sold myself for two hundred rubles. They registered me as a peasant and now are sending me off as a recruit. I hope," he said with an air of importance, "that as soon as there is a war I will rise to the rank of general. And if there is no war, I will line my pockets as much as I can manage to do, and, crowned with laurels, will retire to my fatherland."

I shrugged my shoulders more than once while listening to this tramp; and with a pained heart lay down in my cart, set off on my journey.

---

* thirty-six pounds—Trans.

ZAVIDOVO

The horses were already harnessed to the cart, and I was preparing to depart when suddenly a great commotion arose outside. People began running from one end of the village to the other. Outside I saw a military man in a grenadier hat who proudly strutted about and, holding a raised whip, shouted: "Quickly, horses! Where is the elder? His Excellency will be here in a minute. Present the elder to me now. . . ." Doffing his hat at a hundred paces, the elder ran at top speed in response to the summons. "Quickly, horses." "Right away, little father. An order for post horses please." "Take it. And hurry up, or else . . ." he was saying, raising the whip over the head of the trembling elder. This unfinished speech was as full of expression as Aeolus's speech to the winds "Or else . . ."[117] in Virgil's *Aeneid*. And cowed by the sight of the scourge of the all-powerful grenadier, the elder felt the might of the threatening warrior's hand as vividly as the mutinous winds felt over them the power of Aeolus's forceful trident. Surrendering the order for post horses to the latter day Polkan,[118] the elder said: "His Excellency and his honorable family require fifty horses, and we only have thirty on hand, others are out."[119] "Make them, old devil. And if there are no horses, I will disfigure you." "But where can I get them, if they are nowhere to be had?" "He's still talking. . . . But I will have these horses. . . ." And he grabbed the old man's beard and began mercilessly beating him on the shoulders with the whip. "Have you had enough? Well there are three fresh ones," said the judge, a stickler of the post station, pointing to the horses harnessed to my cart. "Unharness them for us." "If the master will give them up." "How can he not give them up? He'll get the same from me that you've had. And who is he?" "Don't know, some. . . ." What honorific he gave me, I do not know.

Meanwhile I walked outside and stopped the brave precursor of His Excellency from fulfilling his intention to force me to spend the night in the post station by unharnessing my horses.

My spat with the Polkan of the guards was interrupted by the arrival of His Excellency. Even from afar one could hear the shouts of drivers and clatter of horses galloping with all their might. The rapid beating of hooves and the rotation of wheels invisible to the eye so thickened the air with a cloud of dust that His Excellency's chariot was concealed by an impenetrable cloud from the gazes of the coachmen awaiting him as if he were a thundercloud. Don Quixote, for sure, would have seen something miraculous here, since the dust cloud that swirled under the eminent person of His Excellency suddenly stopped and parted, and he appeared before us gray-faced from dust looking like progeny born looking black at birth.

Between my arrival at the post station and the time when horses were again harnessed to my cart at least an entire hour passed. But the carts of His Excellency were hitched up in no more than a quarter of an hour . . . and away they galloped on the wings of the wind.

Still, my nags, even though they looked superior to the ones privileged to carry the person of His Excellency, ran at a moderate trot since they did not fear the grenadier's knout.

Blessed are the grandees of autocratic governments. Blessed are those decorated by ranks and sashes. All nature obeys them. Even senseless beasts cater to their desires and, lest they grow bored of yawning while on the way, gallop without sparing their legs or their lungs and often die of the effort. Blessed are—I will repeat—those whose appearance draws everyone to reverence. Among those who tremble when menaced by the lash, how many know that the one in whose name they threaten him is in the court grammar labeled "without voice"? That in all his life he could say neither A . . . nor O . . .?*[120] That he is indebted for his prominence to someone whom he is ashamed to name? That in his heart he is the basest creature? That deception, perfidy, treachery, fornication, poisoning, thievery, robbery, murder cost him no more than drinking a glass of water? That his cheeks never reddened out of shame, perhaps only out of rage or from a slap? That he is a friend to every court stoker and the slave of anyone barely cutting a figure at court? But he is a sneering overlord to everyone ignorant of his baseness and obsequiousness. Eminence without true merit resembles village sorcerers. All peasants respect and fear them, thinking that they are masters of the supernatural. These impostors rule over them, however they want. But as soon as anyone unmoved by the grossest superstition turns up in the crowd of worshippers, their deceptions are exposed. Such clairvoyants do not dwell in the places where they work their

---

* See the manuscript Court Grammar of Fonvizin.

wonders. In the same way, anyone who dares to expose the sorcery of grandees should also beware.

But how could I catch up with His Excellency? He raised a column of dust which disappeared as soon as he flew past, and on arriving in Klin I found that even the memory of him had perished with the noise he made.

KLIN

"It was in Rome, the city, Prince Euphemius there lived once upon a time. . . ." This singer of this folk song titled "Alexei the Man of God" was a blind old man sitting by the gate of the post station and surrounded by a crowd mostly of children and youths. His hoary head, closed eyes, the look of calm visible on his face compelled those looking at the bard to stand before him in awe. While his tune was artless, its accompanying tenderness of elocution penetrated the hearts of his listeners. They were better attuned to take in nature than the ears of inhabitants of Moscow and Petersburg, trained in harmony, take in the ornate chant of Gabrielli, Marchesi, or Todi. None of those present remained unaffected by a deep shiver when the singer of Klin, as he reached the departure of his hero, barely recited his narrative, his voice breaking moment by moment. The place where his eyes used to be filled with tears emanating from a soul made sensitive by misfortunes, and streams of these poured down his cheeks. O Nature, how powerful you are! Looking at the old man cry, women began to weep; from the lips of youth flew off its habitual companion, the smile; on the face of adolescence appeared diffidence, a true sign of a painful if unknown feeling. Even a manly age, so habituated to cruelty, acquired a solemn appearance. “O Nature!,” I cried out again.

How sweet is a benign feeling of grief! How it renews the heart and its sensitivity. I wept after the gathering at the post station, and my tears were as sweet to me as tears wrenched from my heart by Werther. . . . O my friend, my friend! Why did not you too see this picture? You would shed tears with me, and the deliciousness of shared feeling would have been far sweeter.

At the end of the recital, everyone present gave the old man something, as it were, in reward for his labor. He received rather indifferently all the half- and quarter-kopecks, all the pieces and chunks of bread, each time augmenting his thanks with a bow, crossing himself, and saying to the giver: “May God grant you health.” I did not want to leave without being sent on my way with a prayer by this elder who was, of course, agreeable to heaven. I wanted his blessing for the fulfillment of my journey and my aspiration. It seemed to me—and I always have this wish—that the benediction of sensitive souls facilitates the path of progress and removes the thorn of doubt. Drawing near him, I placed a ruble in his trembling hand, my hand also trembling from the doubt whether I was acting from vanity. Crossing himself, he did not have a chance to utter his usual blessing to the donor, distracted as he was by the unusual sensation produced by what was in his palm. And this wounded my heart. “How much more a quarter-kopeck given to him pleases him!” I told myself. “He feels in it an ordinary human sympathy for sorrows; in my ruble he perhaps senses my arrogance. He does not offer his blessing to it.” Oh, how petty I then seemed to myself, how I envied those who gave the old man after his singing a quarter-kopeck and a chunk of bread! “Is not this a five-kopeck coin?” he said, directing his speech vaguely, just like his every word. "No, grandfather, this here is a ruble," a boy standing close to him said.—"Why such alms?" the old man said, lowering the hollow spots of his eyes and seemingly trying to imagine in his head what was lying in his palm. "What good is it to a man who cannot use it. If I were not deprived of sight, how great would be my gratitude. If I had no need, I could provide it to an indigent. Ah, if I had had it after a fire that took place here, the wail of my neighbor's hungry chicks would have ceased if only for one day. But what's it to me now? I can't even see where to put it. It might even provide the occasion for a crime. There is not much gain in stealing a quarter-kopeck, but many people would willingly pocket a ruble. Take it back, kind sir: with your ruble you and I might create a thief." O truth! when you are a rebuke how harsh you are to a feeling heart. "Take it back, I really do not need it, and I am not worth it now, since I did not serve the sovereign portrayed on it. It pleased the Creator to deprive me of my bearings when I was still vigorous. I patiently abide His chastisement. He visited me for my sins. . . . I was a soldier, took part in many battles with the enemies of my fatherland, and I always fought boldly. But one should be a warrior only out of necessity. Rage always filled my heart at the beginning of a battle. I never spared an enemy lying at my feet and did not grant mercy to the disarmed when he asked for it. Exalted by the victory of our arms, as I aimed for punishment and spoils, I fell, deprived of sight and feeling by the cannonball that flew past my eyes while still in all its force. O ye who come after me, be manly but remember humanity!"—He returned my ruble and calmly resumed his place.

"Take your holiday pie, grandfather," a woman of about fifty said to the blind man when coming up.—How rapturously he took it with both hands. "Here is true benefaction, here true alms. For thirty years in a row I have been eating this pie on holidays and Sundays. You have not forgotten the promise you made in your childhood. Does what I did for your late father deserve your remembering me until my death? I, my friends, saved her father from the beating that itinerant soldiers often give to peasants. The soldiers wanted to confiscate something from him; he began to argue with them. The affair took place behind the threshing areas. Soldiers began to beat up the peasant. I was the sergeant in the same company as these soldiers and happened to be there. I came running when I heard the peasant's cry and saved him from the beatings; perhaps even from something worse, not that one can guess beforehand. This is what my present benefactress remembered when she saw me here in my beggarly state. This is what she remembers every day and every holiday. My deed was not large, but it was kind. And a kind deed pleases God; He never allows it to go for naught."

"Will you really insult me so in front of everyone, dear old man, and will you reject my alms alone?" I said to him. "Are my alms the alms of a sinner? Even so, they can be of use to him if they serve to soften his cruel heart." "You distress a heart already distressed long ago by the punishment of nature," the elder said. "I was unaware that I could offend you by not accepting a handout that could cause harm. Forgive me my sin, but give me, if you want to give me something, give me what can be useful to me. . . . We had a cold spring, my throat was sore; I did not have a smallest scarf to tie around my neck. God had mercy, the illness passed. . . . Do you not have a little old scarf? When my throat gets sore, I will tie it around; it will warm my neck, and my throat will stop hurting. I will remember you, if you need the recollection of a beggar." I took the scarf from my neck and put it around the blind man's neck. . . . And I took my leave.

When I was returning through Klin, I did not come across the blind singer again. He died three days before my return. But my scarf, as the woman who brought him pies on holidays recounted, he put around his neck after he fell suddenly ill shortly before his death, and they laid him in his coffin with it. Oh! should anyone feel the value of this scarf, he will also feel what passed in me when I heard this.

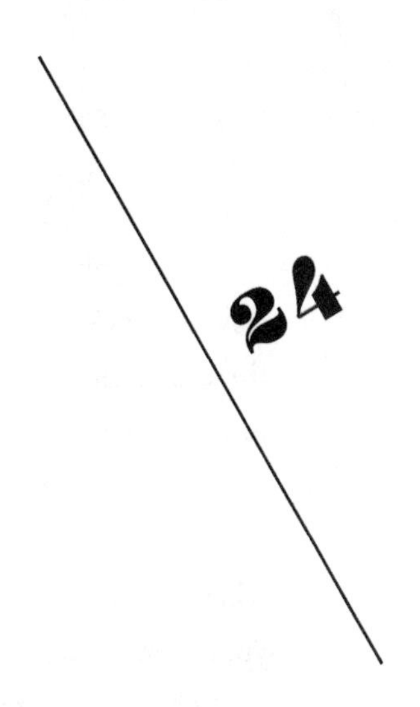

PESHKI

No matter how much I wished to hasten the completion of my journey, hunger—as the saying goes—smashes stone walls,[121] and it forced me to enter the post hut and, until I could gain access once more to ragoûts, fricassees, pâtés, and other French food invented to poison the stomach, to dine on the old piece of roast beef that traveled with me as stores. Having dined this time much worse than many colonels (not to mention generals) sometimes dine on long marches, I, according to praiseworthy common custom, poured into a cup the coffee prepared for me and assuaged my capriciousness with the fruits of the sweat of miserable African slaves.

Spotting the sugar in front of me, the hostess who was kneading dough, sent a small boy to me to ask for a little piece of this food of boyars. "Why boyars'?" I said to her, giving my remaining sugar to the child. "Can you, too, really not use it?" "It is boyars' because we do not have the means to buy it, while boyars use it because they are not the ones who furnish the money. It is true that our steward, when he goes to Moscow, buys it, but he, too, pays with our tears." "Do you really think that whoever uses sugar makes you weep?"

"Not everyone, but all noblemen, yes. Is it not your peasants' tears that you drink when they eat the same bread as we do?" As she said this, she showed me the composition of her bread. It consisted of three-quarters of chaff and one quarter of unsifted flour. "And even in the current bad harvests we thank God. Many of our neighbors are worse off. How much good can it do you, boyars, that you eat sugar while we go hungry? Children are dying, adults die too. But what can you do—you grieve for a while, you grieve but do what your master orders." And she began to put bread loaves into the oven.

This rebuke, uttered not angrily or indignantly but with a deep feeling of stirring sorrow, filled my heart with grief. For the first time I examined carefully all the tools of the peasant hut. For the first time I turned my heart to something that it had previously only glided over.—Four walls covered halfway atop with soot, as was the entire ceiling. The cracked floor, covered with dirt at least a *vershok** thick; the oven, although lacking a chimney, was the best protection from the cold, and its smoke filled the hut every morning in the winter and summer; window frames over which a bovine membrane was stretched allowed in a dingy midday light; two or three pots (lucky is the hut to have in one of them every day any meatless cabbage soup!). A wooden bowl and round platters called plates; a table hewn with an axe which is scraped clean for holidays. A trough to feed pigs or calves when there are any, and to sleep together with them, gasping air in which a burning candle looks as if it were in fog or behind a curtain. If lucky, they have a barrel with *kvass* tasting like vinegar and outside there is a bathhouse in which, when they do not steam in it, cattle sleep. A hempen shirt, footwear given by nature, leg

---

* one and three-quarters inches.—Trans.

wrappers and bast shoes to go out in.—Here is what is considered to be in all fairness the source of the state surplus, strength, power. But here also can be seen weakness, deficiencies and abuse of laws, and their, so to speak, rough side. Here can be seen the greed of the nobility, larceny, our tyranny, and the defenseless state of the poor.—Greedy beasts, insatiable bloodsuckers, what do we leave to the peasant? Just what we cannot take away: air. Yes, air alone. Often we deprive him not only of bread and water, a gift of Earth, but also of light itself.—The law forbids taking away his life.—Forbids only when it is done quickly. How many ways there are to take it away gradually! On the one side, you find near omnipotence; on the other side, defenseless vulnerability. For in relation to a peasant, the landlord is a lawgiver, judge, executor of his own decision, and, as suits him, plaintiff against whom the defendant dares not speak. This is the fate of someone in chains, this is the fate of someone locked in a fetid dungeon, this is the fate of a bullock in a yoke. . . .

Cruel-hearted landowner, look at the children of the peasants subjected to you. They are almost naked. Why? Was it not you who imposed over and beyond fieldwork a quitrent on those who gave them birth into pain and sorrow? Is it not you who allocated for your own profit flax that was still unwoven? What do you care about the fetid rag which your hand, accustomed to luxury, loathes to lift? It is scarcely fit to use for wiping the beasts that serve you. You take even what you do not need despite the fact that the uncovered nakedness of your peasants will be a reproach to you. If in this world there is no judge over you—well, you will come before the Judge respecting no persons, who once gave even you conscience, a guide to the good that your dissolute reason, however, long ago ousted from its dwelling, your heart. But do not flatter yourself that you have impunity.

This vigilant guardian of your actions will catch you when you are alone and you will feel His punishments. Oh! if only these were of any use to you and to your subordinates. . . . Oh! if only man could confess his deeds to an implacable judge, his conscience, by entering frequently his inner self. Changed into an immobile pillar by a thunderous voice, he would not permit himself secret malefactions; ruination, devastation would become rare . . . and so on, and so on, and so on.

25

CHORNAYA GRYAZ

Here I saw another exceptional example of the tyranny of the nobility over the peasants. A wedding party was passing through. But instead of a happy procession and the tears of a timid bride, destined soon to be turned into rejoicing, on the face of those destined to enter into matrimony could be seen sadness and grief. They hate one another and are being dragged by the power of their master to an execution—to the altar of the Father of all blessings, the giver of tender sentiments and joys, the architect of true happiness, the creator of the universe. And His servitor will accept an oath coerced with force and will confirm a marriage! And this will be called a holy union! And this sacrilege will remain as an example to others! And this irregularity in the law will remain unpunished! . . . Why be surprised by this? A hired hand blesses the marriage. The town governor district commander, appointed to keep the law, is a nobleman. Each of the two has an interest in the matter. The first does it for the sake of receiving reward; the second so that, even if abolishing violence that shames mankind, will himself not forfeit the flattering advantage of despotically ruling over his equals.—O bitter fate of many millions! Your ultimate condition is still hidden from the gaze even of my grandchildren. . . .

I forgot to tell you, reader, that the Parnassian judge with whom I dined at the inn in Tver made me a gift. His mind has already tested its powers on many things. How successful his attempts have been you can judge for yourself—but tell me in my little ear what you think. If while reading you should feel like a doze, then close the book and go to sleep. Save it for insomnia.

An Oration About Lomonosov

The loveliness of the evening after a hot summer's day chased me from my cell. I directed my steps beyond the Nevsky Monastery and rambled for a long time in the grove that lies behind it.* The sun had already hidden its face, but the light curtain of the night was scarcely perceptible on the blue vault of the sky.† While returning home I walked past the Nevsky Cemetery. Its gates were open. I entered. . . . In this place of eternal silence, where the firmest brow will certainly frown at having thought that here must be the end of all brilliant exploits, in this place of unshakable tranquility and steadfast equanimity, it seems hardly possible that arrogance, vanity, and haughtiness can coexist. But the magnificent sepulchers? They are doubtless signs of human pridefulness, but also the signs of man's desire to live forever. Is this, however, the eternity that man so desires? . . . It is not a column erected over your mortal coil that will preserve your

* Ozerki

† June

memory for the most distant posterity. It is not a stone with a carving of your name that will advance your glory into the next centuries. It is your language, living forever and ever in your creations, the language of the Russian tribe that you have renewed for our tongue that will fly on the lips of the people beyond the infinite horizon of centuries. Let the elements, raging conjointly, open the depths of the earth and swallow this magnificent city from which your loud singing resounded to all ends of vast Russia; let some fierce conqueror exterminate even the name of your beloved fatherland: but as long as the Russian language strikes the ear you will live and never die. If it falls silent, your glory will also burn out. It is gratifying to die this way—gratifying. But if anyone knew how to calculate the measure of this posterity, if the finger of divination assigns a span to your name, is not this eternity? . . . This I exclaimed in rapture, stopping before a column erected over Lomonosov's remains.—No, it is not this cold stone that recounts that you lived for the glory of the name of Russia; it cannot say what a man you were. May your works tell us about it, may your life tell us why you are famous.

Where are you, O beloved friend! Where are you? Come to converse with me about the great man. Come that we may weave a crown for this cultivator of the Russian language. Let others, fawning before power, extol strength and might with their praise. We—we will sing a hymn to the service done for society.

Mikhailo Vasilyevich Lomonosov was born in Kholmogory. . . . Since he was born to a man who could not give him an education through which his understanding would be sharpened and adorned by useful and pleasant knowledge; limited by virtue of his station to spend his days among people whose intellectual horizon did not extend beyond their trade; destined to divide his time between fishing and attempts to receive payment for his labor—young Lomonosov's mind could not attain the scope that he acquired when laboring on natural experiments, nor could his voice reach that sweetness which it acquired from consorting with the pure Muses. From the education in his parental home, he took something modest that was in fact the key to learning—a knowledge of reading and writing; and from Nature—curiosity. And this, Nature, is your triumph. Avid curiosity, instilled by you in our souls, aspires to the knowledge of things; and a heart burning with the love of glory cannot abide the shackles confining it. The heart roars, boils, groans, and, smashing the shackles in a single blow, flies headlong (nothing to stop it) to its purpose. Everything is forgotten, the mind has only this purpose; by this we breathe, by this we live.

Not letting the coveted subject out of his sight, the youth amasses a knowledge of things from the most meager streams of the source of learning flowing down to the lowest levels of society. Lacking the supervision needed to make rapid progress in knowledge, he hones and adorns memory, the primary strength of his mind, in such a way as to sharpen his reason. The narrow scope of knowledge he could acquire in his birthplace was unable to slake his parched spirit, but rather more ignited in the youth an insuperable striving for learning. Blessed is one who at the age when for the first time the tumult of passions takes us out of a state of insensibility, when we near a condition of maturity, whose aspiration turns to the understanding of things.

Incited by an avidity for knowledge, Lomonosov leaves his parental home; goes to the capital city, comes to the dwelling of monastic Muses, and takes his place among the number of youths dedicating themselves to the study of the liberal arts and theology.[122]

Knowledge of languages is the gateway to learning, but it looks like a field seeded with thistle and like a mountain covered by daunting rocks. The eye does not find here a pleasantness of arrangement, and the traveler's feet do not find calm smoothness for resting, nor is there a greening shelter for the tired person. So it is that a student, having approached a new language, is accosted by diverse sounds. His larynx grows tired by the unaccustomed gurgling of breath emitted from it, and his tongue, forced to twist in a new way, is exhausted. The mind then seizes up, reason grows weak without activity, imagination loses its wings; only memory stays alert and sharpens and fills all its crannies and nooks with the images of hitherto unknown sounds. In learning languages, everything is disgusting and burdensome. If hope did not reassure one that, after habituating one's hearing to unusual sounds and mastering alien pronunciation, the most pleasant subjects would open up, it would be impossible to expect anyone to want to embark on such a daunting path. But once these difficulties have been overcome, how many times will perseverance in labors endured be rewarded. New views of nature are revealed, a new chain of fantasies. Through the learning of an alien language, we become citizens of the region where it is spoken, we converse with people who lived many thousand centuries ago, assimilate their ideas, and the inventions and thoughts of all peoples and ages we combine and render in a single connection.

Persistent application in the learning of languages made Lomonosov a fellow citizen of Athens and Rome. It was thus that his perseverance was rewarded. Like a blind man, unseeing of the light since coming out of his mother's womb, when, owing to the skilled hand of an eye doctor, the majesty of the daytime luminary begins to shine for him—with a rapid glance he runs through all the beauties of nature, marvels at its variety and simplicity. Everything captivates him, everything amazes. He feels its grace more vividly than do eyes accustomed to seeing, experiences delight, and goes into raptures. It was thus that Lomonosov, after receiving tuition in the Latin and Greek languages, devoured the beauties of ancient orators and poets. With them, he learned to feel the niceties of nature; with them, he learned to perceive all the contrivances of an art always concealed under the lively forms of poetry; with them, he learned to express his feelings, to give body to thought and soul to the inanimate.

If my powers were sufficient, I would represent how the great man gradually ensconced in his understanding foreign ideas that, transformed in his soul and mind, appeared in a new form in his works or gave birth to entirely different notions previously unknown to the human intellect. I would represent him searching for knowledge in his school's ancient manuscripts, chasing after the semblance of knowledge everywhere its repository seemed to be. Often he was deceived in his expectations. But thanks to frequent reading of ecclesiastical books, he laid the foundation of the gracefulness of his style. Such was the reading he proposes to all who wish to acquire the skill of writing the Russian language.

Soon his curiosity received ample satisfaction. He became the pupil of the celebrated Wolff.[123] By jettisoning the rules of Scholasticism or, better, the delusions taught to him in religious academies, he established firm and clear steps for ascending to the temple of philosophy. Logic taught him to reason; mathematics to arrive at conclusions and reach certainty only through evidence; metaphysics taught him speculative truths that often lead to error; physics and chemistry, which he learned diligently, perhaps for the sake of an elegant power of imagination, led him to the font of nature and revealed to him its mysteries; metallurgy and mineralogy, offshoots of the previous disciplines, drew his attention to them, and Lomonosov wanted to understand the rules regulating these disciplines.

An abundance of fruits and products compelled people to exchange them for those that were scarce. This generated trade. Great difficulties in the barter trade stimulated thought about symbols that would represent all wealth and all goods. Money was invented. Gold and silver, as the most precious metals because of their perfection, previously having served for decoration, were turned into symbols representing all forms of wealth. And in all truth, it was only then that this insatiable and vile passion in the human heart for riches was ignited, which like an all-devouring flame grows stronger as it feeds. Then man left his primeval simplicity and his natural practice, tillage, and made over his life to the furious waves or, disdainful of hunger and desert heat, crossed these to unknown countries in prospect of riches and treasure. Then, contemptuous of the light of the sun, the living creature descended into the grave and, breaking open the interior of the earth, dug a burrow for himself like a terrestrial reptile foraging at night for its food. So it was that man, while secreted in the chasms of the earth, sought glittering metals and, by imbibing the poisonous fumes coming out of the earth, shortened the span of his life by half. But in the same way that poison, once chronic, becomes itself a necessary habit for man, so the mining of metals, while shortening the days of the miners, is not repudiated owing to its deadliness; rather, the means to extract more metals, by the easiest means, are devised.

This indeed was what Lomonosov wanted to learn actively and for the fulfilment of his intention he went to Freiburg. I imagine that I see him approaching the shaft through which metal extracted from the bowels of the earth flows. He takes a flickering beacon designed to light the way for him in crevices to which the rays of sun never extend. He has taken the first step. "What are you doing?" screams Reason to him. "Can it be that nature has distinguished you with talents only in order that you use them for the destruction of your brothers? What are you thinking when you descend into this chasm? Do you seek to discover a better skill to extract silver and gold? Or do you not know what evil they have caused in the world? Or have you forgotten the conquest of America? . . . But no, descend, learn the subterranean artifices of man and, upon returning to your fatherland, have enough fortitude to offer advice to cover over and flatten these graves where thousands are buried alive."

Trembling, he descends into the aperture and soon loses sight of the life-bearing orb. I wish I could follow him in his subterranean journey, collect his musings, and present them with the same coherence and in the same order in which they germinated in his mind. The picture of his thoughts would be entertaining and instructive for us. On passing through the first layer of earth, the source of all vegetation, the subterranean traveler found it unlike the next ones: it differed from the other ones most of all by its fecund power. Perhaps he concluded that the earth's surface is composed of nothing other than the decomposition of animals and plants, that its fertility, nutritious and restorative power, had its origin in indestructible and primordial particles of existence of every kind, which do not change their essence but rather change only the appearance generated from random combinations. Progressing further, the traveler saw the earth consistently arranged in layers. In these layers, he sometimes found the vestiges of animals living in the seas, found the vestiges of plants and was able to conclude that the layered sedimentation of the earth took its beginnings from the fluid state of the waters, and that the waters, displaced from one part of the earthly globe to the other, gave the earth's interior its very appearance. This uniform arrangement of layers, as it retreated from his view, sometimes looked to him like a compound of many heterogeneous strata. From this he concluded that fire, a ferocious element, had penetrated the bowels of the earth and, encountering a countervailing liquid, raged, disturbed, shook, knocked down, and hurled everything that attempted in vain to resist it with its counterforce. After disturbing and mixing diverse layers, fire with its torrid breathing triggered in the primary metals the force of attraction and unified them. There Lomonosov saw these inherently inanimate treasures in their natural state, recalled the greed and misery of peoples and, with a broken heart, left this gloomy dwelling of human insatiability.

Applying himself to natural philosophy, he did not forsake the beloved study of poetry. Even in his homeland, an occasion showed him that Nature had designated him for greatness, that he would not wander along the ordinary pathway of human progress. The *Psalter* transposed by Simeon Polotsky into verse revealed to him a natural mystery about himself, showed that he, too, was a poet. When conversing with Horace, Virgil, and other ancient writers, he determined long ago that Russian versification was quite uncongenial to the euphony and graveness of our language. When reading German poets, he found that their style was more fluent than the Russian, that feet in poetic lines were distributed according to properties of their language. And so, he decided to attempt a composition in new verses, having first established rules for Russian poetry that were based on the euphony of our language.[124] He implemented this by writing an ode on the Russian army's victory over the Turks and Tatars and on the capture of Chocim, which he sent from Marburg to the Academy of Sciences. The singularity of its style, the power of expression, depictions that almost breathed, astonished those reading this new composition. And this firstborn child of an imagination propelled along an uncharted path, together with others, served to prove that once a people is directed toward perfection, it advances toward glory not along one trail, but along many pathways at the same time.

Force of imagination and lively sensation do not thwart scrutiny of detail. In providing examples of euphony, Lomonosov knew that elegance of style is based on rules intrinsic to the language. He wanted to extract them from the very language, not, however, ignoring that custom always provides the primary example of word combinations, and that expressions derived from a rule become correct through usage. By analyzing all parts of speech and coordinating them with usage, Lomonosov compiled his *Grammar*. But not contented only with teaching the rules of the Russian language, he also affords an idea about human speech in general as the most noble endowment after reason, given to man to communicate his thoughts. Here is a summary of his *General Grammar*: language represents thoughts; the instrument of language is voice; the voice is modified by formation or enunciation; various modifications in the voice express different ideas; therefore language is a depiction of our thoughts through the formation of voice by means of the organs designed to that end. Departing from this premise, Lomonosov defines as indivisible the parts of speech whose representations are called letters. The combination of these indivisible parts produces syllables, which apart from the distinction of their vocal formation, are further differentiated by stress, as it is called, which is the basis of versification. The joining of syllables produces root words, or the signifying parts of word. These represent either a thing or its action. The verbal representation of a thing is called a *name*; the representation of an action, a *verb*. Other parts of language function in the depiction of relations of things each to the other and connect them in conversation. But the first two are essential and can be called the principal parts of language, whereas the others can be considered auxiliary. In discussing different parts of speech, Lomonosov discovers that some of them are not fixed. A thing can occupy different positions in relation to other things. The representations of such positions and relations are called *cases*. Every action occurs in time; and, therefore, verbs are also arranged according to the times in order to represent the time in which the action takes place. Finally, Lomonosov speaks about a combination of parts of speech that produces speech.

Beginning with so philosophical a consideration of language in general, based on the very nature of our bodily constitution, Lomonosov sets out the rules of the Russian language. How could they be mediocre if the mind that sketched them was led through grammatical thickets by the torch of ingenuity? Do not scorn this praise, great man. Your *Grammar* alone did not build your fame among your fellow citizens. Your services to the Russian language are manifold; and in this unglamorous labor you are venerated as the first founder of the veritable rules of our language and as the explorer of the natural arrangement of every kind of word. Your *Grammar* is the antechamber of your *Rhetoric*, and both of them are guides to grasping the beauties of the way your creations are uttered. Proceeding to teach the rules, Lomonosov intended to guide his fellow citizens on the thorny paths of Helicon, showing them the road to eloquence by outlining the rules of rhetoric and poetry. But the brevity of his life allowed him to complete only half of the undertaken labor.

Born with tender feelings, endowed with a powerful imagination, prompted by love of honor, a man erupts from the milieu of the people. He ascends the Tribune. All eyes are on him, everyone waits impatiently for his oration. Applause or mockery bitterer than death itself awaits him. How could he be mediocre? Such a man was Demosthenes, such a man was Cicero; such was Pitt; such now are Burke, Fox, Mirabeau, and others.[125] The rules of their speeches derive from circumstances, the sweetness of enunciation derives from their feelings, the power of arguments derives from their wit. Marveling at men so outstanding in the art of speech and analyzing their speeches, coolheaded critics thought that it was possible to outline rules for wit and imagination, thought that the path to enticement could be set out with laborious prescripts. Here is the origin of rhetoric. In following unwittingly his imagination, improved as it was by his conversation with ancient writers, Lomonosov similarly thought that he could communicate to his fellow citizens the ardor that filled his soul. And although the labor he undertook for this was in vain, yet the examples adduced by him to reinforce and explain his rules can undoubtedly guide anyone bent on pursuing the glory to be gained through the literary arts.

But however vain his work proved in teaching the rules of what is better felt than learned by rote, to those who love the Russian language Lomonosov left proper examples in his compositions. In them, the lips that sucked the sweetness of Cicero and Demosthenes flowered into grandiloquence. In them, in every line, in every punctuation mark, in every syllable (why can I not say in every letter?) can be heard the harmonious and concordant sound of a euphony that is so rare, so inimitable, so natural for Lomonosov.

Endowed by nature with the invaluable right to influence his contemporaries, endowed by nature with the power of creation, immersed in the thick of the popular mass, a great man acts upon it but not always in the same direction. He is similar to natural forces that, acting from the center, by extending their action to all points of the circumference, make their effect perpetual everywhere. So, too, Lomonosov who, affecting his fellow citizens variously, opened the collective mind to various pathways of knowledge. Enticing the collective mind to follow him, unweaving an entangled language into grandiloquence and euphony, he did not leave it as a scant source of literature lacking ideas. He would tell the imagination: soar to the limitlessness of dreams and possibilities, collect bright flowers of inspiration, and, guided by taste, decorate with them even the intangible. And so again Pindar's trumpet that resounded during the Olympic games, like the psalmodist, emitted praise to the Supreme Being. On a trumpet, Lomonosov announced the greatness of the Everlasting One sitting on the wings of wind, preceded by thunder and lightning bolts and revealing to mortals His essence, life, in the sun.[126] Moderating the voice of Pindar's trumpet, he used it to sing the fragility of man and the narrow confines of his understanding. In the infinite abyss of the worlds, like a small speck of sand in the sea waves, like a spark barely scintillating amid the never melting ice, like the finest dust in the fiercest whirlwind—what is the human mind?[127]—It is you, O Lomonosov! my raiment cannot disguise you.

I do not envy you the fact that you flattered Elizabeth with encomium in verse. This was consistent with the common practice of flattering tsars who, not infrequently, far from deserving the praises sung in harmonious voice, scarcely deserve the plinking of a *gudok*.[128] And if it were possible without giving offence to truth and posterity, I would forgive you for the sake of a soul grateful for her generosity to you. But he will envy you, the writer of odes who cannot follow your tracks, he will envy a delightful picture of popular calm and peace, this strong defense of towns and villages, solace of tsardoms and tsars;[129] he will envy the innumerable beauties of your language; even if someday he happened to equal the constant euphony of your poetry, although nobody has yet managed this. And so what if everyone succeeds in outdoing you for sweet singing, so what if your thoughts in the eyes of our descendants seem disordered, your poetry not overabundant in essence! . . . But look: on the expansive tiltyard to the end of which the eye cannot reach, among the crowding multitudes, in the lead, in front of everyone, opening the gates to the tiltyard—it is you. Anyone can be famed for their achievements, but you were the first. Even the Almighty cannot take away what He gave you. He begat you before everyone else, begat you to become a leader, and your glory is the fame of a leader. O! you who labored fruitlessly thus far to understand the essence of the soul and how the soul acts upon our corporality, this task that lies before you as a test is difficult. Tell us how the soul acts upon another soul, what kind of connection is there between minds? If we know how the body acts upon a body by touch, tell us how the intangible acts upon the intangible, producing substance; or what kind of contact there is between nonsubstantial entities. That it exists, this you know. But if you know what kind of action a great man's mind has upon the collective mind, then you also know that a great man can beget another great man. There is the laurel crown of victory. O! Lomonosov, you created Sumarokov.

But if the influence of Lomonosov's poems could achieve a majestic advance in the education of his contemporaries' poetic understanding, his eloquence made no perceptible or obvious mark. The flowers picked by him in Athens and Rome and so successfully transplanted in his words—the force of Demosthenes's expression, the eloquence of Cicero—he used in vain, since they remain cloaked in the murkiness of the future. And who, satiated on the prolific grandiloquence of your laudatory orations, will thunder in a style that is not even yours yet will be your disciple? This moment can be distant or near, the wandering gaze, straying in the uncertainty of the future, finds no footing where to stop. While we may not find a direct heir to Lomonosov's rhetoric, the impact of his euphony and the resonant pauses of his nonpoetic speech was pervasive, nonetheless. Even if his civic oratory may have had no disciple, its influence was felt on the general character of writing. Compare what was written before Lomonosov and what was written after him, and the impact of his prose will be evident to everyone.

But do not we err in our conclusion? Long before Lomonosov, we find in Russia eloquent shepherds of the Church who by preaching the word of God to their flock taught it and themselves were renowned for their sermons. It is true that they existed, but their language was not Russian. They wrote the way it was possible to write before the Tatar invasion, before Russians entered into contact with the European peoples. They wrote in the Slavonic language. But you who saw Lomonosov himself, and perhaps learned eloquence from his works, shall not be forgotten by me. When in defeating the proud Ottomans the Russian army surpassed the expectations of everyone who cast an indifferent or envious eye over its exploits—you, summoned to give solemn thanks to the God of war, the God of strength, O! you, in the rapture of your soul, invoked Peter at his grave that he come to contemplate the fruits of his planting: "Arise, Peter, arise!" When you charmed my hearing, and my hearing then enchanted my sight, that was when it seemed to everyone that in coming to

Peter's grave you, invested with higher powers, wanted to resurrect him. That would be the moment when I, too, would have declared to Lomonosov: "Look, look, even here we see your cultivation." But if he could teach you language. . . . In Platon there is Plato's soul, and how to charm and to understand us his own heart taught him.[130]

Servile gestures are incompatible not only with what may arouse our veneration but even when we love. While doing justice to the great man, we shall, therefore, not consider him God the creator of all, we shall not cherish him as an idol to be worshipped by society, and we shall not collude in implanting any kind of prejudice or false assumption. Truth is the highest divinity to us, and if the Almighty should want to change its image by revealing Himself not through truth, our face will be averted from Him.

Consonant with the truth, we shall not search in Lomonosov for a great historian, we shall not compare him to Tacitus, Raynal, or Robertson; we shall not put him on the level of Marggraf or Rüdiger since he worked in chemistry.[131] If he liked this science, if he spent many days of his life in studying the truths of natural science, his pathway was but the pathway of a follower. He roamed along well-worn ways and in the innumerable riches of nature found not a single blade of grass that eyes better than his had not looked at. He did not scrutinize even the crudest catalyst in matter that his predecessors had not discovered.

Can we juxtapose him with someone who merited the most flattering inscription that a man can see beneath his portrait? The inscription, etched not in flattery but a truth daring to be powerful: "Here is one who wrested thunder from heaven and the scepter from the hand of tyrants." Do we place Lomonosov next to him because he researched the power of electricity in its effects; and that he was not repelled from its study after seeing how his teacher was mortally struck down by its power?[132] Lomonosov knew how to produce electrical power, knew how to deflect thunderbolts, but in this science the architect is Franklin, Lomonosov just a craftsman.

But if Lomonosov did not achieve greatness in his investigations of Nature, he depicted its magnificent works in a style both pure and articulate. And while we do not find in his works about the natural sciences a graceful teacher of natural philosophy, we nonetheless find a teacher of language and a permanent model worthy of imitation.

And thus, by giving the great man his due, by placing Lomonosov's name in an aura worthy of him, we do not seek to arrogate for him merit for what he did not do and what he did not influence; or only to get carried away by frenzy and enthusiasm by using uninhibited language. This is not our goal. We want to show that in the domain of Russian literature the one who blazed a path to the temple of fame is the prime mover in the achievement of glory, even when he could not enter the temple. Is not Bacon of Verulam worthy of remembrance solely because he was able to say how to multiply branches of learning? Are brave writers who rise up against ruin and dominion not deserving of appreciation even if they were unable to deliver humanity from chains and captivity? And we do not reverence Lomonosov because he could not understand the rules of theatrical poetry and languished in epic; because he was out of his depths in the poetry of sensibility; because he was not always discerning in his judgment; and because even in his odes he sometimes put more words than thoughts. But listen: before the beginning of time when existence had no foundation and everything was lost in eternity and immeasurability, everything was possible for the Source of power, all the beauty of the universe existed in His thought since there was no action, no beginning. And then when the all-powerful hand intruded matter into space set it in motion. The sun shone forth, the moon took light, and rotating celestial bodies formed on high. The first jolt of creation was omnipotent. All the wonders of the world, all its beauty are only consequences. This is how I understand the action of a great soul upon the souls of contemporaries or descendants; this is how I understand the action of mind upon mind. In the trajectory of Russian literature, Lomonosov is the first. Envious crowd, be gone; it is for posterity to judge him, it is not hypocritical.

But, dear reader, I have got carried away chatting with you. . . . Here already is Vsesvyatskoye. . . . If I have not bored you, wait for me by the city boundary and we can see each other upon my return journey. For now, farewell.—Coachman, drive on.

MOSCOW! MOSCOW!!! . . .

NOTES

DEDICATION

The line is adapted by Radishchev from the narrative poem *Tilemakhida* by V. K. Trediakovsky (1703–1769), a poetic version of the French writer and educationalist Cardinal Fénelon's didactic novel *Télémaque* (1699), widely read as a conduct book and used as a manual for teaching virtue to princes and kings. The line comes from a part of the poem in which evil rulers in hell see themselves in the mirror of Truth. Trediakovsky rendered Fénelon's *Télémaque* in the equivalent he devised to the classical hexameter: a line that combined trochees and spondees and had six stresses. It can be interpreted as a *dolnik*. Trediakovsky's hexameter was later adopted by Nikolai Gnedich (1784–1833) in his seminal translation of the *Iliad* (1829) and by Vasily Zhukovsky (1783–1852) in his translation of the *Odyssey* (1842–46).

A.M.K.

Aleksei Mikhailovich Kutuzov (1749–1797), a friend from youth and Leipzig, known for his philosophical character and involvement in Freemasonry.

1. DEPARTURE

1. Cf. Matthew 5:4: "Blessed are they that mourn; for they shall be comforted."

2. SOFIA

2. Radishchev refers here to the decrees of 1782 that regulated the order of dispensing horses at the post stations.

3. The stationmaster, fourteenth class in the Table of Ranks, organized the provision of postal coaches and horse relays. This provincial petty clerk stuck in a backwater was made famous in Pushkin's story "The Stationmaster" (1831). For more on the Table of Ranks, see endnote 9.
4. Folk songs became prized in the eighteenth century as genuine expressions of popular culture. A number of important collections of ethnographic materials, folklore, and popular songs were published in Russia.

3. TOSNA

5. Radishchev is referring to Catherine's 1787 journey to Crimea and Ukraine.
6. The Service Archive (*razriadnyi arkhiv*), established in 1711, contained the service records of all service people (*sluzhilye liudi*) for the sixteenth and seventeenth centuries. Service records of eighteenth-century servitors were kept in the Heraldry Office.
7. Rurik was the legendary founder of the Rurikid dynasty, who, according to Russian chronicles, ruled in Novgorod beginning in 862. His descendants ruled in Kiev beginning in the early tenth century. Vladimir Monomakh reigned in the twelfth century and was famed for his wisdom and advice to princes.
8. *Mestnichestvo* was the Muscovite system of precedence governing ritual occasions and reflecting individual and family status among the nobility from the fifteenth to the late seventeenth century. A reform introduced in 1682 by Tsar Fyodor Alexeyevich, the older brother of Peter the Great, abolished *mestnichestvo*, shifting power to military interests away from the landed nobility. The law eliminated the superiority of Moscow nobility over that of the provinces.
9. The Table of Ranks was a list of positions in the military, civil, and court services introduced by a 1722 law to govern state servitors' promotion through the ranks. It played a critical role in overhauling the service class and allowed Peter to replace the Muscovite service elite with a new class of servitors. It forcefully reconfirmed every nobleman's obligation to serve the Crown and the state. Divided into fourteen grades or classes, from the first (highest) to the fourteenth (lowest), the Table defined the status of every servitor and his position vis-à-vis his peers. It also made it possible for commoners to be ennobled through ascending the hierarchy of ranks, making the hereditary nobles resentful.
10. According to Catherine the Great's legislation of 1785, which instituted fundamental reforms in the nature of service to the Crown and the treatment of nobles, a register was to be kept in every province of the genealogy of the local nobility, with the ancient aristocracy (as distinct from the newer service nobles) listed in the final part.
11. Piter remains a familiar name for St. Petersburg; the usage first emerged in the late eighteenth century.

12. Prostrations or small bows from the waist were part of the etiquette of respect and deference as well as shows of piety in church.

4. LYUBANI

13. Quitrent (*obrok*): a tax imposed on a serf for using the land allocated to him by the landowner. It was considered a lighter obligation than the corvée.
14. Schismatic or Old Believer (*raskol'nik* or *starover*): a member of a movement of religious purists that arose in Russia in the middle of the seventeenth century. Schismatics rejected the reforms of Patriarch Nikon, which aimed to bring Russian religious practices closer to Greek. Radishchev refers here to the Schismatics' refusal to keep religious holidays, including Sunday.
15. One point of contention between the Schismatics and the Orthodox believers was how to make the sign of the cross, with two fingers or three. Here the peasant indicates that he is an Orthodox believer by claiming that he uses three fingers to cross himself.
16. The peasant is referring here to corvée (*barshchina*), unpaid work on the landowner's land. It was considered to be the more onerous obligation.
17. Poll tax (*podushnye*): a tax that peasants had to pay to the state; it was calculated according the number of male members (souls or *dushi*) in the household.
18. State peasants worked on lands owned by the state. Although they, too, had to pay various taxes, they enjoyed many freedoms (most importantly, personal) denied to peasants belonging to an individual landowner.

5. CHUDOVO

19. Sisterbek: presently Sestroretsk, a town to the north of St. Petersburg on the northern shore of the Gulf of Finland.
20. Paphos and Amathus: ancient cult sanctuaries of Aphrodite on Cyprus.
21. Claude-Joseph Vernet (1714–1789): a painter celebrated in the second half of the eighteenth century for his maritime paintings and large canvases depicting shipwrecks as sublime events in which the terrible drama of the disaster contrasts with the still beauty of the moonlit sea; a number of his paintings were in the Hermitage.
22. The last Turkish War in the Archipelago: Russo-Turkish War of 1768–74, in particular the victory of the Russian fleet in Chesme Bay in July of 1770.
23. Subedar: an Indian officer rank in British India. The travails of Clive of India, who established the dominance of the East India Company in Bengal, was discussed in contemporary historical writing by, among others, Abbé Guillaume-Thomas de Raynal, in his *Histoire philosophique et politique des établissements et du commerce des Européens dans les deux Indes* (1777) and Voltaire in his *Fragments historique sur*

l'Inde (1773). The British were attacked in 1756, leading to the fall of Calcutta and the death of more than one hundred British prisoners stifled in cells (giving rise to the name the Black Hole of Calcutta).

24. Oranienbaum: the oldest of the imperial palaces around St. Petersburg. Located to the west of St. Petersburg on the southern shore of the Gulf of Finland, it features formal gardens and terraces. In 1743, Elizabeth commissioned Giambattista Pittoni to build a palace for her nephew, the future Peter III. In the 1760s, Pittoni built the Chinese Palace for Catherine II as her official country residence.

6. SPASSKAYA POLEST

25. Polkan, Bova: characters in the Russian woodblock print (*lubok*) *The Tale of Bova the King's Son*. Originally, Pulicane (a chimeric character, half-human, half-horse) and Buovo in the Italian version of a fourteenth-century chivalric romance *Li Reali di Francia nei quali si contiene la generazione degli imperadori, re, principi, baroni e paladini con la bellissima istoria di Buovo di Antona* by Andrea da Barberino. In 1799–1802 (?), Radishchev wrote a long poem, *Bova*, of which only the introduction and canto 1 survive. Nightingale-Robber: in East Slavic mythology, a monstrous creature that kills with its terrifying whistling.
26. Governor-general (*namestnik*): according to the 1775 Provincial Reform Law (*Uchrezhdenie o guberniiakh*), the state's chief administrator in charge of two or more provinces.
27. Bolshaya Morskaya: a street perpendicular to Nevsky Prospekt in St Petersburg, near the Admiralty. Naval staff lived there (hence its name "Large Maritime Street").
28. Radishchev plays on the idiom "*ne zhit'e, a maslenitsa*": "life is a regular feast (or Shrovetide)."
29. The clerk's wife refers to payments he takes for the exchange of paper and copper money, which costs less, for silver and gold.
30. The physiological workings of sensibility and the mind, as Radishchev knew, were explored in eighteenth-century thought by various schools (mechanical, chemical, theological).
31. A possible reference to Denis Diderot's *Letter on the Blind for the Use of Those Who Can See (Lettre sur les aveugles à l'usage de ceux qui voient)*, a discussion of visual perception inspired by success in the surgical removal of cataracts.
32. Captain James Cook (1728–1779): British navigator, cartographer, and explorer in the Pacific, author of an important set of scientific journals. He perished in Hawaii, probably murdered during an uprising, although different accounts circulated.
33. The Goths were East Germanic peoples who toppled the Western Roman Empire in the fifth century AD; the Vandals sacked and looted Rome in the sixth century and made extensive conquests in Southern Europe and North Africa.
34. Castalia and Hippocrene: two of the three creeks favored by the Muses.

7. PODBEREZYE

35. Praskovya (Paraskeva): "Friday" in Greek; St. Paraskeva Pyatnitsa (name day November 10) is a mythological figure in East Slavic tradition that combines Christian and pagan features.
36. Radishchev's interlocutor lists five of eight subjects (classes) taught in seminaries. Kuteikin, a character in *The Minor* (*Nedorosl'*, staged in 1782, published in 1783) by Denis Fonvizin (1744/1745–1792), refers to his unfinished seminary education, informing the other characters that he reached the sixth ("rhetoric") class of the eight classes that comprised seminary education before leaving the school. Radishchev's seminarian ironically mentions the next class, "philosophy," after which seminarians ostensibly leave without taking the last class, "theology."
37. Hugo Grotius (1583–1645): a Dutch philosopher, political theorist, and jurist. Charles de Montesquieu (1689–1755): a French political philosopher. William Blackstone (1723–1780): an English jurist and politician. The works of all three were in Radishchev's library.
38. Court almanac (*pridvornyi kalendar'*): a yearly publication (beginning in 1745) that published the names of courtiers promoted in rank as well as lists of recipients of awards.
39. Louis Claude de Saint-Martin (1743–1803): a French esoteric philosopher and mystic, the founder of Martinism, a form of Christian mysticism focused on the fall of man and the process of his return to grace.
40. Emanuel Swedenborg (1688–1772): A Swedish theologian and mystic.
41. Frederick the Great (1712–1786): the king of Prussia from 1740 to his death. A proponent of enlightened absolutism, he modernized the Prussian bureaucracy, reformed the judicial system, and encouraged religious tolerance.
42. Akibah (Akiva) ben Yosef (c. 50–135): a prominent Jewish scholar and sage, the author of copious commentaries to the Talmud.
43. Bayle's Dictionary: Radishchev quotes *The Historical and Critical Dictionary* (*Dictionnaire historique et critique*) by Pierre Bayle (1647–1706), one of the most important works of rational skepticism of the European Enlightenment. In editions that contain a chapter on Akibah (and not all do), Bayle gives the dialogue in Latin with an English translation in which parts of the body are omitted and indicated with a long dash. Radishchev is more explicit and ironical.

8. NOVGOROD

44. In the 1780s, Radishchev read various historical sources and made numerous notes. The nature of government in Kiev and, especially, Novgorod was one of his particular interests because he believed that both were republics governed by princes invited and dismissed by the *veche*, a popular assembly of all residents,

proving for Radishchev that medieval Russia practiced direct democracy. For a full publication of Radishchev's notes, see Irina Reyfman, "Istoricheskie zametki A. N. Radishcheva," in *Filosofskii vek. Al'manakh*, vol. 25, *Istoriia filosofii kak filosofiia*, part 2, ed. T. V. Artem'eva and M. I. Mikeshin (St. Petersburg: Sankt-Peterburgskii Tsentr Istorii Idei, 2003), 235–50.

45. Mayor (*posadnik*): the head of the civilian government in Novgorod. The military commander (*tysiatskii*) oversaw the militia troops and the police. Both were elected officials.
46. *Veche*: see note 44.
47. Ivan Vasilyevich: a composite image of two Ivans, Ivan III (reigned 1462–1505) and Ivan IV the Terrible (reigned 1547–84), both of whom were instrumental in subjugating Novgorod to Moscow. Ivan the Terrible is believed to have personally participated in the so-called massacre of Novgorod in 1570; hence the later mention of the cudgel.
48. What follows comes from the notes Radishchev made while reading various historical sources, including V. N. Tatishchev's *Russian History* (*Istoriia Rossiiskaia*), G. F. Miller's "Brief Report on the Origins of Novgorod" ("Kratkoe izvestie o nachale Novagoroda"), and *Nestor's Chronicle with His Successors . . .* (*Letopis' Nesterova s prodolzhateliami . . .*). For a description of Radishchev's sources, see Reyfman, "Zametki A. N. Radishcheva po russkoi istorii," 227–34.
49. The merchant class was not hereditary but was defined by voluntary membership of one of the three guilds. Beginning in 1785, a qualification for joining the third was declaring a capital sum of one thousand to five thousand rubles; the second, five thousand to ten thousand rubles; and the first, ten thousand to fifty thousand rubles. Those who declared capital of more than fifty thousand rubles received the status of eminent citizens (*imenitye grazhdane*). There were other ways to achieve this status.
50. Johann Kaspar Lavater (1741–1801): a Swiss writer, philosopher, physiognomist, and theologian best known for his *Physiognomische Fragmente zur Beförderung der Menschenkenntnis und Menschenliebe* (4 vols., 1775–78), in which he propagated the theory that human character was expressed in the structure of skull and face. His work was very popular in the late eighteenth century and was translated into English by Thomas Holcroft as *Essays on Physiognomy for the Promotion of the Knowledge and the Love of Mankind* (London: G. G. J. & J. Robinson, 1789).
51. Blackening one's teeth was fashionable in Russia up to the early nineteenth century.

9. BRONNITSY

52. Perun: God of sky, thunder, and storms in Slavic mythology.

53. Radishchev has adapted the lines from Joseph Addison, *Cato, a Tragedy* (1712), act V, scene 1, verses 26–30:

> The stars shall fade away, the sun himself
> Grow dim with age, and nature sink in years,
> But thou shalt flourish in immortal youth,
> Unhurt amidst the wars of elements,
> The wreck of matter, and the crush of worlds.

10. ZAITSOVO

54. The future assessor's service record is questioned by Krestyankin. According to the Table of Ranks regulations, the military service accorded hereditary nobility to commoners beginning with the lowest fourteenth class (this changed under Nicholas I, in 1846). In contrast, in civil and court service a commoner had to achieve the rank of the eighth class to receive hereditary nobility. Radishchev's Krestyankin excludes court service from this rule, given that the lower ranks in the court service, in his exaggerated presentation, were occupied by stokers, lackeys, and butlers. Cf. "Vydropusk," where Radishchev includes the argument against treating the court service as equal to civil service.
55. Lavater: see note 50.
56. The Zaporozhian Host (*Zaporozhskaia Sech'*): a military commune founded by the Cossacks in the late sixteenth century to the south of the rapids on the Dnieper. The Cossack society consisted of groups of several hundred men each, who lived and ate together. Corporal punishment was widely used—hence Radishchev's comparison.
57. Peasants with land (*odnodvortsy*): in Muscovite Russia, the servitors of the lowest rank who were rewarded for their service by a small parcel of land. In the eighteenth century, their status was ambiguous: like state peasants, they paid taxes and had to serve the military (fifteen years instead of twenty-five); like noblemen, they had the right to own land and serfs and were free from corporal punishment.
58. The Summer Garden (*Letnii sad*), the Baba: parks in St. Petersburg. The first was imperial; the other belonged to the courtier A. A. Naryshkin. Both parks were open to the public.
59. Officials in the ranks of first to fourth class as were there wives and widows, were to be addressed "Your Excellency"; fifth to eighth, "Your High Ancestry"; ninth to fourteenth, "Your Honor."

11. KRESTTSY

60. Boyar: a member of the feudal aristocracy, a group that by the late eighteenth century had declined, making the term old-fashioned.

61. Knowledge of English, unlike French and German, was unusual in the eighteenth century. Radishchev had at least a good reading knowledge.

13. VALDAI

62. Lada: Slavic goddess of love, most likely invented in the late eighteenth century; see Mikhail Chulkov, *Dictionary of Russian Superstitions* (*Slovar' russkikh sueverii*) (St. Petersburg: 1782), 189.
63. Leander: in Greek mythology, a lover of Hero (see the following note). He had to swim the Hellespont at night to visit her and drowned one stormy night.
64. Hero: in Greek mythology, a priestess of Aphrodite, a beloved of Leander (see the previous note). Distraught, Hero drowned herself as well.

14. EDROVO

65. Annushka, Anyutushka, Anyuta, and Anyutka are all diminutives of Anna.
66. Pretender: Emelyan Pugachev (1742–1775), leader of the 1773–75 peasant rebellion executed in 1775, styled himself as the Emperor Peter III and was therefore a Pretender to the throne.
67. "You already know how to love": cf. Nikolai Karamzin, "Poor Liza" ("Bednaia Liza," 1792): "Peasant women too know how to love" ("I krest'ianki liubit' umeiut"), a line that became proverbial. While it is likely that Karamzin had read the *Journey* when he wrote his famous story, there is no proof he had.
68. Vanya, Vanka, and Vanyukha are all diminutives of Ivan.
69. Piter: see note 11.

15. KHOTILOV

70. "And we, the sons of glory, we, glorious by name and deeds among the peoples of the Earth": the original plays on the similarity of the words *slava* (glory) and *slovuty* (known, glorious) and *slaviane* (Slavs). This false etymology was popular in the eighteenth century. See, for example, the beginning of Vasily Trediakovsky's "Discourse on the Primacy of the Slavic Language Over Teutonic" ("Rassuzhdenie o pervenstve slavenskogo iazyka pred tevtonicheskim," published in 1773).
71. "Change your name and the story talks about you": a quotation from Horace, *Satires*, I.1. 69–70: "Mutato nomine, de te fabula narratur" ("With the name changed, the same tale / Is told of you").
72. A reference to the Pugachev rebellion; see note 66.
73. Table of Ranks: see note 9.

16. VYSHNY VOLOCHOK

74. "Cursed is the ground in its needs" (*Prokliata zemlia v delakh svoikh*): a slightly changed quotation from Genesis 3:17: "Cursed is the ground for thy sake."
75. Monthly allocation (*mesiachina*) of food, normally dispensed to house serfs.
76. In Christian traditions, including Eastern Orthodox tradition, Easter week (*Svyataya nedelya*) is the period of seven days from Easter Sunday through to the following Saturday. Lent ends on Easter Sunday, and the following week is the time when food containing meat or milk is allowed. One can detect irony in the traveler's tone.

17. VYDROPUSK

77. The nymph Egeria: in Roman legend, a divine consort of Numa Pompilius, Rome's second king (reigned 715–673 BC) and a figure much written about in the eighteenth century as a legislator; Egeria was said to have counseled Numa on laws and religious rituals.
78. Manco Cápac (died 1107): the first Inca ruler of Peru, the founder of the Inca Empire.

18. TORZHOK

79. Mitrofanushka (Mitrofan): a character in Fonvizin's comedy *The Minor*. The minor of the title, he is comically ineducable. For more on this comedy, see note 36.
80. Johann Gottfried von Herder (1744–1803): a German philosopher, poet, and literary critic. Radishchev here translates, with some omissions and additions, a fragment of his 1780 "Vom Einfluss der Regierung auf die Wissenschaften und der Wissenschaften auf die Regierung" ("On the Influence of the Government on the Sciences and the Sciences on the Government").
81. The word *klobuk*, the headgear of Orthodox monks (here, a metonymy for ecclesiastical censorship) is absent in Herder's original and added by Radishchev.
82. Paragraph 480 of Catherine II's Instruction to the Legislative Commission contains, among other things, this principle: "Words are never to be considered a crime, unless they lead to or are linked to or follow a lawless act."
83. See notes 14 and 15.
84. Radishchev's main source for this account is vols. I (part 1) and II (part 2) of Johann Beckmann, *Beiträge zur Geschichter der Erfindungen* (Leipzig, 1786–1805).
85. Protagoras (c. 490–420 BC): a pre-Socratic Greek philosopher, ostensibly the author of the statement "Man is the measure of all things."

86. Titus Labienus: an historian in the time of Augustus, an opponent of monarchy. He committed suicide after his writings were burned on the order of the Senate. His works were later restored on the order of Caligula.
87. Benito Arias Montano (1527–1598): a Spanish orientalist and theologian. He was accused of heresy but eventually acquitted in 1580. Radishchev's motivation in citing him in the context of Roman censorship is unclear.
88. Titus Cassius Severus (d. 32 AD): Roman writer and orator, an advocate of freedom of speech. He was exiled to Crete and his works were banned after his death.
89. Aulus Cremutius Cordus (d. 25 AD): Roman historian, whose works were burned under Tiberius, the Roman emperor who succeeded Augustus, on the order of the Senate.
90. Antiochus IV, Epifanius (215–164 BC): Hellenistic king of the Seleucid Empire from 175 BC until his death; unlike his predecessors, he tried to suppress Judaism by force.
91. Diocletian (Gaius Aurelius Valerius Diocletianus Augustus, 244–311): the Roman emperor from 284 to 305; a persecutor of Christians.
92. Arnobius of Sicca (d. c. 330): an early Christian writer.
93. Radishchev refers to the Council of Nicaea (325) called by Constantine the Great (reigned 306–337), the first Roman emperor converted to Christianity. Arius (256–336), a Libyan presbyter and ascetic, was relegated to anathema by the council as a heretic for his arguing for the supremacy of God the Father.
94. Theodosius II (401–450): Eastern Roman emperor. In 431 he called the Council of Ephesus that condemned as a heretic Nestorius (386–450), the Archbishop of Constantinople (428–431).
95. Eutychus (c. 380–456): denounced as a heretic by the Council of Chalcedon in 451.
96. Pandects of Justinian: a compendium of writings on Roman law compiled by order of the Eastern Roman emperor Justinian I (reigned 527–565) in the sixth century AD.
97. Abelard (Pierre Abélard, 1079–1141 or 1142): a French scholastic philosopher, theologian, and logician. In 1141, Pope Innocent II (1130–1143) excommunicated Abelard, confined him in a monastery, and ordered his books to be burned.
98. Maffeo Ghirardi (or Gherardi, 1406–1492): Patriarch of Venice from 1466 to his death.
99. *Codex diplomaticus*, published by Gudenus, volume IV: *Codex diplomaticus anecdotorum, res Moguntinas, Francicas, Trevirenses, Hassiacas, finitimarumque regionum nec non ius Germanicum et S. R. I. historiamvel maxime illustrantium*, ed. Valentin Ferdinand, Freiherr von Gudenus, et al., 5 vols. (Göttingen, Frankfurt, and Leipzig, 1743–68).
100. The words in brackets are restored based on the Latin original from which Radishchev was translating: "*tenore presentium districte precipiendo mandamus* . . ."

101. Pope Alexander VI (Borgia/Borjia, 1431–1503): elected Pope in 1492. Radishchev compares him to Tiberius (see note 89).
102. William Caxton (c. 1422–1491): an English merchant and writer, who pioneered printing in England. The book cited by Radishchev is *A Book of the Chesse Moralysed* (*Le jeu d'échecs moralisés*), attributed by Caxton to Jean de Vignay, who in fact had translated it from the Latin original by Jacopo da Cessole.
103. Secret Chancery (*Tainaia kantseliariia*): body of political investigation established by Peter the Great in 1718.
104. Thomas Wentworth, Earl of Strafford (1593–1641): English statesman, supporter of Charles I. The Long Parliament abolished the Star Chamber.
105. As there is no firm evidence that Radishchev quotes from American revolutionary documents, the translation is from Radishchev's wording
106. Wilhelm Ludwig Wekhrlin (1739–1792): a German writer and journalist. The magazine *Gray Monstrosity* (*Das graue Ungeheuer*) was published from 1784 to 1787.
107. Joseph II (1741–1790): Holy Roman Emperor from 1765 and sole ruler of the Habsburg lands from 1780 until his death. He reformed the legal system, abolishing brutal punishments and the death penalty in most instances, and also experimented with the reform of serfdom in his lands (claiming to see in Catherine the Great a model). He also ended censorship of the press and theater.

19. MEDNOE

108. Burkhard Christoph von Münnich (1683–1767): a German general who in 1721 was invited to Russia to work on engineering projects in the newly acquired northern territories. Eventually, he became a field marshal and a prominent political figure during the reign of the Empress Anna Ioanovna (r. 1730–1740), niece of Peter the Great.

20. TVER

109. The traveler's interlocutor refers to the adoption by Russians of the syllabo-tonic versification system, usually called "the reform of versification," which replaced the syllabic versification ("the Polish cladding") practiced from the beginning of the seventeenth century. In the earlier system, the poetic line was determined by the number of syllables in the line, usually at least twelve, with no fixed pattern of stressed syllables. In the new syllabo-tonic system, the line of verse was determined by the number of fixed syllables arranged according to a regular pattern of unstressed and stressed vowels (the tonic element). Vasily Trediakovsky (1703–1769), Mikhailo Lomonosov (1711–1765), and Alexander Sumarokov

(1717–1777) were instrumental in carrying out this reform. In the following paragraphs, both their positive and negative contributions to this reform are discussed.

110. The traveler's interlocuter expresses regret over predominance of iambs in eighteenth-century Russian poetry, mentioning Lomonosov's predominantly iambic transpositions of psalms and chapters 38–41 of *Job*, Sumarokov's iambic tragedies *Semiramis* (*Semira*, written and staged 1751, published 1768) and *Dimitry the Pretender* (*Dimitry Samozvanets*, staged and published 1771), and Mikhail Kheraskov's iambic epic poem *Rossiada* (1770–78).
111. Vasily Petrov's translation of the *Aeneid* (1781–86) and Ermil Kostrov's translation of cantos 1–6 of the *Iliad* (1787) are also written in iambs.
112. On Trediakovsky and his *Tilemakhida*, see the note to the dedication at the beginning of this book.
113. The first translation of Voltaire's *Henriade* into Russian was done in unrhymed iambics by Yakov Knyazhnin (1740 or 1742–1791), published in 1777.
114. Radishchev wrote "Liberty" ("Vol'nost'") in the early 1780s and first published it, with significant cuts, in his *Journey*. Despite the criticism of iambic meter in "Tver," it follows the tradition originated with Lomonosov's "Ode on the Capture of Chocim" (written in 1739, significantly revised for its first full publication in 1751) in using both iambic tetrameter and a ten-line stanza. In early manuscript versions of the *Journey*, after "Liberty" was included a metrically innovative "Creation of the World" oratory (*pesnopenie*).
115. *Veche*: see note 44.
116. Radishchev took an interest in the constitutional arrangements of the new American republic, curious about the relationship between states and a federal government. He also disagreed with Montesquieu and Rousseau that only small states can enjoy good government. See A. N. Radishchev, "Razroznennye zametki," in his *Polnoe sobranie sochinenii*, vol. 3 (Moscow, Leningrad: Izd. AN SSSR, 1952), 47, item no. 7. This was in a way his response to their argument.

22. ZAVIDOVO

117. Radishchev's mistake: it was Neptune who used this expression addressing the winds in Virgil's *Aeneid* (see Book I, 135: "Quos ego—"). Radishchev quotes Virgil's poem in Vasily Petrov's translation, where these words are translated as "Ia vas! . . ."
118. Polkan: see note 25.
119. The address "His Excellency" signals that the passing bureaucrat is of the third or fourth class, which entitles him to six horses per carriage. The requirement of fifty horses satirically implies that he either travels in eight to ten carriages or wants more than six horses per carriage.

120. Radishchev refers to Denis Fonvizin's satirical *General Court Grammar* (*Vseobshchaia pridvornaia grammatika*, 1786). Fonvizin (and Radishchev after him) puns on phonetic terms: *glasnye* (vowels, but also having a voice, able to speak out) and *bezglasnye* (voiceless, not able to speak out).

24. PESHKI

121. The original uses an idiom "*golod—ne svoi brat*" ("hunger isn't one's brother"), which means that hunger is difficult or impossible to ignore.

25. CHORNAYA GRYAZ

122. Slavo-Greco-Latin Academy: a religious school on Moscow founded in 1685 (classes began in 1678) and converted by Peter the Great to a state institution of higher education in 1701. Lomonosov was accepted as a student in January 1731 and left in late 1735, after he was selected, along with eleven other students, to be sent to Germany to be trained in mining. In 1734, he spent a year studying at the Kiev Academy.
123. Christian Wolff (1679–1754): German natural philosopher and mathematician. Lomonosov studied mathematics, physics, and mechanics under his supervision until his departure in July 1739 for Freiberg to study chemistry and metallurgy.
124. Before departing for Germany, Lomonosov bought Trediakovsky's 1735 *New and Brief Method for Composing Russian Verse* (*Novyi i kratkii sposob k slozheniiu rossiiskikh stikhov*), in which Trediakovsky proposed first steps in reforming the syllabic versification system dominant in Russia at that time. Lomonosov's copy of Trediakovsky's book survived with Lomonosov's extensive marginalia (the copy is preserved in the Archives of Academy of Sciences in St. Petersburg, fond. 20, op. 2, no. 3).
125. All the figures listed here were renowned as orators. The Athenian Demosthenes was a statesman and a legendary rhetorician; the Roman Cicero was a senator and an important intellectual; (William) Pitt the Elder, a British prime minister in the mid-eighteenth century, was famed for his organlike voice. The figures from Radishchev's generation are Edmund Burke, the Irish parliamentarian, philosopher, and enemy of the French Revolution but supporter of the American colonies; Charles James Fox, notorious as an antislavery campaigner and supporter of the French Revolution; and the comte de Mirabeau, a French revolutionary activist. These three figures used their eloquence to whip up political assemblies.
126. A reference to Lomonosov's transposition of Psalm 103 (Orthodox Psalm 104); written before 1749, first published in 1784.

127. A reference to Lomonosov's 1748 "Evening Meditation on the Greatness of God on the Occasion of Great Northern Lights" ("Vechernee razmyshlenie o Bozhiem velichestve pri sluchae velikogo severnogo siianiia"). In this deist poem, Lomonosov discusses several hypotheses explaining the aurora borealis.
128. *Gudok*: a primitive chordophone instrument mostly used in the seventeenth and eighteenth centuries by Russian jugglers (*skomorokhi*).
129. A reference to Lomonosov's "Ode on the Day of the Ascension to the All-Russian Throne of . . . the Empress Elisaveta Petrovna, the Year 1747" ("Oda na den' vosshestviia na vserossiiskii prestol . . . imperatritsy Elisavety Petrovny 1747 goda"), 1747.
130. Pyotr (Platon after becoming a monk) Levshin (1737–1812), the Metropolitan of Moscow from 1787 to 1812, a theologian and a gifted rhetorician. Radishchev refers to his 1772 oration given on the occasion of the Russian naval victory of Chesme. Radishchev also implies Levshin's connection to Plato (Platon in Russian tradition) through his adopted name.
131. William Robertson (1721–1793): a Scottish historian; Andreas Sigismund Marggraf (1709–1782): a German chemist; Andreas Rüdiger (1673–1731): a German natural philosopher and physicist.
132. Radishchev is referring here to Georg Wilhelm Richmann (1711–1753), a Baltic German physicist, a member of the St. Petersburg Academy of Sciences. He was electrocuted while experimenting with lightning.

R

RUSSIAN LIBRARY

Between Dog and Wolf by Sasha Sokolov, translated by Alexander Boguslawski
Strolls with Pushkin by Andrei Sinyavsky, translated by Catharine Theimer Nepomnyashchy and Slava I. Yastremski
Fourteen Little Red Huts and Other Plays by Andrei Platonov, translated by Robert Chandler, Jesse Irwin, and Susan Larsen
Rapture: A Novel by Iliazd, translated by Thomas J. Kitson
City Folk and Country Folk by Sofia Khvoshchinskaya, translated by Nora Seligman Favorov
Writings from the Golden Age of Russian Poetry by Konstantin Batyushkov, presented and translated by Peter France
Found Life: Poems, Stories, Comics, a Play, and an Interview by Linor Goralik, edited by Ainsley Morse, Maria Vassileva, and Maya Vinokur
Sisters of the Cross by Alexei Remizov, translated by Roger John Keys and Brian Murphy
Sentimental Tales by Mikhail Zoshchenko, translated by Boris Dralyuk
Redemption by Friedrich Gorenstein, translated by Andrew Bromfield
The Man Who Couldn't Die: The Tale of an Authentic Human Being by Olga Slavnikova, translated by Marian Schwartz
Necropolis by Vladislav Khodasevich, translated by Sarah Vitali
Nikolai Nikolaevich and Camouflage: Two Novellas by Yuz Aleshkovsky, translated by Duffield White, edited by Susanne Fusso
New Russian Drama: An Anthology, edited by Maksim Hanukai and Susanna Weygandt
A Double Life by Karolina Pavlova, translated and with an introduction by Barbara Heldt
Klotsvog by Margarita Khemlin, translated by Lisa Hayden
Fandango and Other Stories by Alexander Grin, translated by Bryan Karetnyk
Woe from Wit: A Verse Comedy in Four Acts by Alexander Griboedov, translated by Betsy Hulick
The Nose and Other Stories by Nicolai Gogol, translated by Susanne Fusso